# THE GUARDIANS' LIGHT

## THE RISE OF THE THREE

A Novel by
# M.J. BELL

MJB Publishing, Inc., LLC

# Books by M.J. Bell

### Chronicles of the Secret Prince Fantasy Trilogy:
*Book 1:* **Before the Full Moon Rises**
*Book 2:* **Once Upon a Darker Time**
*Book 3:* **How Dark the Light Shines**

### Next Time I See You
*A time travel suspense thriller*

### The Guardians' Light
*The Rise of the Three*

# THE GUARDIANS' LIGHT

## THE RISE OF THE THREE

*For Tiffany Lopo and Lisa Moore, whose love and support helped bring this story to light.*

*And for my readers, who are the reason I keep writing.*

# PROLOGUE

The slushy, pelting rain turned the world outside the small SUV into a dark, hostile blur. The vehicle, which was speeding down the road way too fast for the conditions, hit a puddle of standing water and hydroplaned across the rain-slick road into the oncoming traffic lane.

The driver, Ukani, cranked the wheel hard to the right to correct the skid.

The metal guardrail, the only barrier between the SUV's five occupants and the steep embankment beyond, screeched in protest as the vehicle scraped along its side. Then, somehow the tires miraculously reconnected with solid asphalt and the SUV surged on.

Minutes later, the SUV swerved again into the oncoming lane as it rounded another bend.

Jenn, sitting in the passenger seat, clutched the dashboard with both hands. "Slow down! You're going to kill us all."

Ukani ignored her and kept his attention on the intermittent glimpses of road through the swish of the windshield wipers. He had very little experience dealing with humans like the one sitting beside him, and even less experience driving in a downpour on some godforsaken road in the middle of nowhere Oregon, and his patience was wearing thin.

He threw a glance into the rearview mirror at the three toddlers strapped into car seats in the back. Two of them had their eyes closed, but the one in the middle stared back at him with old-soul eyes that held much too much wisdom for a three-year-old.

Ukani shot Jenn a glare and barked over the drumming of the rain for her to check on the kids.

Jenn looked over her shoulder and smiled sweetly at the little girl with the biggest, roundest blue eyes. "It's okay, sweetie. Close your eyes and go to sleep. We're almost there. Then we can have some fun, okay?"

Jenn's smile disappeared the second she turned back to the front. "How much longer before we can stop?"

Ukani's jaw twitched. "I don't know. This road is shit!"

He glanced up at the S in the corner of the rearview mirror and sneered. They were supposed to be heading west, but thanks to the twists and turns, it seemed they were constantly backtracking instead of moving forward.

"This rain's a fucking nightmare too," he added, increasing the pressure on the accelerator in hopes of making up time.

Jenn squeezed her eyes together as the back end of the vehicle fishtailed in response.

They had been traveling for over eighteen hours with only a few short bathroom stops, and the strain was taking its toll on all of them. Ukani had factored in losing time on the backroads of Oregon, but he hadn't anticipated how poorly maintained the roads would be. But then, nothing had gone right with this mission from the minute he took the kids, and he was beginning to second-guess his plan.

In addition to his other problems, his mind control over Jenn was weakening. The evidence of that being her growing agitation and continuous questioning as to why he felt it necessary to flee with the kids instead of going to the police.

"You need to listen to me," Jenn said, reiterating what she'd been saying for the last two hours. "You're not thinking this through clearly. I know it must of been a shock for you to find your sister and her husband dead. That would be hard for anyone to see. But you've had time to think about what you did." She paused, her eyes going wide as if realizing she had misspoken. "... I mean, what you're doing. If you really want what's best for these kids, you'll turn around and go to the authorities."

A low growl rumbled in Ukani's throat.

Jenn hurried on. "I'm sure the cops will understand you did what you did if you explain that Abigail and James were already dead when you got to the house. And that you only took the kids because you were afraid the murderer would come back. I mean, heck, you're the only family they have left now. It's a natural instinct for you to want to protect them. But running away across state lines is bad. It brings the FBI, too. And if someone sees us with these kids and turns us in, you might not get a chance to tell your side of the story. They may even think you had something to do with the murders."

Ukani gnashed his teeth and gripped the wheel tighter. *When this is done, I'm going to hunt down and kill every last one of those Sons of Ea bastards.*

He hated the Sons more than he hated humans, and almost as much as he did the Pleiadians, the alien forefathers of the Sons. It was because of the Sons he was in this situation now and forced to deal with this stupid, whining human.

The first time Ukani found the Guardians three years ago, they were still babies and still with their Pleiadian parents. But before he could turn the Three over to the Anunnaki, the Sons showed up. Like the Pleiadians, the Sons take their oath to protect the Earth from alien invaders very seriously. Ukani, a Dracuzian and natural born killer, managed to take out a good number of them, but he was only one man and there were over two dozen of them. In the end, they got away with the babies and Ukani had to start the search all over again.

He never doubted he could find the Guardians a second time, though it took him longer than he expected. But who would have thought the Pleiadians would give up their children to humans and let them be raised as human children in the suburbs of Denver?

At least this time around, the Sons hadn't gotten wind of his plan. Though, at the moment, he would almost rather deal with them than this stupid human he had brought along to handle the kids.

Ukani had found Jenn in a bar in downtown Denver where she had gone to celebrate a friend's engagement. Her plain-Jane looks and soft-spoken demeanor had set her apart from the other women in the bar and had drawn his attention. He had been on the lookout for someone to watch over the kids on the cross-country trip, and when he heard she was a pre-school teacher that sealed the deal.

As he expected, Jenn had easily fallen under his mind control and had been as malleable as clay. Up until yesterday when he told her to stay in the car as he went into the house of his supposed sister to pick up his nieces and nephew for a fun weekend. If she had only done as she was told, she wouldn't have heard Abigail scream or the crash of the end table when James flew into it after the bullet hit him in the chest. And she wouldn't have come running into the house.

It had taken every ounce of Ukani's willpower not to shoot Jenn right there on the spot. It was only the fact that he hated kids, especially these three, and that he needed someone to care for them on the long trip to Crater Lake, that she didn't end up dead, too.

Ukani was barely able to stash the gun under his coat before Jenn saw it. He then had to spend a great deal of effort to get her back under his spell and convince her the Smiths were already dead when he walked in.

But now, her constant nagging was wearing on his nerves and he wished he had just shot her in the head back at the house.

"I'm not going over it again with you," Ukani said through clenched teeth. "The police couldn't protect my sister. They won't be able to protect these kids, either. And I've already told you, it takes too much time to go through channels to get custody. That would leave the kids vulnerable and give the murderer plenty of chances to get to them. Do you really want to see them dead too?"

"Of course not! But … please … you don't understand," Jenn pleaded. "I'm sure by now an Amber Alert has been issued. Since you're not from America, you may not understand what that means, but I can tell you that people here, especially law enforcement agencies, take an Amber Alert seriously. The kids' pictures will be spread across the entire country and everyone will be looking for them."

She paused, her eyes pleading with him.

"If you're worried they won't believe your story," she went on, "we could just leave the car in a parking lot, or somewhere along the road, and call in an anonymous tip. Then, as soon as the kids are picked up, you could show up and claim them. You said you're the only blood relative they have now, so I'm sure they'd turn them over to you. And this way you wouldn't be breaking any laws. You wouldn't be implicated in the murders, either."

She placed her hand on his arm. "Please … you have to see how bad it will look if the cops stop us and find these kids in the car."

Ukani yanked his arm away. This was one of the many reasons he hated dealing with humans. They always acted more on emotion than logic.

"Why do you think we're traveling these shitty back roads? We've come this far and no one has recognized the kids yet. We're almost to our destination now, and I don't want to hear any more about it."

"But that's just it!" Jenn exclaimed. "There's no place we can take these kids that they won't be recognized if there's an Amber Alert in place. And what good are you going to be to them if you're accused of murder … and theft?"

Ukani flinched. *Shit!*

Jenn smirked. "Oh yeah … I saw those bags filled with gold bars that you took from the house."

"I said *enough!*"

His shout roused one of the sleeping toddlers. The little girl started to whimper and Jenn shot him a glare cold enough to frost the windshield.

"Now look what you've done." She reached back to comfort the girl, but the seat belt restricted her movement. She unlatched the buckle, got up on one knee, and leaned over the seat. "Shhh," she whispered, tucking the blanket up under the child's chin, then patted her chest.

Just as the toddler's eyes drifted closed again, the car hit a large pothole. The jolt threw Jenn off balance. She groped for the back of the seat.

Ukani cranked the wheel hard to the right and the SUV veered onto the gravel shoulder.

The back of Jenn's head smacked hard into the windshield, leaving a large circular spiderweb crack in the glass. Her body went limp.

The front bumper of the SUV smashed into the guard rail again. Ukani clenched his jaw and twisted the steering wheel hard to the left. The rain looked like miniscule meteors through the glow of the headlights as the SUV careened across the road and plowed into another rail, which buckled as if made of cardboard.

The vehicle flipped, slamming the roof onto the rocky bank. The windshield shattered and Jenn flew out through the opening. The small squeak of her last breath was drowned out by the screech of tearing metal as the SUV cartwheeled over and over down the steep embankment, finally coming to a jolting halt upright in the middle of a small creek that still had ice and snow lining its banks.

⊿⌐⅄

The deafening roar of the wind rushed through Ukani's head as he came up out of darkness. He opened his eyes and lifted his head, a movement he immediately regretted as an excruciating pain seared through his skull. He winced in agony and went stiff, hoping the pain would pass. It didn't.

He blinked to focus his eyes, but something wet dripped into the right one. He reached up, wiped it away, and stared in bewilderment at the dark red liquid that covered the fingertips of his gloves. He then noticed he was soaking wet and freezing.

*What the hell? Where am I?*

He tried to push himself up, but a strap running horizontally across his chest held him back. He looked down and frowned, his mind too muddled to process what was holding him in place. He lifted his gaze and stared blankly at the steering wheel, now partly covered in a white piece of fabric. The crease in his brow deepened as he tried to make sense of it. It took several seconds more before he realized what he was looking at. At that same moment, the memory of going off the road came back to him.

Ukani craned his neck toward the passenger seat and held his breath as another shooting pain sliced through his head. He closed his eyes and concentrated on his breathing, filling his lungs with air, then slowly blowing it out through his mouth until the black fog swimming at the edge of his mind receded some.

Cautiously, he opened his eyes and waited until his vision focused on the empty passenger seat. "Jenn?"

Without moving his head, he shifted his gaze to the opening where the windshield had been. His eyes then narrowed as the memory of her being ejected through it played in his mind.

*Shit!* Her death meant nothing to him, but the thought of having to manage the kids all by himself infuriated him.

He inhaled sharply at the thought of the Guardians and jerked around to look in the back seat. Another piercing pain blurred his vision for a moment. He held his breath until the wave of nausea passed.

The three car seats were lined up as before with the toddlers still safely strapped in. All three appeared to be unconscious and unscathed and were tightly gripping each other's hands. The air around them rippled like water after a pebble had been dropped in—a telltale sign a force field had been activated.

"Son of a bitch," Ukani mumbled turning back to the front.

He wiped the blood from his gloves onto his pant leg and fumbled to unhook his seat belt. His fingers were numb from the cold and it took several attempts for him to get it free. He then had to use all the strength he could muster to push the crushed door open. It took another monumental effort and a great deal of sweat to gingerly move his frozen legs.

The sky was a lighter shade of gray than before, which indicated the sun had risen and it was morning. But the ping of rain still bounced off the roof and hood of the SUV.

Ukani grimaced as he placed his left foot down and the icy water of the creek seeped in through the tongue of his boot. He steeled himself and planted his right foot next to his left and stood.

An intense pain shot up his right leg and nearly doubled him over. He grabbed for the door, lifted his foot out of the water, and blew breaths through his teeth until the pain was tolerable. But his head continued to swim.

Ukani cursed again. Nothing had gone as it was supposed to since he had picked up the Guardians, and now he had a broken ankle on top of everything else.

Keeping a firm hold on the door, he tentatively placed his foot down in the water and added weight a little at a time until he was standing straight. His high-top leather boots were stiff enough to keep the bone stable, and the knife he always kept tucked in the side of the boot acted as a splint. The glacial water also helped and was turning his foot numb. Still, it hurt like hell.

He squared his shoulders and stood tall. Pain was another inconvenience he would rather not have to deal with, but it had never stopped him before. He knew he had to get out of there before the car was found, and the only way to do that was on foot.

Ukani moved his body slowly to avoid straining anything else and looked around to get his bearings.

He had chosen Crater Lake for the transfer of the Guardians not only because the Anunnaki kept several of their spacecrafts hidden deep within the water of the lake, but because he'd been told few people visited there at this time of year. From the looks of it, that information was accurate. But then again, the rain prohibited him from seeing much past a few yards.

"Son of a bitch!" he growled, pounding his fist against the doorframe.

The girl in the middle car seat jumped, but her eyes remained closed.

Ukani ran his hands through his hair. He was stronger than the average human, but the road was at least twenty-five feet above him, and climbing a steep, rocky hill on a broken ankle was outside even his abilities. But that wasn't what concerned him most.

The bigger issue was how to get the three kids out.

He turned west, in  the direction of the lake, and stared into the forest of fir trees, hoping for some kind of inspiration. The only thing that came to him was Jenn's warning that if the police found him with the kids, he could be thrown into prison for the rest of his life, which for him probably wouldn't be all that long. The Anunnaki didn't tolerate failure and had enough people inside the prison system to ensure his untimely demise. And though he didn't fear death, he wasn't ready to die yet.

That left only one plausible option—leave the Guardians behind. He hated the thought of that, but he could come back and retrieve them once he got his ankle fixed up. Or if they'd been found in that time, he could go to the police station and claim to be their uncle, as Jenn had suggested.

"Fuck!" Ukani yelled to the trees. He had searched so long for the Three he didn't want to end up empty handed a second time.

But as he thought about it, he realized there was a plus side to this option. When the police got here and only found Jenn and the kids, that would make it appear she had perpetrated the crime on her own. They might even be more sympathetic to him then when he showed up as the grieving uncle.

He narrowed his eyes at the SUV, which was registered to Jenn. He'd always made sure to wear gloves whenever he got into it, so the only place his DNA could possibly be was on the deployed airbag.

"Fucking primitives," Ukani mumbled to himself as he pulled the knife from his boot and cut the fabric off the steering wheel. He wadded the material up and stuffed into his pants pocket, then grabbed one of the toddlers' blankets lying on the floor behind the driver's seat and meticulously wiped down the steering wheel, the dashboard, and the driver's-side door for any errant blood splatter from his nose and the large gash across his forehead. Fortunately, none of his blood had gotten on the seat belt or the cloth seats.

Lastly, he adjusted the driver's seat to fit a person of Jenn's height, to further the illusion she was by herself. Although, the missing airbag would tell anyone with half a brain there was someone else in the car with her. But he hoped, because this was the middle of nowhere, that the police force here wouldn't have much experience with real crimes and see this as just another unfortunate car crash.

But even if they were to notice the missing airbag, he felt confident they couldn't tie him to anything. Jenn's friends only knew him by his alias, Seth Nassar.

Ukani gritted his teeth, limped to the back of the vehicle, and wrenched open the hatch. The zipper on one of the two duffle bags holding twenty-five one-kilo gold bars each had split open and the bars were scattered amongst the toys and clothes from the kids' bags. The gun he'd used to kill the Smiths was missing, too.

He scanned the embankment, but the rain was still coming down in sheets, and even with his exceptional eyesight, he couldn't pick out a thing. It didn't matter, though. The gun was of no importance to him and couldn't be traced back to him, either. And if it was found, that would be one more piece of evidence against Jenn.

Turning back to the SUV, Ukani gingerly pulled a hoodie over his head and slipped on a jacket on top of that. As an afterthought, he threw Jenn's handbag up to the front to make sure the police would have no trouble identifying her.

He then collected the scattered gold bars and stuffed them, along with the blanket he'd used to wipe the car down, into the duffle bags. A soft moan escaped his lips as he hefted a bag over each shoulder.

Then, with his backpack in his hand, he hobbled alongside the SUV.

He paused at the back seat window to give one last longing look at the three toddlers. His yellowish skin, wide-set hooded eyes, short flat nose, and wide mouth reflected back to him on the glass.

The girl in the middle opened her eyes and squeezed the hands of the other two. They, too, opened their eyes, and all three stoically stared back at the man.

"I've found you twice. I'll find you again. Mark my words on that," Ukani hissed, then turned and sloshed through the water of the creek without a backward glance.

SOFIA

# ONE

*January 13th, Fifteen years later.*

A crack opened in the shroud of clouds covering the night sky, letting a stream of light from the waxing moon shine through a hole in Sofia's bedroom blinds. It hit her directly in the face. She flopped over to her other side with a groan but had no sooner settled back into her pillow when her cell phone vibrated with her morning alarm.

She blew out a long weary breath, rolled to her back, and stared up at the large water stain on the ceiling a couple feet above her. She cocked her head to one side, then the other, and squinted until the edges of the multiple layers of brown and yellow solidified into an image. It was different every day, depending upon the moon's position in the sky and the shadows created by the angle of the slats of the blinds. Sometimes, it was a bear, other times a clown, a buffalo, a horse, and on rare occasions a dragon, which was her favorite. Today it was definitely a dragon. That usually meant it was going to be a special day, and those were few and far between.

Sofia's chest tightened with expectation as she threw her legs over the side of the bunkbed and jumped down, landing as quietly as a cat. As was customary, she looked over her shoulder to make sure she hadn't aroused her roommate, Meredith, who slept in the lower bunk.

Meredith wasn't a pleasant person to deal with on a good day, but if Sofia happened to wake her before it was time, her bunkmate's unpleasantness tripled. Sofia had discovered this the hard way two days after she moved into her current foster home, when she accidently bumped Meredith's arm while pulling the bunkbed ladder into position to climb down. She'd never seen anyone move as fast as Meredith did. Before she even knew what was happening, she was sprawled on the floor in the hallway, the bedroom door was locked, and she wasn't able to get dressed for school, which made her late for her first day at Urbandale High.

But dealing with Meredith types was nothing new to Sofia. There was always at least one mean girl in every foster home she'd ever been in. And she'd been in plenty. But she quickly learned the best way to handle them was to stay out of their way. Unfortunately, not all of her foster brothers and sisters, especially the younger ones, could do that. And Sofia, being Sofia, would step in and become their protector, which ironically earned *her* the label of being a "troublesome child."

Sofia wasn't actually troublesome, though. She was just incredibly intelligent and confused as to why people treated others so horribly. It also wasn't in her nature to sit back and watch an injustice go by without speaking her mind or taking some sort of action. Not surprisingly, that seldom sat well with most adults, especially those in authority, which as it turned out, was another huge issue of Sofia's. She couldn't stand it when people told her what to do—particularly people who never took the time to really get to know her and only pretended to care about her.

Fortunately, the stars finally took pity on her and gave her a break by placing her with Poppo and Nana Miller, an elderly couple who were kind and patient and took in foster kids not *only* because of the money, but because they truly wanted to provide a real home to a few of the lost. They were the complete opposite of what she had previously experienced in her other ten foster homes, and the last two years would have been pure bliss if Meredith hadn't been in the picture.

Gathering up her clothes and boots, Sofia tip-toed out of the room and closed the door with a soft click. She showered and dressed quickly without waking anyone else in the household, then grabbed a bottle of water, a granola bar, and her down jacket on her way out the door.

The gritty mounds of crusty snow, dating back to the first snowfall of winter, were now pristine white from snow that had fallen throughout the night. Most people in Iowa were sick of winter by the time January rolled around, but Sofia loved fresh snow and the way it looked like diamond dust in the glow of the streetlights.

With a smile on her face and humming softly to herself, she shuffled her way to the park down the street like she did every morning and went straight to her favorite swing. She sat down on the frozen strip of rubber and stared through a break in the clouds at the constellation Pleiades. As always, the soft sounds of Rachmaninoff's *Rhapsody on a Theme of Paganini* began to play in her head and colors danced in her mind, the piano notes generating soft waves of teal, the strings ripples of lavender.

She had always preferred the darkness and silence of the night to the blazing sun and noise of the day. The shiny pinpoints of light in the sky, especially those of the Seven Sisters, always gave her a warm sense of peace, and that was something she had so little of in her life.

This quiet time was also the only time visions of her parents— her real parents— appeared to her. That was the main reason she got up at this ridiculous hour of the morning.

Sofia couldn't explain how she knew the image of the couple, who had the same high cheek bones and electric blue eyes with blazing yellow circles around the pupils that she did, were her real parents. Her birth certificate said she was born to a James and Abigail Smith. She had no recollections of the Smiths, though. None whatsoever.

That had bothered her for years. And though she'd never thought of herself as cold and uncaring, she began to wonder if maybe she was, because not even a photo of them she had found on the Internet sparked a memory. She had stared at the picture a long time, trying to feel something … anything, but it was like her memory had been wiped and the couple felt as irrelevant as every other couple she passed on the street on a daily basis. The only feeling she could muster was a bit of sadness when she read the Smiths had been murdered. That was news to her, too.

She was thirteen when she had her first vision of the couple she believed to be her real parents, and just like that, as if the image had rebooted her mind, all kinds of memories began to flood in. For the first year, the memories gave her a terrific headache in the lower back of her head, but that didn't stop her from seeking them out. A little pain was nothing compared to the joy she felt recalling the sound of their voices, the twinkle in mother's eyes when she was happy, and the way the yellow circle around her mother's pupils would turn to liquid gold when she was mad. The dearest memory she had was of her mother coming into her room in the middle of the night, cradling Sofia in her arms and singing a haunting tune in a language Sofia didn't understand.

The memories convinced Sofia she was right about these two people being her parents, but she asked her social worker, Stephanie, for confirmation just to be sure. The middle-aged woman with sagging jowls seemed annoyed, and, just like always when she didn't want to give an answer, Stephanie brushed the question off with a well-rehearsed reply of, "Foster children make up fantasy parents all the time. It's nothing to worry about as long as you don't get obsessed with the fantasy."

But Sofia knew she wasn't making her parents up. She wasn't obsessed, either. She just wanted the truth and to know more about them. And most of all, she wanted to find them and be wrapped in the love she could literally feel every time the visions came to her. Or at least she assumed the tender looks on their faces that put a yearning in her heart and turned her stomach upside-down was love. No one else had ever looked at her like that or made her feel that way. But then no one else had ever truly loved her. Mostly, people treated her as if she was just a pariah.

Slowly, the clouds merged together and blocked out the dots of starlight. Sofia shivered with the cold as a brisk gust of air whipped up the loose snow and blew it into her face. She adjusted the scarf around her neck, looked down at the time on her phone, and let out a wistful sigh. She didn't want to leave even though her fingers felt like icicles, but she knew from experience the walk to the Dunkin Donuts for her morning shift would take longer than usual with the icy sidewalks. She lifted her face to the dark sky one more time and blinked off the snowflakes that had started falling again.

"Just two more months and I'll be eighteen. Then no one can

keep me from looking for you," Sofia whispered, squinting up at the sky in hopes of getting one more glimpse of the constellation through the clouds, but the snow was coming down too heavily.

She let out another soft sigh and pushed back the apprehension that always came with the thought of her birthday. While most teens looked forward to turning eighteen to get out from under parental control, she dreaded it. Not because she didn't want to be able to make decisions for herself, but because foster kids like her were chucked out of the system as if they were pieces of trash when they turned eighteen. It didn't matter that she would still be in high school on her birthday. But then her life had never mattered, so why should this be any different?

*I'll only have to get by for five months. I can do that. Then, once I'm at college in Cambridge, no one'll know where I came from. I'll be just another student like everyone else,* she thought, rubbing her hands together to get the circulation back.

She heaved herself up to her feet, her frozen joints slow to move, slung her backpack over her shoulder, and headed toward the donut shop.

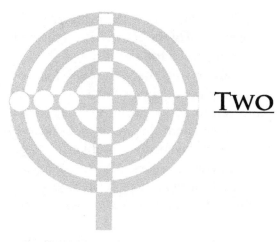

# TWO

*February 13th*

Ukani plodded across the red clay tennis courts at the Katameya Heights Resort, ignoring the angry protests of the players, which abruptly faded to nothing when he stopped on the sideline of the court where Makin Daher was playing a doubles match.

Daher, an intimidating man who carried himself like royalty, not only owned the club but was listed by Forbes Magazine as the wealthiest man in the world. He also had the reputation of being ruthless with those who displeased him.

Ukani was living proof of that and had the scars to show it.

The last time the two had met was on the day Daher sent Ukani to the gold mines in South Africa. That was almost fifteen years ago. Fifteen years of laboring eighteen hours a day in insufferable heat and toxic fumes. Fifteen years of regretting his decision to leave the Guardians in the wrecked car in Oregon. Fifteen years of plotting what he'd do if he were to ever get out of the mines. Though he never actually expected that would happen.

Daher was one of the Elite in the Anunnaki hierarchy, and that alien race of pillagers of planets were not known to give out second chances. Yet here Ukani was, and he couldn't help but wonder what had changed.

Ukani gritted his teeth to hide his aggravation and stoically stood at attention, waiting to be acknowledged.

Daher played on, giving no sign he was aware the Dracuzian had arrived, even though Ukani's giant shadow cast a dark stain across almost half the court.

When at last the match ended, Daher marched to the sideline with a familiar, intense look on his bronzed face. His scrawny assistant, Tabari, bolted across the court after him, carrying a towel, a bottle of water, and a tablet.

Daher's lip curled in disgust as his gaze moved over Ukani's ill-fitting, shabby clothes and emaciated appearance.

"You're still alive," he said without preamble, yanking the towel from Tabari's hand and mopping his perpetually furrowed brow. "I'm surprised by that. The survival rate in the mines has always been poor. It makes me wonder now if that's been the case because we've been sending down the wrong people. If all Dracuzians can tolerate the conditions as well as you, maybe I should consider sending more of them in."

Ukani pressed his lips together and remained silent. Daher was just trying to rile him, and he was determined not to give the Anunnaki a single second of satisfaction.

The corner of Daher's mouth twitched with amusement as he tossed Tabari the towel. He then turned and strode toward the golf cart waiting outside the perimeter fence.

Ukani blew out a weary sigh and followed, jogging to keep within a few feet of the cart as it sped toward the sprawling clubhouse.

Daher barreled through the doors of the Trophy Lounge and went straight to the best table in the room—the one with no other table within ten feet of it and sat by a window that provided a full view of the pool.

Ukani staggered in after him but came to an abrupt halt as an array of aromas from the kitchen hit him like a tsunami. Hunger pangs ripped through his stomach reminding him that his last piddly meal of a small bowl of rice had been over forty-eight hours ago. He swallowed back the urge to run and grab some food off the plates and forced his feet to move on across the room instead. He came to a stop behind the chair that faced Daher and focused his gaze on the blue water of the pool to keep from looking at the tempting dishes streaming out of the kitchen.

As before, Daher acted as if Ukani wasn't there and barked at a waiter who had just set a glass of melon juice in front of him to bring him a rare steak. Then, with a wave of his hand, he dismissed all those hovering around.

As his minions hustled away, Daher lifted the glass to his lips and studied Ukani over the rim as he sipped the sweet nectar.

Ukani stood straight, even though his muscles quivered with exhaustion and his stomach rolled with hunger.

Daher leisurely dabbed his mouth with a napkin and meticulously draped it over his lap before sitting back and steepling his fingers over his chest. "You must be wondering why I summoned you," he said at long last.

Knowing it was a rhetorical question, Ukani remained silent.

"You were the only one able to track down the Guardians before," Daher continued. "I don't know how you did it when no one else could, but I don't need to know. I just need you to do it again."

Ukani's pulse accelerated, but being a master of the blank stare, he showed no sign of the small seed of hope that had sprouted within him.

"After you killed the humans caring for the Guardians and bungled the mission to deliver them to me, the Guardians were placed in a human organization called Child Protective Services. Normally, that wouldn't have been a problem for me, but the Pleiadian scums got there first and wiped out all trace of the Three in the system. They quite effectively turned the Guardians into ghosts, and none of my political ties or anyone I've sent has been able to find out what happened to them. Not a single Dracuzian has gotten so much as a sniff of them, either."

Daher snorted in disgust. "Why the ancients didn't wipe out the Pleiadians before they left Earth millenniums ago, I'll never understand. That was definitely a mistake, but one I've made sure to rectify. I'm happy to say your fellow enforcers have eliminated all full-blooded Pleiadians on Earth, except for the three Guardian, who we know are still somewhere in the United States. We also know they're not using their given names, but that's the only information we've been able to ascertain."

He paused and stared at the glass of juice for a long-drawn-out minute, then swiveled his high-back wicker chair around to face the window. There was another long, uncomfortable silence before he spoke again.

"It's beautiful here, isn't it?" Daher didn't wait for a reply. "I must say, I've grown quite accustomed to the plush, easy lifestyle of this planet. The wealth here is almost equal to the planet, Inanna, and it's all wasted on these humans, who have no idea what they're sitting on or how rare it is. The Pleiadian dogs should be charged with high crimes and exiled from this galaxy for allowing humans to progress in their technology and weaponry to the point I now need a contingent of soldiers to take the Earth back. And I can't bring those soldiers in as long as the power grid is on and shielding the planet."

Daher suddenly swung back around and slammed his palms on the table with such force the vase, which held a single rose, tumbled over and soaked the tablecloth with water. His minions jumped but no one dared approach to clean up the mess.

"I became the richest, and thus the most powerful man on Earth, in less than a year. Because of this, humans call me a genius. A handful of them even treat me as a god, but I know they don't truly accept me as one. They only do it to gain my favor and reap the rewards. The general masses have no clue I *am* their god or that my ancestors were the ones who genetically created the *homo sapiens.*" His nostrils flared. "It's past time for me to reclaim what is rightfully mine and teach these inferior beings the truth. Every man, woman, and child on this planet should bow down on their knees and worship *me,* not those made-up mystical beings they've been duped into believing created this world."

He spoke only loud enough for Ukani to hear, but his tone held the same punch as if he were screaming.

Ukani kept his back straight, determined not to show any intimidation, as Daher's steely eyes drilled into him. But it wasn't easy. The Anunnaki were masters of the penetrating glare, like that of an eagle, which is why they were often depicted as such in ancient drawings.

"The Guardians will soon turn eighteen," Daher said, sitting back in the chair. "That's the magical age when the Child Protective System spits them out and abandons them. No one will care what happens to them or will block our way any longer ... except possibly those interloping Sons of Ea. But according to my spies, they don't know who the Guardians have become, any more than we do. That's why I brought you here. You found the Guardians before. I want you to do it again. I'm tired of this waiting game. I need that power grid turned off so I can take back this planet and return these pathetic humans to the status for which they were created—Anunnaki slaves."

Daher's words swirled inside Ukani's head, but it took what little energy he had left to stand upright, and he was having trouble putting two words together to make sense of them.

At that moment, the waiter returned with a steak the size of the plate and set it in front of Daher. Ukani swayed at the sight and smell of the rare-cooked beef. He clenched his fists as a sharp pain pierced his stomach, but he couldn't stop the saliva from leaking out the corner of his mouth and dribble down the side of his chin.

Daher picked up his knife and fork, appearing not to notice Ukani's discomfort. He cut into the steak, then hesitated, laid the utensils down, and pushed the plate across the table toward Ukani. "Sit. Eat."

The last thing Ukani intended to do was surrender and give Daher another win. But he hadn't had real food in such a long time. A low growl rumbled in the back of his throat as his hunger took over and the last of his resistance melted away. He collapsed into the chair and tore into the piece of meat with his razor-sharp teeth, stuffing as much as he could into his mouth out of fear that Daher was toying with him and would take the steak back.

Ukani emptied the plate in record time, swallowing huge bites that had barely been chewed. To his surprise, another steak miraculously appeared in front of him once he finished the first. He made it halfway through the second before his stomach, which had grown accustomed to one meager meal a day of thin porridge and stale South African mealie bread, began to protest.

Ukani swiped the back of his hand over his mouth and sat back, savoring the taste of the blood and meat that coated his tongue, as well as the knowledge that Daher must be desperate to be this generous.

He squared his shoulders but kept his face blank and looked Daher in the eyes. "Tell me what you know of the Guardians' lives."

By the time Daher finished filling Ukani in, a plan to lure the Three into the open had begun to formulate in the Dracuzian's head. The plan was a bit unconventional, but he'd learned a lot about humans in his years on Earth and he knew their weaknesses. The biggest challenge would be convincing Daher, who was more systematic, to go along with it.

Ukani rested his elbows on the table. "Just to be clear, you're saying the Three have had no Pleiadean influences and know nothing of their heritage or full potential. They've grown up thinking they're human."

Daher nodded.

Ukani's brow furrowed. "I don't see how it's possible they could have stayed hidden all these years. At some point in their lives, their inherent abilities that aren't human would have had to come out. Someone should have noticed."

"Yes, I agree," Daher replied. "Which is why I've been monitoring all social and media outlets closely, looking for signs of phenomena outside the norm, or of persons exhibiting a talent outside the limits of a human. To date, there've been no sightings or reports of any such abnormalities, which leads me to speculate they haven't fully accessed their powers yet because they haven't had anyone to train them.

"At the very least, though, *they* should be aware of their superior physical prowess," Daher added. "Why they haven't shown that to the public puzzles me and makes me think they must have completely yielded to the human philosophy and belief that anyone who's different is bad, and they're afraid of becoming outcasts."

Ukani nodded as he digested Daher words. Then his wide mouth stretched into a semblance of a smile. "That is good. Humans have two main priorities: money and power. That's what we'll use to snare them."

Ukani leaned forward as his idea solidified in his mind. His voice was rusty, but the words still gushed out.

"You've made it clear you don't want to wait. But with no leads and no Pleiadians left to gather information from, tracking the Guardians in the conventional manner could take years. So, what about this ..." He took a breath. "You produce a TV reality show and bring the Guardians to you. Reality shows are still as big as they were fifteen years ago, right?" he asked and waited for Daher to nod before he continued.

"Good. The concept of the show will be a wealthy person who's dying," Ukani lifted his hand to indicate Daher, "looking for an apprentice to run his businesses after he's gone. It's a well-known fact you have no family or heir, and also that you hate governments, so getting the humans to buy into this concept shouldn't be a problem."

Daher, clearly not following, frowned. "I don't see how a reality show or me pretending to be on death's bed is going to get the Guardians to come to us."

"The novelty of being on a TV show, plus the prize, will appeal to their human teachings and also to their age group. We'll announce the show in all the newspapers across the country and have people send in applications to be on it."

Daher cut in, "Newspapers are a thing of the past. Humans have cellphones and tablets and social media for their news now."

Ukani shrugged. "I'm out of touch with this world's current technology, but human greed has been consistent since their creation. That's not ever going to change. Your people can take care of the fine details. The announcement just needs as much exposure as possible."

He swallowed hard, knowing the next part was crucial, but also knowing it would be what Daher would have the biggest issue with.

"The key to ensuring we get the Guardians' attention will be the payout." He cleared his throat. "As I mentioned, you'll state that the winner will become your apprentice. That alone, though, won't be enough to get the results you're going to need. The prize must be something irresistible, like …" His mouth went dry and it was hard to get the next words out. "… the winner will become your sole heir and inherit your entire estate."

Daher visibly stiffened and his yellow eyes turned frostier than normal.

Ukani rushed on. "I'm not saying you'll actually have to turn anything over to them. It's just the bait we dangle out there to pique their interest. You'll have to put up some cash to pull it off right, but for someone with your wealth, it'll amount to no more than pocket change. You won't even notice a dent in your bottom line. Trust me. And any promises you make to draw the Guardians in will mean nothing once you apprehend them and become the supreme ruler of Earth."

Daher's glower stayed in place a long moment before he inclined his head for Ukani to continue. An unspoken threat remained in the air between them, though, and Ukani knew if he didn't tie things up quickly, the day could turn deadly.

Ukani shifted in his seat. "You know that humans are easily swayed and hear only what they want to hear. So, maybe we don't even have to specifically state the winner will become your heir. We just insinuate it. Then, we help start the rumors and that belief will spread like Scaxol spores on a windy day. And if, as you say, the Guardians think like every other human, they'll believe it. We'll then invite them to come on the show and the Sons of Ea won't even know what's happening."

Ukani paused to give Daher a moment to process the idea, but the Anunnaki's eyes remained hard and his face unreadable.

Several more agonizing seconds passed before Daher finally muttered, "If this plan is so irresistible to humans, there will be hundreds of thousands, if not millions of applications coming in. How do you propose picking the Guardians out of those kinds of numbers?"

Ukani breathed a silent sigh of relief. If Daher was questioning his methods, it meant he was at least contemplating the idea and not just throwing it out. He lifted his chin and his voice took on a more confident tone.

"We may not know all the changes the Guardians have gone through in the last fifteen years, but we know three things about them that cannot have changed: they have Rh null blood, blue eyes, and a March 10th birth date." He held his hand up as Daher opened his mouth. "I know that is not their true date of birth. But when I was tracking them before, I discovered the Pleiadians had put March 10th on the fake birth certificates they supplied the Smiths at adoption, which made it the official date on record. We can also put in a stipulation that we're only taking applications from eighteen-year-olds who live in the United States.

"The combination of birth date and blue eye filter will eliminate a good portion of the applications that come in. We'll also ask for blood type, even though it's obvious the Guardians don't know they have Rh null blood. If they did, you would have already found them because their names would be on a list humans keep of those with that rare blood type. But asking for blood type will still help eliminate a good number of applications. And those who leave that box blank will then be brought in to participate in a challenge designed to single out the Three."

"What kind of challenge?" Daher asked.

"I was thinking a maze or something that would require inborn Pleiadian powers to finish," Ukani said and sat back.

Daher studied his steepled fingertips as he tapped his index fingers together.

The undigested steak churned uncomfortably in Ukani's stomach as the minutes passed in silence.

"The Pleiadeans have never been interested in accumulating riches." Daher voice was so low Ukani wasn't sure if the Anunnaki was talking to himself or not. "Each one of them could have been a billionaire if they so wanted. Instead, they wasted their advanced knowledge and put it towards helping the humans progress."

Daher shifted his gaze to Ukani. "What makes you so certain the Guardians are different, and this scheme will attract them?"

Ukani hesitated to find the right words. He had no way of knowing for sure that the Three would take the bait. It seemed logical to him to assume that since they were raised as humans, their ideologies would be human. Their brains, however, were still Pleiadean, which meant their thirst for knowledge would be insatiable. They'd be seeking out the best education available and those kinds of schools in the human world were expensive. The prize money would be a quick way for them to get what they want. But still, it was pure speculation and he knew that Daher did not want to hear that.

Ukani cleared his throat. "The Guardians may have Pleiadian blood, but for the majority of their lives they've been brainwashed by a species that continually place the need for power above all else. That kind of power takes money most humans don't have.

"You stated you don't want to spend years tracking them down, so your only other option is to draw them out of hiding. This plan is the best shot at doing that in the shortest amount of time."

Daher's face was an unreadable mask as he glared at Ukani, his index fingers tapping the same rhythm as before.

Finally, after what seemed like another eternity, he turned to Tabari and gave a nod. Tabari rose without question and hurried away as Daher turned back to Ukani.

"All I can say is you better be right," Daher snarled. "The Guardians have caused me enough trouble as it is. I want this finished." He stood, placed his palms on the table, and leaned over them. "Those Three are the only ones on Earth that can shut down the power grid. Every second humans remain in control of this planet they use up and destroy more its natural resources. If I don't get Earth back soon, there'll be nothing left but a useless, barren wasteland. What good will it be to me then?"

Daher straightened his back. "I sent you to the mines the last time you failed me, yet you somehow endured. If you disappoint me again, I'll see you dropped into a live volcano, which I guarantee you won't survive. In other words … this is your final chance. Don't mess it up."

Daher's words rang through Ukani's head as the Anunnaki turned and stomped away. Once Daher and his entourage disappeared through the doorway, he too got up and walked out.

Threats were nothing new to Ukani. But what Daher didn't know was Ukani didn't care if he lived or died. He felt no allegiance to the Anunnaki either. His planet of Dracuz had been conquered by the Anunnaki centuries ago and his people had been bondsmen to them ever since. From the day he was born, he'd been a slave, the same as humans started out being—a different kind of slave, but still a slave.

He didn't need an incentive to find the Guardians, either. His reputation as the number one Elite Enforcer had been stripped from him when he failed to deliver the Three fifteen years ago. In his mind that was far worse than death.

Finding the Three was more of a matter of principle than a survival tactic, and he planned to do whatever it took. Even if that meant giving up his life to ensure the label of "failure" wouldn't be attached to his name for the rest of eternity.

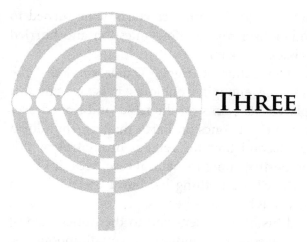

# THREE

*March 3rd*

Winter didn't seem to want to give up this year. A heavy snow had fallen overnight once again and when Sofia arrived for her morning shift, a long line of customers were already waiting not so patiently for their coffee and donuts. She quickly donned an apron and took her place behind the cash register.

Sofia knew most of the customers by name, as well as their standard order and never had trouble carrying on a casual banter about the weather and the goings-on in their small world, one that did not expand too far outside of Urbandale, Iowa. Seldom did anyone mention news of the rest of the country, but today everyone seemed to be in a buzz about a national news story that had appeared on all the media outlets.

Sweet, little, retired Louise Richardson hustled up to the counter when it was her turn and gushed, "Have you heard about *Road to Riches*, the new reality show Makin Daher is sponsoring?"

At the mention of Daher's name, Sofia's mouth filled with the taste of rotten eggs and the faintest crease appeared between her eyebrows.

Having a taste associated with a name wasn't a new sensation for her, although it usually only happened with names of people she knew, such as when someone called out her best friend's name, Maddie, she would taste bubble gum. Her soon to be ex-roommate,

Meredith, would bring on a sour taste.

"I wish I was fifty years younger," Louise went on without giving Sofia a chance to answer. "Or there had been a stranger wanting to give me a chance at a fortune like this when I was young." She leaned across the counter and lowered her voice, though she still spoke loud enough for most everyone in the vicinity to hear. "Everyone says that man is a genius, but if you ask me, he's a certifiable nut case!"

Sofia knew from experience that if she showed any sign of interest, Louise would go off on a tangent, so she just nodded.

But Louise, who seemed to be extra-excited about the news, needed no encouragement to go on. "What about you? You're eighteen now, right? Are you going to send in an application?" She cackled and waved her hand in the air. "What am I saying? Of course you are! You're such a bright girl. Do you know they're saying the winner will become Daher's heir and will get his entire fortune? Who in their right mind would pass up an opportunity like that?"

The next man in line cleared his throat loudly.

Louise ignored him and added, "I'm sure you would have no trouble at all passing the mustard, dear."

Sofia shot the man a sympathetic smile as she punched Louise's usual order into the register. "I actually hadn't heard anything about the show until I got to work this morning. But I'll be sure to check into it as soon as I get off. Did you want chocolate or glazed this morning?" she asked, hoping to move Louise along. Louise was in no hurry, though.

"Oh … umm, let's go with … hmm," Louise's mouth twisted as she thought. "I think maybe chocolate this morning." She returned to the topic of the reality show without missing a beat.

"Gosh, you'd have to think tens of thousands of people are going to want to get their hands on that money. I mean seriously, who wouldn't?" Louise gave Sofia a wink.

"They actually haven't *said* outright that the winner is going to become Mr. Daher's heir, but everyone knows that's what's going to happen." Louise's brow crinkled. "That's why I don't really understand why he's put such a strict age limit on it. I mean, what eighteen-year-old knows how to handle that kind of money? It wouldn't surprise me one bit if the winner goes off and throws a big party and wastes every cent of it on souped-up cars and big fancy mansions. Ooo ... I wonder if the Daher mansions go to the winner too?"

"I'm certain Mr. Daher knows what he's doing and has a reason for it." Sofia glanced at the ever-increasing line as she pushed the donut at Louise. "Your coffee will be right up, Mrs. Richardson."

Sofia turned her smile on the man next in line. "What can I get you, sir?"

Undeterred, Louise took a step back and waited for the man to give his order before continuing. "You, of course, aren't like most other young people. You'd be smarter than that. You *are* going to send in an application, aren't you?"

Sofia smiled at Louise as she handed the man his receipt. "I'll certainly look into it, Mrs. Richardson. Have a nice day now," she said with a hint of finality in her voice and turned to the next customer in line.

⌰⊁⍀⊀⎐⏃⎐⌇

Sofia shivered as much from anxiety as from the icy wind as she waited for the stoplight to turn green. It seemed the majority of customers had wanted to discuss the Road to Riches show and she wasn't able to get out of the coffee shop until well past her usual time. To make matters worse, the sidewalks were too icy to run on, and she could feel the hands of the clock inching toward 8:00 a.m. with each cautious step she took.

Of all days to be late, too, it had to be on a day that her first-hour class was AP calculus. The teacher, Mr. Gates, was a stickler for students being on time. He'd warned her the last time she'd come in after the bell that if it happened again, he would take points off her grade. She didn't know if he would actually carry through with the threat since she was the top student in the class, but she couldn't afford to test him. She was counting on the college credits this class gave her.

Keeping her eyes on the ground, she walked as fast as she could and was approaching the portico at the school entrance when she sensed Maddie coming up fast behind her. A few seconds later, a cell phone appeared in front of her face.

"Ohmigod, have you heard?" Maddie squealed, waggling the phone.

Sofia caught a glimpse of Makin Daher's stern face on the screen as she pushed Maddie's arm aside. *Oh God, not you too.*

"I'm going to be the next billionaire! But don't worry, I'll share … with you, anyway." Maddie ignored Sofia's sour look and prattled on breathlessly as she matched Sofia's pace. "We'll have matching mansions, or better yet … matching yachts. Wouldn't that be so cool?" She let out an exaggerated sigh and linked her arm through Sofia's to slow her down. "Can you even imagine someone handing you over a fortune like that?"

Sofia was not in the mood to hear any more talk about some stupid reality show. "Nothing is free, Maddie. Your chance of getting that money is about the same as me making the swim team."

"You can't say that. You don't know," Maddie replied undaunted. "And besides, that's a totally horrible comparison. You don't know how to swim and you're scared of water, so there's no possibility you'd ever get on the swim team."

Sofia rolled her eyes. Maddie had been her best friend since Sofia moved to Urbandale High the beginning of junior year, and that was saying a lot. She usually didn't let her guard down enough to make even casual friends. But though she cared deeply for Maddie, she didn't have time for scatterbrain dreams at the moment, which Maddie always had in abundance.

Sofia walked a little faster. "Exactly … I'll never get on the swim team, and you'll never become Daher's heir."

"Heir?" Maddie let out another squeal. "I didn't hear the winner would become his heir. That's even better! And I have as good a chance as anyone else. There can't be *that* many eighteen-year-olds in the U.S., so … the odds are with me."

Sofia didn't slow down. "There are 30.6 million people between the ages of eighteen and twenty-one according to the most recent census data."

Maddie huffed. "How do you even know stuff like that?"

The sound of the bell cut off Sofia's response.

She flinched, pulled her arm free, and barked, "So help me God, if you've gotten me in trouble with Mr. Gates, I'll never talk to you again!"

She bolted through the doors and ran down the nearly vacant

hall to the sounds of her backpack bouncing against her back and the soles of her wet Walmart brand tennis shoes squeaking on the tile floor.

At the door to the classroom, she tentatively peered through the small, square window before she pushed the door open and slipped inside. Mr. Gates had not yet arrived, which was out of the ordinary, but a lucky break for her. She slid into a seat at the back of the room with a sigh of relief and a silent thank you to the heavens.

Several minutes later, Mr. Gates rushed in, red in the face and calling for everyone to be quiet as he made his way to the front of the room.

"Please turn to chapter fifteen," he stated over his shoulder as he hastily scribbled an equation on the whiteboard before turning to face the class. He looked out over the top of his glasses, which were sitting low on his nose, and snapped the cap back on the marker.

"The derivative of a function $f$ is given by this equation." He swung his arm toward the whiteboard. "Who can tell me on what intervals $f$ is decreasing here?"

A girl in the front row immediately raised her hand. "Have you heard Makin Daher is putting on a reality show and some eighteen-year-old is going to get all of his billions?"

The class erupted in a surge of excited whispers and a few giggles.

Mr. Gates placed his hands on his desk and leaned forward. Though his expression didn't change, the girl's excitement quickly slid off her face.

"You, Ms. Brown, are an honor student, as is everyone in this room. That being said, I'd like to think each one of you is smart enough to realize your chances of winning this *said* billion dollars—he added air-quotes around the word *said*—are only slightly better than that of winning the Powerball jackpot. And I know you are well aware of those odds since we've previously covered that topic.

Mr. Gates walked out from behind his desk. "I'd also like to think that you and your fellow classmates will be spending your time and energy on getting into the right college, which will give you the knowledge needed to make your own millions, and not on some ludicrous scavenger hunt looking for sunken treasure."

An audible intake of breath and a buzz of murmurs circulated the room at the mention of a sunken treasure.

A boy in the third row piped up, "Is that one of the challenges Daher's putting in the show?"

Mr. Gates's dark gaze drilled into the boy, then slowly moved around the room student by student, pausing an extra moment when he came to Sofia. He then snorted and shook his head in disgust.

"There'll be no more talk of Daher or any game show in this classroom. And let me add, you'll all be wise to put this matter out of your heads for good. Now … who can tell me on what intervals is $f$ decreasing?"

Sofia's hand was the only one to shoot into the air.

When the second the bell rang at the end of the ninety minutes, the students hastily rose from their desks and rushed out of the room as if someone had released a cage of rattlesnakes.

Above the buzz of talk on the chances of getting on the show, Mr. Gates called, "Sofia, I need to speak with you a moment."

Sofia's stomach sank and her hand stalled in mid-air as she went to lift her backpack onto her shoulder. How in the world had Mr. Gates found out she was late?

She blew out a weary sigh and shuffled to the large desk at the front of the room. At times like these she wished she could be more like Maddie, who could spew out an excuse for anything on the spur of the moment. She, on the other hand, couldn't pull off a lie to save her life.

She stood in front of the desk, nervously shifting from one foot to the other as the last of the students filed out and Mr. Gates finished writing in a lesson planner.

Once the door snapped shut, he set his pen down and pulled an envelope out from under the book.

"This arrived in yesterday's afternoon mail. The office asked me to deliver it to you this morning."

The high school's administration had granted Sofia permission to use the school's address on her college applications due to the atypical circumstance of not knowing where she would be living once she turned eighteen. Her gaze went straight to the Massachusetts Institute of Technology logo in the top left-hand corner.

In less than a heartbeat, the worry of being kicked out of class was replaced with a new anxiety—what was inside the envelope?

The tightness in Sofia's stomach moved into her chest. She felt faint.

She had set her mind on MIT back in middle school and had since talked herself into believing her whole future depended on getting into this particular prestigious school. She looked up at Mr. Gates for an encouraging smile, but with more than five decades of practice, he had mastered the ability to never show emotion. Even when the tone of his voice made it clear he was frustrated with a student or furious with the class, his face was a blank mask, as it was now.

She tentatively reached out for the envelope and ran her tongue around her mouth to bring back the moisture that had all but vanished. But her salivary glands flat out refused to go to work and her mouth remained as dry as Nana Miller's crumbly cornbread.

Her hand trembled as she took a letter opener from Mr. Gates, and her fingers were all thumbs as she ran the thin piece of metal under the flap. It took another bit of fumbling for her to get the sheet of paper out. She then took a deep breath, steeled her back, and unfolded the letter.

*Dear Ms. Kaye,*

*On behalf of the Admissions Committee, it is my pleasure to offer you admission to the Massachusetts Institute of Technology for the fall semester.*

That was as far as she got before the words blurred together. She had waited so long to see those words on paper and for a moment she forgot to breathe. But though her heart was near to bursting with joy, her stomach was still clenched tight.

She still had one more hurdle to get over to fulfill her dream and it was just as big a one as the acceptance was, if not bigger. Since she had no college fund set aside for her, she needed MIT to give her a full-ride scholarship from their endowments or the acceptance would do her no good.

She blinked rapidly to clear her vision and quickly scanned the rest of the letter, stopping at the financial aid paragraph. The amount of tuition help they offered was a hefty amount, but it was still twenty-five thousand dollars short of what she would need. Even if she got every other scholarship she had applied for, it wouldn't add up to the required amount.

Sofia put her hand on the desk to steady herself as a powder keg of emotion imploded in her chest.

At the same moment, a pile of folders stacked on a filing cabinet behind Mr. Gates tipped over and homework assignments scattered all over the floor.

As Mr. Gates stooped to collect the papers, she hastily stuffed the letter into the side pocket of her backpack and bent to help.

"Sofia," Mr. Gates said in a tone that caused her hand to pause. "I know going to MIT was extremely important to you."

She sucked her bottom lip in through her teeth and bit down hard. He had no way of knowing how important MIT was to her. Or how desperate she was to be free of the stigma of being someone no one wanted.

"I know your GPA and qualifications are more than enough to get you into that school, so I'm going to take a wild guess by your reaction and say you didn't get the full ride you were hoping for."

He hesitated for her acknowledgement, but she gave nothing away.

"I understand you may think this is the end of the world, but I'd like to point out there are other far less expensive schools that offer an excellent education. I'm sure you're already aware of that, but what you may not know is the potential I see in you. I believe you can become a game-changer as long as you don't give up hope. Or worse … go off on some half-baked treasure hunt in hopes of getting the money you need. The Daher fortune may be tempting and sound like the solution to all your financial woes, but I've always found that if something sounds too good to be true, it usually is."

Once the last few papers had been gathered, Sofia stood, hoping Mr. Gates couldn't tell her knees were wobbling.

Mr. Gates studied Sofia as he arranged the papers into an orderly pile again. "Mr. Daher has a notorious reputation as a narcissist and an unscrupulous man. Most people who have had dealings with him have come out on the short end. I believe this new venture will turn out to be the same, and I fear the price the winner will pay will exceed any monetary reward they receive."

"I don't have any desire to be a contestant on any TV show,

if that's what you're worried about, Mr. Gates," Sofia said, then internally grimaced at the raspiness of her voice.

Mr. Gates sat down in his chair and narrowed his eyes at Sofia's bent head as if trying to read her thoughts. "I'm happy to hear that. Please let me know if there's anything I can do to help you sort through your college options."

He picked up his pen and opened his planner, which she knew meant she was dismissed.

"Yes, sir. Thank you again, sir," she mumbled and hustled out of the room, elbowing her way through the crowded hall to the girl's bathroom. There, she collapsed on the floor in the back corner, hugged her knees and rocked back and forth.

She had always been a fighter. One had to be to survive the foster care system. But there was a limit to how much disappointment one person could handle, even her. She clenched the stone pendant that hung on a chain around her neck, placed her forehead on her knees, and gave in to the tornado of emotions whirling inside her. She didn't cry any tears, though. That was another freaky thing about her that set her apart from everyone else—her eyes didn't produce tears. Instead, her nose would run like a facet and turn bright red, which was far worse than puffy red eyes.

She allowed herself to mourn exactly sixty seconds, then wiped the back of her hand across her drippy nose and tilted her head back to stare up at the ceiling.

"You're *not* going to break me. I'm going to find a way to go to MIT, so you can just go and screw with someone else's life," she whispered forcibly to the invisible entity that seemed to be controlling her life.

That was her belief anyway. No one could have as much bad luck as she'd had unless someone or something was intentionally jerking her around. Or she was just plain cursed. Either way, she wasn't going to lose this time. Not without putting up a fight anyway.

⏂⚹⊠⟍⊽⫙⫙⟍⫚⫙⫚⟍

The cafeteria was already packed by the time Sofia walked in, but she knew Maddie would have gotten there early and secured a spot for their little group just like always. She wove her way through the rows of tables, keeping her head down to hide her red nose, and ignored the calls of, "Hey Rudolph."

She wiggled in between Maddie and Benjamin, the token boy in their group. Chloe and Bella, two other misfit girls that had no one else to hang out with, were alternately rattling off information they had found on their phones about the Road to Riches show.

"… must be eighteen by March 30th to be eligible," Chloe read.

"Chosen candidates will need to be available for an extended competition in which they'll show their forward thinking, versatility, problem solving, and strength," Bella added, reading on.

"I wonder what that means?" Maddie cut in. "An extended competition?"

"Probably, like every other reality show that's ever been on, they'll have the people go through a bunch of different tests and challenges," Bella said. "From what it says here, the winners could be tied up for weeks … maybe even months."

"That's okay with me," Maddie said. "Spending a couple months to become an heir to billions … piece of cake."

Sofia snorted. "Yeah, well that's one more reason why I'm out."

"What?" Maddie turned in her seat. "You're joking. Right?"

Sofia shook her head.

Maddie's face scrunched up as if Sofia had just told her she was dropping out of school. "Nooo! You *have* to apply for this. You're the smartest, most creative person I know. Out of all of us, you have the best shot of being chosen. And I don't want to do this without you. Come oonnn … do this with me, pleeease," Maddie pleaded.

"Oh, for the love of God, will you just stop already!" Sofia shouted, slamming the palms of her hands on the table.

The whole room went silent for a few seconds. Then the light above the table gave a soft pop and went out. The shocked look on Maddie's face quickly turned to hurt and Sofia's anger faded as suddenly as it had come.

She looked down at her hands. "I'm sorry. I'm … I just got my acceptance letter from MIT."

An eruption of grasps sounded around the table, but instantly died when Sofia looked up.

"I didn't get a full ride, so I won't be able to go unless I get other scholarships and grants to fill in the rest of the money." Her voice was hoarse with emotion. "I'm going to have to ask for extra hours at work, too. Or maybe get a second job. So, for sure, the last thing I can afford to do is go off for weeks on some wild goose chase."

She took in a deep breath. "I *won't* let them take MIT away from me. It's my dream, and the only way I'm ever going to get out of here and make something of myself."

"Oh, hon, I'm *sooo* sorry. I know how much you were counting on going there," Maddie said sympathetically, then brightened. "But don't you see? If you're named Daher's heir, you'd be able to afford MIT or any other college you wanted."

Sofia opened her mouth, but Maddie rattled on before she could spit out her objections.

"Seriously, just listen for sec. Filling out an application's not gonna take much of your time or keep you from work or applying for more scholarships. As far as the taking time off … you don't have to worry about that unless you're selected. And who knows, by then things could be different. So really, what you can't afford to do is to let this opportunity slip through your hands."

Maddie placed her hand on Sofia's arm, batted her eyes innocently, and pursed her full lips into a pout, which Sofia knew was her technique to get what she wanted. And though it worked most of the time, it always cracked Sofia up. She covered her mouth with a napkin and feigned a cough to keep from laughing out loud, but Maddie wasn't fooled.

"Laugh all you want. We'll see who's laughing when I'm rolling in money because I put in my application!" Maddie said indignantly as she removed her hand and turned back to her lunch.

"I'm sorry. I wasn't laughing at you."

Maddie shot Sofia a sideways glare.

"I was laughing at the ridiculousness of this whole thing. I mean, seriously … what billionaire gives away all his money? That kind of stuff only happens in the movies. I'll betcha in the end it's gonna come out that this was all just one big publicity stunt."

Maddie blew out a loud breath. "Why do you have to be so cynical all the time? It wouldn't be all over national news if it weren't for real."

"I'm not being cynical. I'm being practical," Sofia shot back in defense. Then added in a gentler tone, "You're the dreamer, I'm the pragmatist. If you want to waste your time sending in an application, then you definitely should. And that'll cover me too, 'cause you already said you were going to share with me." She flashed Maddie a grin.

"Ooo, you guys," Bella cut in. "I was just looking through the application. It wants a photo and your blood-type. That's kinda weird. Why would they want that?"

Maddie and Chloe both turned toward Bella and leaned over her arm to see the application for themselves.

Sofia rolled her eyes to the ceiling and turned to Benjamin, whom she assumed was on her side about the heir scam since he hadn't piped in. To her surprise, he got up and rushed around the table to look over Bella's shoulder with the others.

Sofia shook her head and picked up her peanut butter and honey sandwich. "The whole flippin' world has gone crazy!"

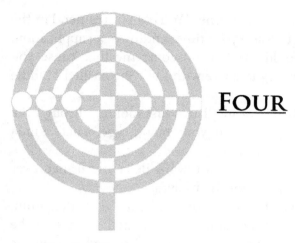

# FOUR

*March 10th*

S ofia lay on her bed and watched the illuminated numbers on the clock sitting on the chest by the bedroom door tick off one by one. When they flipped over to midnight, the official start of her birthday, her heart stalled for a second.

This was it. The big one-eight. The day that marked the end of three-square meals a day and a place to live. She rolled onto her back and stuffed her fist in her mouth to hold back the scream building in her throat.

A crack opened in the middle of the water stain above her head and snaked across the ceiling to the opposite wall.

Why couldn't she be like all the other kids? She'd been trying hard her whole life to be normal, but it was now time to face facts—she wasn't normal and never would be. The kids in one of her old elementary schools used to say she was a witch. Maybe they were right. Maybe that was why bad things kept happening to her. And maybe she deserved all of it.

Sofia shook her head and sniffed back her drippy nose. Things would be different once she got to MIT. *If* she got to MIT. She still had to make it through the next five months and get at least one of the grants she'd applied for. But then she would ditch this place and her horrific past for good.

*Five months. That's really not that long. I can do it,* she told herself, as she had so many times before.

When the numbers on the clock read 3:00, she rolled to her side and silently jumped down from her bunk. There was no point in staying in bed any longer when she knew sleep was not going to come. She dressed in the dark and didn't look back as she walked out of the house and that chapter of her life forever.

The sparkling snow that had mesmerized Sofia two days earlier had been transformed into a black, gritty field of ice by foot traffic and car exhaust. It matched her mood perfectly and crunched under her boots like glass shards as she lumbered to the park one last time, lugging a black trash bag filled with all her earthly possessions.

She deposited the bag on the merry-go-round and collapsed next to it, pressing her back onto the cold metal. She had packed her few meager belongings last night before Meredith got home in order to avoid the unpleasantness of a fight over whose stuff was whose. She didn't really have anything of value other than her stone pendant, which she doubted anybody would want but her, but Meredith loved to mess with her, and she couldn't take the risk of losing what little she had left.

A twinge of guilt for slipping out of the house before the Millers got up laid heavy in the pit of Sofia's stomach. Nana and Poppo had been good to her over the last two years. Better than any of the other foster parents she'd ever had, anyway, and she hated the thought they'd think she was an ungrateful little snot for sneaking away in the dead of the night. She had to, though. She detested the "G" word and couldn't bear going through another fake emotional departure scene. She'd had enough of those to last her ten lifetimes already. She did appreciate the Millers, though, and to show them she made a DVD of one of her dances she'd choreographed to the Rihanna song, *Farewell*. She'd left it on the counter next to the coffeepot, along with a thank you note, and hoped it would be enough because she didn't have anything else in her to give.

A part of Sofia understood that the Millers' decision to turn her out wasn't totally their fault. They were on a limited budget and dependent on the money they received from foster care to supplement their income. Another part of her, though, couldn't help but feel if they really cared about her as much as they claimed, they could have at least let her crash on the sofa through the few remaining months until college started instead of kicking her out to fend for herself on the streets.

Sofia stared up at the constellation, but neither the stars nor the usual haunting notes of *Rhapsody on a Theme of Paganini* that instantly filled her head could penetrate the deep depression that had settled over her. Her gaze automatically moved to a star that sat above and to the left of the brightest of the Seven Sisters. Not many people could pick it out of the haze of the constellation without a telescope, but she could.

"Are you really out there?" she whispered to the air.

She had asked that question a thousand times over the years—mostly directed toward her biological parents, sometimes toward other civilizations in the galaxy. Tonight, the question was for her parents. She wanted to believe they had given her away for a good reason—a tragic incident or special circumstance that had forced their hand. She felt sure if she could just figure out what that catalyst had been, she'd be able to find them. And she really wanted to find them, because now more than ever, she needed someone to care.

The starlight suddenly blurred into a big fuzzy glob. She had struggled to survive for so long and she was so very tired of fighting. On top of that, she hadn't slept a wink all night, so her eyelids felt like lead and she was just plain tired of her life. She squeezed her lids together to give her eyes a moment of relief.

The next thing Sofia knew, her pocket was vibrating.

She jerked and her eyes sprung open wide. The grogginess in her brain took a moment to clear before she realized where she was. Without rising, she wrangled her phone out of her coat pocket and stared at the time on the screen. It showed 5:03. She sighed and dropped it beside her on the merry-go-round.

She'd always considered herself an optimist through and through, but at the moment it was hard to see anything good with the brown cloud of homelessness hanging over her head. She bit down on her trembling bottom lip and squeezed her eyelids tightly together again.

A bright flash exploded behind her eyes and a sharp pain pierced the back of her head. She sat up with a gasp and pressed her fingers into the nape of her neck, then froze as the number 03032003 appeared in front of her.

She had learned a long time ago she had a neurological

condition called synesthesia. It was the reason certain names had a taste associated with them and she heard music in her head whenever she looked up at the stars. It was also why she saw different colors when specific instruments played. Another part of that condition made numbers, as well as the days of the week and the months of the year, appear in front of her as three-dimensional images. Whenever a number was spoken out loud, or even when she thought about one, she would see the number in its own specific spot on a spatial "map" around her body.

The strange thing was, Sofia had not been thinking about numbers. And seeing them had never caused her pain like this before.

Adding to the weirdness, the number wasn't where it should have been on the "map," but was twisted into a spiral cone, each number growing smaller as the spiral went down. The number also wasn't white on a dark navy background, which was how numbers usually appeared to her. Instead, these numerals were a neon purple color except for the threes, which were bright red. And the first number three was stretched out vertically twice the size of the others.

She blinked rapidly and shook her head to set them right. All that did was intensify the pain in the back of her head and made it throb twice as hard.

Just when she thought her head was going to explode, her phone buzzed and rattled on the cold metal. She flinched.

Another flash lit up the back of her eyes and the numbers vanished along with the pain.

"Ohmigod," she breathed, sending a white cloud of breath into the air as she gingerly touched the back of her head.

The spot felt hot even though her hair was stiff with cold, but it wasn't the least bit tender now.

*Shit! I'm losing my frickin' mind.* She lifted the collar of her coat up around her ears and tilted her head back to look up at her star— the only consistent thing in her life.

"You're all I've got left now. Please, don't you leave me too."

Sofia sadly gazed around the playground, knowing it was the last time she would be coming here. The peeling paint on the jungle gym, rust-colored stains on the slides, and the swing seat with one side hanging to the ground from a broken chain looked as desolate as she felt.

"Happy birthday to me," she whispered as she listlessly pushed herself to her feet. She picked up her phone and stuffed it back into her pocket. Then, she hefted the trash bag over her shoulder and trudged off toward the Dunkin Donuts, trying not to think about all that she had lost.

# FIVE

*April 30th*

Sofia's phone vibrated in her pocket with an incoming text, but her hands were occupied with a tray of fresh donuts that she was adding to the display case. Friday nights were typically busy in the donut shop, with people coming in to stock up for the weekend. This night was no different. By the time she finally got a second to check the message from Maddie, it was almost closing time.

*Come over to the food court when you get off,* the text read.

Sofia dropped her chin to her chest and sighed. Most every other senior in the school had chosen to slack off their final semester before graduation. But that wasn't Sofia's style. Instead of playing and enjoying the camaraderie of those she'd roamed the halls with and would most likely never see again, she had signed up for every AP class available to rack up extra credits for college. She'd also added an extra shift at the Dunkin Donuts four days a week after school on top of her six-days-a-week early morning hours. That, coupled with her heavy load of homework and the dance classes she taught at a local dance studio on Saturday mornings, didn't leave much time for sleep. She'd really been looking forward to just going home and crashing.

But her current "home" was Maddie's house, so there was no way she could say no.

She let her head fall back and stared at the ceiling, longing for the day she wouldn't have to be dependent on others. She hated being an imposition to everyone in her life, and though her friends insisted she wasn't, she knew she was. She could feel it. Though she tried to stay away from the house as much as possible, and whenever she was there, she did what she could to help out, the old saying, "Guests, like fish, start to smell after three days" ran in a constant loop inside her head. She could only imagine by the end of summer she'd have no friends left at all.

Thankfully, Sofia's co-workers offered to close up the shop for her, so she was able to leave earlier than usual. As she staggered down the few blocks to the mall, she prayed Maddie would also take pity on her and let her skip out on whatever plans had been put together for the rest of the evening.

The food court was packed with teenagers as it typically was on a weekend night. The noise of everyone talking over each other and trying to be heard above the music blaring through the speakers pounded in Sofia's head as her stomach rumbled from the combination of savory smells coming from the rows of fast-food stands. She had studied through her dinner break instead of eating, and the buzz she'd gotten from a coffee and donut she'd had for breakfast had long since worn off. She needed real food, but she was too cheap to spend money on it.

Maddie and the group, which included Bella's newest boyfriend, were sitting at a table across from the candy shop. For two seconds, Sofia thought about turning around and walking away, but Maddie caught a glimpse of her and waved her over before she had the chance. Sofia's shoulders drooped under the weight of her backpack, which suddenly felt like it weighed a hundred pounds, and her feet dragged as she wove her way through the crowd.

As if on cue, the second Sofia dropped down on the empty chair next to Maddie, the chatter at the table ceased and everyone suddenly became intently interested in their phones. Any other time that would have set off alarms that something was up, but tonight their odd behavior barely even registered in Sofia's tired brain.

Maddie bounced around in her seat and asked in a voice that was a little too sweet, "So, how was your day?"

Sofia sat up straighter and swallowed hard as she watched

Maddie's mouth curl into the all-too-familiar smile she used when she wanted to manipulate people.

"It was fine," she hesitantly replied.

"Gosh, I don't know how you do it. School … working so much." Maddie interlaced her fingers on top of an envelope lying on the table in front of her and glanced over at Chloe, who nodded, as if to say, "Go on."

"I, um …" Maddie paused, as if trying to get up the courage to utter the next words.

A memory of the weird way Maddie's mom had acted that morning flew into Sofia's mind, and the permanent invisible band around her chest tightened a little bit more.

Maddie reached out and put a hand on top of Sofia's.

Sofia's breath caught in her throat.

"Please remember that I love you, and I only ever have your best interests at heart," Maddie said.

*Oh God.*

"This came in the mail for you yesterday." Maddie tipped her head toward the envelope as she slid it toward Sofia. "It's from the law firm that's handling the Road to Riches show."

Sofia blinked, not following what Maddie was saying. She looked around the table for clarification, but the other four silently stared back at her with the same anxious expression that was on Maddie's face.

"When we all filled out our application, I sorta filled one out for you too," Maddie said, giving Sofia's hand a squeeze. "None of the rest of us have gotten a reply back. Just you. So, we think maybe you've been selected."

Still not following, Sofia looked down at the envelope. Her gaze moved from her name to the printed logo of the law firm of Conway and Vik in the top left corner. The crease in her brow deepened.

"Open it!" Chloe shrieked. "We've all been dying to know what it says."

Little by little the realization that Maddie wasn't going to kick her out of the house as Sofia feared began to sink in. She looked up at her friends, their faces pale with guilt, and suddenly, the truth hit her.

*Ohmigod!*

"You sent in my name without my permission?" she asked to verify the facts.

"I know we …" Maddie darted a look at her friends, then looked back. "*I* should have asked, but I was afraid you'd say no. And you of all people need this more than anyone else. It just didn't seem fair to leave you out."

Sofia pulled her hand out from under Maddie's. "If I recall, I specifically told you I didn't have time to mess with this stupid scam."

Bella piped in: "It's not a scam. It's all over national news and social media."

"Come on, Sofia, Maddie was only trying to help," Benjamin added.

"I really was," Maddie gushed to confirm her motives. "You've been stressing out about getting enough money to go to MIT. It makes me tired just watching you kill yourself working all these extra hours on top of the extra classes you're taking to make that happen. I only wanted to give you a chance to get what you wanted for a change. Please don't be mad."

Sofia knew she should be mad that Maddie went behind her back, but compared to being kicked out on the street again, having an application for a reality show put in in her name was barely a blip in her life. She closed her eyes, inhaled deeply, and swallowed the lump of relief that clogged her throat. When she looked up again and saw the nervous expressions around the table, it was all she could do to keep from laughing out loud.

She cleared her throat. "I'm not mad." She then squared her shoulders and lifted her chin. "But if you *ever* do anything like this again, I swear I'll strangle each and every one of you. And I'm not kidding. This was so not cool."

She tried to hold a stern look, but the sense of relief coursing through her wouldn't let it stick.

Maddie let out a small squeal and threw her arms around Sofia's shoulders. "I just knew you would understand." She pulled back. "Now, open it so we can see what it says!"

Sofia looked down at the envelope. She was a little curious about what was inside herself, but she'd never admit that to her friends. She hesitantly picked the envelope up. A tingle ran through her fingertips and up her arms. She sucked in a breath, then very slowly turned the envelope over, slid her thumb under the flap, and moved it across to slit the top.

"Ohmigod, come on! You're killing me," Chloe exclaimed, her excitement bubbling out of her.

Sofia pressed her lips together to hide her smile. She wasn't intentionally trying to torture them, but she didn't mind knowing that she was. They so deserved it.

Keeping that thought in mind, she leisurely pulled out the letter and unfolded it. Inside was a first-class airline ticket, which she hardly gave a second glance to, as a strange, glowing purple symbol in the top left corner of the letterhead grabbed her attention. The symbol had a similar look and shape as the tattoo on her left shoulder blade.

The smile tugging at the corner of Sofia's mouth slipped away.

The design had come to her in a dream one night and reminded her of a large pinwheel-type lollipop, the kind she always wanted as a kid but never got. It had stuck in her head, and when Maddie offered to pay for a tattoo for her eighteenth birthday, she knew that was exactly what she would get.

"What's it say?" Bella asked leaning halfway over the table.

Maddie pushed down on Sofia's hand and stuck her nose in to read the letter. A moment later, she let out a squeal, grabbed the airline ticket, and held it up for all to see.

"She's made it to the first round of the challenges! They're flying her first-class to Nice, France, on June 22nd."

The cry that erupted around the table jolted Sofia out of her trance. She tore her gaze away from the symbol and looked up in surprise.

Everyone was talking at once and throwing out questions faster than she could comprehend. But her head was full of her own questions: Why did the symbol look so much like her tattoo? And why did it fill her with an intense feeling of homesickness?

Maddie threw her arms around Sofia again. "You know I had a really good feeling about this when I sent in your application. I just knew it was finally going to be your time! I'm so happy for you. A little jealous maybe too. But if this could only happen to one of us, you deserve it the most."

Sofia's brow creased in confusion. She had no idea what Maddie was talking about. Looking down at the letter, she hurriedly skimmed the lines of the first paragraph. When she looked up again, her face was even paler than usual.

"They want me to go to France." As soon as she said the words out loud, a tug-of-war started within her between wanting to go and knowing it wasn't logical to run off on a vacation when she still didn't have enough money for college.

"We know! It's so wonderful," Bella said. "I've *always* wanted to go to France. It's the most romantic country in the world, you know," she added, smiling flirtatiously up at her boyfriend.

Sofia slowly shook her head from side to side. "I can't go."

The excitement at the table died as abruptly as if a cone of silence had been dropped over them.

"Sure, it'd be awesome if this really was a solution to my problems. But it's not," her voice cracked. "It's a pipe dream. No one's gonna make a worthless foster kid like me their heir. So taking off work would be a huge waste of my time, not to mention I'd lose out on all my wages while I was gone."

A hint of disappointment gripped her as she those words came out of her mouth. She pushed it aside, swallowed hard, and turned to Maddie, who was staring at her as if she had lost her mind.

"I appreciate what you tried to do. You've been looking out for me ever since I got here, and I love you for that. But you of all people know how much going to MIT means to me. I can't give up on that and go traipsing around the world no matter how fun it sounds. You understand, don't you?"

Before Maddie could answer, Chloe cut in. "You can't be serious."

"Stop being a fuckin' moron, Sofia," Benjamin added. "This is a once-in-a-lifetime proposition. Taking a month off doesn't mean you can't still go to college." Benjamin's tone was harsher than Sofia had ever heard him use before. "Worst-case scenario is you don't start til the winter semester. That's not a game-changer. But going to France might be. Shit, I'd give my left nut for an opportunity like this. Everyone else in this room would too, and you're just going to throw it away? Come on … I know you're smarter than that. Or I thought you were anyway."

Sofia winced as his stinging words slammed into her brain. Next to her, he was the smartest one in their group and she'd thought he'd understand the most out of all of them since his college finances were just as uncertain as hers. It hurt that he wasn't siding with her. But what bothered her even more was knowing what he said held a measure of truth.

"Benjamin's right," Maddie gushed, jumping on his point. "No one in their right mind would turn this down. You think you aren't gonna win, but look … you've already made it farther than the rest of us. I have faith in you. We all do." She looked around at the others for support.

They all quickly nodded their heads in agreement.

Sofia pressed her fingernails into the flesh of her palms to hold back the tidal wave of emotions rolling through her. Her brain was telling her it would be a waste of time, but she couldn't shake the feeling that she really needed to do this.

Mental and physical exhaustion crashed down on her all at once and it was suddenly hard for her to even stay upright. She dropped her head into her hands.

"I don't want to talk about this right now. I'm so tired I can't even think."

Maddie perked up. "Does that mean you'll be willing to consider it later?"

Sofia blew out a weary sigh, knowing Maddie wouldn't let it go until she relented. "I'll *think* about it after I get some sleep."

Excited exclamations erupted around the table again.

Chloe, barely able to hold it together, asked, "What does the letter say about the competitions?"

Maddie tugged the letter out from under Sofia's elbow and started reading it out loud to the others.

Sofia raised her head and caught sight of a little girl with a big pink bow tied around her ponytail and wearing a faux fur coat walk by. The girl, maybe five or six-years-old, was licking a pinwheel lollipop bigger than her fist.

An icy prickle ran along the back of Sofia's neck as she watched the girl, or actually the lollipop, walk to the exit doors and disappear.

Sofia wasn't a believer in coincidences, but if this wasn't a coincidence, the lollipop symbol on the letter and now a lollipop just like it showing up, then what was it? A sign she was supposed to participate in this heir search?

The longing she had felt in her chest intensified. She looked back at her friends, who were all huddled around Bella and her phone, oohing and ahhing over pictures of Daher's villa on the coast of Saint-Jean-Cap-Ferrat, France.

"You've got to come see this place," Chloe said, motioning for Sofia to join them. "It says on Google it's the most expensive house in the world."

Sofia ignored Chloe, picked up the letter Maddie had dropped on the table, and stared at the symbol.

"Have any of you guys seen this symbol before?" she asked, pointing to the corner of the page.

All eyes turned to the letter for a split second before going back to Bella's phone.

"What symbol?" Maddie asked indifferently, her eyes rounding at a photo of a bedroom with powder-blue-damask-covered walls and an elegant canopy bed with yards of heavy fabric draping down the four corner posts.

"This one." Sofia tapped the corner of the letter impatiently.

Again, five sets of eyes turned to look.

"The lawyer's logo?" Chloe asked.

"No, not that. This glowing lollipop thing that sorta looks like the tattoo on my back." Sofia put her finger on the center of the symbol.

Maddie's gaze moved from Sofia's finger to her face. "All I see is the law firm's name and address and it doesn't look anything like your tattoo."

"Nooo, I'm not talking about the lawyer stuff. I'm talkin' about the symbol behind it. The purplish ..." Sofia's words trailed off as a concerned look crossed every one of her friends' faces.

She had discovered years ago she could see light and colors others couldn't, but this symbol was so blatantly obvious, how could they not see it?

*Holy shit!* She dropped her head into her hands again and massaged her temples with her thumbs. *Is this it? Have I finally lost my frickin' mind?*

"It's okay, sweetie. You've been working so hard. You're probably just overtired." Maddie gently pulled the letter back and resumed reading it out loud.

With a dozen questions bouncing around inside Sofia's mind, she paid no attention to what Maddie was reading. But when she heard a squeal of, "Omigod," she looked up to find her friends staring at her excitedly again.

Her stomach dropped. "What?"

"Didn't you just hear what Maddie read?" Bella exclaimed. "You're going to get ten thousand dollars for just showing up! That's like three times more than what you'd make working all summer. It looks like Maddie was right all along! This really is your lucky break. And now you have no reason to turn it down!"

Sofia started as the number 10,000 appeared in the air on her left side just above her head, her synesthesia at work again.

At the same moment, Mr. Gates's words of warning also popped into her head: *If something sounds too good to be true, it usually is.*

She opened her mouth to ask to see the letter.

Before she could get the words out, Maddie, who had been silently reading on, exclaimed, "Oh no!"

Sofia's stomach took another nosedive.

"It says you can't tell anyone except your immediate family that you've been chosen as a candidate. If you tell anyone else or the media gets wind that you've been selected, the invitation will be rescinded and the airline ticket will be voided." Maddie looked up, her eyes wide and overbright. "I think we might have just ruined this for you."

"That's ridiculous," Benjamin said. "Why would that matter?" He pulled the letter out of Maddie's hand and quickly scanned it. "Jesus … she's right. It says it's imperative to keep their decision confidential to avoid a media circus."

Sofia swayed as the emotional roller coaster thundered through her again. The ups and downs were becoming too much. If it kept up, she was going to lose what little was left in her stomach.

"Okay, wait. It's going to be all right," Maddie said in her taking-charge voice. "Technically, we *are* Sofia's family. The only one she's got anyway. And none of us are going to say a word about this to anyone else." She looked around the table and waited for nods of acknowledgement from each person. "Sooo … as long as this *never* leaves this room, they'll never know."

Maddie took Sofia's hand in hers. "We're not going to let you down. You're going to go to France and you're going to crush it. Just promise you won't forget who your friends are when you win it all, 'cause we expect you to let us help you spend your money."

Sofia forced herself to chuckle along with the others. She had never been given a break like this before and she didn't know how to handle it. And with her emotions so raw, it took her several seconds to find her voice.

When she finally got herself together, she extended her free hand to Benjamin and squeezed both his and Maddie's hands tightly.

"I love you guys. You're the best." She stumbled over her words. "I … I can't believe this is happening. All I've ever wanted to do was go to college and make something of myself. And now with this … I can do it. I can live my dream." She looked directly at Maddie. "And if the stars do somehow magically align to let me win, you'll be the first one I let ride in my private jet."

Laughter circled the table again, then quickly turned into excited whispers about what everyone thought the challenges might be.

Sofia tried to listen, but her mind drifted back to this sudden stroke of good fortune. After a lifetime of bad luck, it was hard to wrap her brain around the possibility of something like this happening.

She looked down at the lollipop symbol and a sudden thought came to her—what if it wasn't luck at all? What if it's her destiny?

# OLIVIA & ZACHARY

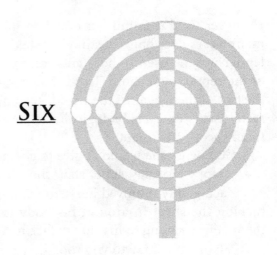

# SIX

*March 10th*

The house was silent and dark, as every window was shuttered by either blinds or curtains. Still, Liv's eyes shot open the second the first light of dawn kissed the horizon just as if an alarm clock had gone off.

On school days, she typically hit the snooze button, rolled over, and went back to sleep for as long as possible, dragging herself out of bed at the last possible second to avoid being late.

But not today. This was the day she had been looking forward to her whole life, and as far as she was concerned, the sooner it got started, the better.

She scrambled out of bed and rushed into the bathroom to brush her teeth and give her long, black-dyed locks a quick comb through.

Then, as stealthily as a cat, she tiptoed down the hall to the last room, gingerly turned the knob, and pushed the door open enough to squeeze through.

The room was as dark as the rest of the house, but Liv had the night vision of a feline and her steps didn't falter. She glided straight to the bed, lifted the thick comforter and slid in between the sheets next to the sleeping body of her brother, Zach.

He tensed as she tenderly slid her arm across his muscled chest and his eyes sprung open wide.

Tiny icicles pierced Liv's heart, but she scooted closer anyway.

He never used to mind her crawling into bed with him. That was many years ago, but she still cherished the vivid memories of the tender way he used to hold and comfort her when the nightmares of the reptile man came. They'd had a special bond back then. Just the two of them against the world, keeping a secret that they weren't really twins or even biologically related, because being twins got them special treatment.

God, what she wouldn't give to go back to that time.

"Happy birthday, super star," she whispered in his ear.

Zach gently removed her arm from his chest and inched away, tucking the sheet in around his body to create a barrier between them before rolling to his side to face her.

"Happy birthday to you too," he whispered back, his voice still croaky from sleep.

Liv swallowed back the lump that had leapt into her throat.

"We've been waiting for this day forever," she breathed. "We're finally eighteen and no one can tell us what to do anymore. We're free to be ourselves!"

A warm smile slid across her face as she reached out to toy with a lock of his hair that had fallen over his forehead.

Zach recoiled at her touch, then raked his fingers through his hair to push it all back, as if wanting to make sure she had no other excuse to touch him.

"That's not the way it works," he replied. "We're the same two people we were yesterday, with the same rules. The only difference is it's going to look even worse if Mom or Dad catches you here in my bed. You know, we've talked about this—"

Liv put two fingers over his mouth. "Yes, but I'm tired of waiting. I love you. It's not fair that we can't be together. You're not my twin brother or even my blood brother. It's time we let the world know that."

Zach lifted her fingers off his mouth and tenderly enclosed her hand in his. "I love you, too. I always will. But not in that way."

His hand tightened around hers as she started to pull it away.

"Come on, you know as well as I do that it's not going to matter that we have different biological parents. Society will always see us as brother and sister." He squeezed her hand. "Besides, we made a pact and both swore we'd never tell. Remember? You know Mom would be crushed if she found out the truth. And our lives would become a fuckin' circus too.

"Look..." Zach's lips curved into a tender little smile that always melted Liv's heart. "... we've only got a few months of high school left. Let's not complicate things any more than they already are, okay?"

Liv's eyes narrowed as she pulled her hand out of his. In the same heartbeat, the sheet, blanket, and comforter flew to Zach's feet and his naked body was fully exposed.

"What the fuck, Livy!" he cried, rearing up and yanking the sheet back up over him.

Liv's heart stalled for a moment. She'd just recently discovered she could move things with her mind, but only small things like pencils and water bottles. Never had she managed to move anything as big or heavy as a full blanket and duvet before and she was just as shocked as Zach.

A fire of desire ignited between her thighs. As the heat swiftly spread through her body, she realized she might have reacted a little too impulsively. But how could she have known he'd be naked beneath the blanket?

"What'd ya do that for?" Zach's eyes held a mixture of shock and barely contained anger.

She held up both hands up, palm side out. "I didn't touch 'em. But since when did you start sleeping naked?"

The ring of yellow around Zach's pupils turned to molten gold, and Liv knew she had gone too far. Before he could say anything more, she swung her long legs over the side of the bed and stormed across the room.

Liv hesitated at the doorway and flipped the light switch on to give him a good view of her firm butt cheeks peeking out from under the flimsy t-shirt she slept in. She could feel his eyes on her backside and slowly turned, arching her back to give him a glimpse of the dark circles of her perky breasts pressing against the thin fabric.

"You're fooling yourself to think the truth won't eventually come out," she spat, the yellow ring around her own pupils sparking just like Zach's had. "And I'll bet you you're wrong about people's reaction when it does. No one's gonna care one way or the other about two adopted kids."

Goosebumps pimpled her arms and every cell in her body screamed for her to jump back into bed with him and kiss him into submission. But she resisted the urge, knowing it would do more harm than good.

"No one's ever going to love you as much as I do," she added. "One of these days, you're going to realize that. Then you'll be sorry for all this time you've wasted." She gave her hair a flip and didn't so much as flinch as the books on Zach's desk tumbled to the floor.

"Hope you have a wonderful birthday, *brother*," she sneered and firmly shut the door behind her.

"Livy!" he called after her.

She ignored him and continued down the hall.

This was not at all the way Liv had planned for this day to start. But to be honest, she wasn't totally surprised by Zach's reaction, either. He had always been the cautious one, trying to appease everyone and doing everything that was expected of him. She, on the other hand, was a wild child and relished the thrill of bucking the system and being the center of attention. She had no qualms about using her special talent of being able to draw people to her and get them to do whatever she wanted. Zach was the only exception. For some reason she didn't understand, he was immune to her spell.

But things were changing. She was eighteen now, and with her new telekinesis ability, a whole new world of possibilities was out there for the taking.

Liv hurried into the bathroom and took the extra time she had planned on spending with Zach on her makeup and hair.

Lastly, she put in a pair of contacts to hide the hated yellow ring around her pupils and stood in front of the mirror admiring her reflection. The girl staring back at her with the peacock blue eyes looked more like a model heading out to a photo shoot than a high school senior, which was the exact look she was going for.

She cocked her head one way, then the other, testing out which pose made her look the sexiest.

"Yeah, that's right … you were stupid for turning this down," she whispered, picturing Zach's mouth dropping open when he saw her.

By the time she got back to her bedroom to dress, her mood had improved immensely. She sighed wistfully as she pushed aside the new sweater she had bought for this day and took out her cheer uniform. The boys' varsity basketball team, which Zach was captain of, was in the Texas State 6A Championship Tournament, which meant the cheerleading squad had to wear their uniforms the entire week. Her new skimpy sweater was right on the line of passing the school's dress code anyway, and she still planned to show it off tonight at the "surprise" party she had foreseen her friends throwing her.

Ten minutes earlier than usual, Liv bounced down the stairs. She slowed her walk as she approached the kitchen and put on her best blank expression, which wasn't easy with the bubbling pot of excitement brewing within her. Her parents always made a big deal out of holidays, especially birthdays. And this being her and Zach's eighteenth, she could only imagine the extravaganza in store for them.

She casually strolled into the kitchen and stopped at the end of the island. Her dad was seated at the table, staring at a tablet in his one hand and gripping the handle of his coffee mug with the other. Her mom's head was in the refrigerator as she rummaged around, pulling out ingredients for a salad she would have later for lunch.

Liv looked from Mom to the empty stove, where the traditional birthday breakfast of Belgian waffles and bacon—her favorite, though she seldom ate it because she was afraid it would make her fat—and ham, Zach's favorite, should have been sizzling away. Her perfectly etched eyebrows drew together in confusion as she scanned the rest of the room for the stack of presents that *always* accompanied the breakfast. The room was as empty as the stove. There wasn't even a card lying at her and Zach's places at the table.

"Morning, honey," Mom called over her shoulder.

"Morning," Liv mumbled through a lump that had suddenly lodged in her throat.

Dad looked up and did a double take. "Wow, don't you look nice today," he said, then quickly looked back down at his tablet.

Liv sniffed back the drips from her nose that were about to fall onto the D of her uniform.

At that moment, Zach sauntered into the kitchen. He went straight to the cupboard and pulled out a box of cereal and a bowl like he did every other day. Mom closed the refrigerator door and handed him a gallon of milk without looking at either of them.

"Morning, honey," she repeated in the same expressionless tone she'd given Liv.

Dad looked up over the top of his reading glasses. "Morning, son. Do you think Coach will be keeping y'all late tonight?"

"He didn't say anything. But I wouldn't think so. He wants us to be fresh and ready for tomorrow."

Mom cut in, "I had to drop my car off at the shop last night, so we'll all have to ride in with Dad today."

Zach nodded and mumbled his acknowledgement through the spoonful of cereal he had just scooped into his mouth.

Liv looked from Mom to Dad, not sure what the hell was going on. Had they really forgotten it was her and Zach's birthday?

"I have an early meeting this morning, too," Mom added, again without looking up. "So we need to get going. Are y'all ready?"

"Yup, I'm ready. Just need to grab my coat," Dad replied. He took another quick sip of coffee, then stood and scurried into the front room.

Mom reached into her purse and pulled out two ten-dollar bills. "I didn't have time to pick anything up for your lunches, so y'all will have to buy today." She laid the bills on the island and made a wide path around Liv to retrieve Dad's abandoned coffee mug from the table.

Liv put her hand on the counter to steady herself.

Zach shoveled the last of the cereal into his mouth and dropped his bowl into the sink just as Dad walked back into the kitchen.

"I'm almost ready." Dad set his briefcase on the table and opened it. "Y'all go ahead and get in the car. I'll be right behind ya."

Mom reached for a paper towel and slowly dried her hands as Zach grabbed up his gym bag and backpack.

Liv was too shocked to move. But as Zach walked by on his way to the garage, he took her arm and pulled her along with him. It wasn't until they reached the door that her defiant nature finally took over. She yanked her arm out of his hold and elbowed him in the chest.

"I'm old enough to walk out on my own, thank you very much," she spat and jerked the door open.

She took one more step, then froze.

Parked in the middle of the three-car garage was a sleek, gun-metal gray Nissan Altima with a giant green and gold bow that matched their school colors in the center of the hood.

Liv let out a high-pitched screech as Zach uttered "Holy shit!" under his breath.

Liv turned to her parents, who were wearing smiles that almost stretched from ear to ear.

"Ohmigod, you guys!" She covered her mouth with her hand and rushed to her mom, hugging her tight. Zach turned and fell into his dad's arms.

"You didn't forget," Liv whispered.

Mom chuckled. "Of course we didn't. How could we? You put a big circle of red hearts around the date on the calendar."

"I wish we could have gotten each of you a car, but we couldn't swing it financially at the moment." Dad pulled back and looked into Zach's eyes. "We figured that most of your time outside of class will be spent at basketball practice anyway, so you wouldn't have that much need of a car."

"It's fine," Zach said, his emotion making his voice sound gruff. "Actually, it's freakin' awesome! Thank you so much."

He and Liv traded places and gave more hugs.

Dad pulled the car keys out of his pocket and dangled them in the air. "So … who's going to have the privilege of being the first to drive her?"

"Livy," Zach said without hesitation and smiled at his sister. "She'll look a lot hotter behind the wheel than me."

Liv let out another squeal and quickly gave her dad another peck on the cheek as she took the keys from his hand and rushed to the garage. A trickle of excitement ran up her spine as her fingertips lightly brushed over the smooth, cold metal of the fender. She reverently slid into the driver's seat, gripped the steering wheel with both hands, and took a deep breath of the new car scent.

The day had started out lousy, but the car had made it a lot brighter.

Now, if she could only get Zach on board, she'd have the life she'd dreamed of having from the time she was six years old.

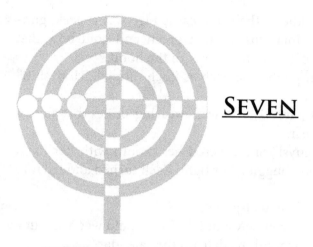

# SEVEN

The pungent smell of body odor penetrated the air as two boys simultaneously pushed up and down to the chants of their fellow teammates circling them. The push-up contest, a weekly ritual initiated a decade ago, was used to determine who got to lead the basketball team through the cheer line and onto the court at the start of the next game.

Technically, the contest was open to any player. But halfway through the season it became obvious no one could compete with Zach Schultze, team captain and shooting guard, and Jamal Martin, co-captain and small forward, and the other players decided they would rather just stand back and watch the show.

In the beginning, Zach had no interest in being part of the challenge. It was his first year at DeSoto High—his dad's new job had moved the family from Houston over the past summer—and being a senior, he didn't feel the need to prove himself. All he cared about was getting through the year with no injuries and as few complications as possible. He had planned to play just hard enough to secure his scholarship to the University of Texas and that was it. However, once Jamal, the previous year's undisputed champ, saw Zach's prowess on the court, he challenged Zach at every possible opportunity.

Zach had declined at first, but after weeks of snide remarks and Jamal being an all-around a-hole, he finally gave in and joined the contest to get Jamal off his back more than anything else. But instead of putting Jamal in his place, Zach's participation had fueled the situation and increased Jamal's competitiveness.

At the count of thirty-five, both boys' speed began to slow. At forty-five, their faces were the color of the ever-present red Tootsie Pop in Coach Dekle's mouth.

Zach glanced at Jamal out of the corner of his eye. Jamal's biceps were visibly shaking under the strain. Zach clenched his teeth against the burn in his own muscles and concentrated on the numbers that floated into his mind as the team called them off one by one.

"Fifty-five. Fifty-six," the circle of boys counted. "Fifty-seven."

Jamal collapsed on the mat. The disappointed groans of Jamal's few supporters were drowned out by roars of the others.

Zach hesitated another heartbeat to see if Jamal was truly out. Then, with the bluish-purple stone pendant he wore around his neck swinging on its chain, he pushed up again.

"Fifty-eight. Fifty-nine. Sixty!" the crowd cheered.

Zach collapsed beside Jamal, pressed his forehead into the mat, and gasped in gulps of air.

The bystanders cheered for another minute before two of them reached down and yanked both boys to their feet.

Zach extended his hand to Jamal in a show of good sportsmanship. Jamal squared his jaw and walked away, purposely knocking hard into Zach's shoulder as he went by.

"Schultze, Martin, my office," Coach Dekle shouted over his shoulder as he turned from the doorway of the locker room and started down the hall.

"Yes, sir." Zach started after Coach, slapping the fronts and backs of his teammates' hands and graciously accepting congratulatory punches in the arm as he passed, leaving Jamal standing in the middle of the room, alone and ignored.

"Sit," Coach said around the Tootsie Pop in his mouth when Jamal finally sauntered into the office several minutes later.

As soon as Jamal was seated, Coach removed the lollipop, making a soft popping sound as if he were pulling it out of a vacuum, and fixed the boys with a penetrating glare.

Zach tensed.

"I know I don't need to tell you how important tomorrow's game is. We have a real good chance of bringing the state championship trophy back home to DeSoto. I'm counting on you two being a big part of that victory. As co-captains and top scorer," he looked directly at Zach, "it's your responsibility to keep the team focused and their heads in the moment. There's no room on my bench for any player who isn't a hundred percent dedicated to the team."

Coach's gaze shifted to Jamal. "To make sure you're both perfectly clear on what I mean by that, I'll put it in simpler terms for you. I don't have the time or patience to deal with any prima donna who's more interested in their own glory than in the team's."

Zach's cheeks, still warm from the exertion of the contest, heated up more. He knew Jamal didn't handle losing well. He also knew he could have stopped as he'd done in previous matches and let Jamal have the victory. But Jamal's endless taunts and constant bullying of the under-classmen had gotten under Zach's skin and he couldn't help himself. He'd gone into today's competition fully intending to knock Jamal down a notch.

Coach rubbed the stubble on his chin. "I've watched the rivalry between the two of you grow throughout the season. I haven't said anything before now because I've always believed competition is good for the soul. You two in particular seem to thrive on it. And you were kickin' ass there for a while, too. But in the last few weeks the other boys have started picking sides and it's affecting their play, which in turn hurts the team. If we go into the semifinals divided, we'll get crucified. I guarantee you that.

"So, I'm here to tell ya this bullshit is going to end right here, right now. The only players getting on the bus for San Antonio tomorrow will be *team* players. And the only competition I want to see take place on the court is between our team and Cypress Falls. If you two can get serious and play as teammates, I'll be happy to have you join us. But mark my words, I'll sit your asses on the bench if any of the shenanigans that have been going on this week in practice shows up on the court tomorrow. Or if I even see a hint of bad blood between the two of you.

"Have I made myself clear?" Coach leaned back in his chair and reinserted the Tootsie Pop into his mouth.

Zach sat up a little straighter and nodded his head. "Yes, sir."

Jamal's nostrils flared and his upper lip turned up in a sneer as he also mumbled, "Yes, sir."

Coach again stared directly at Jamal and added, "If you decide you can't play side by side, Mabrey will get you a box so you can clean out your lockers. Otherwise, drills are in ten. If you *do* come out on my court, I damn well better see a significant attitude adjustment."

With that said, he leaned forward, the spring in his chair squeaking loudly, and shuffled the papers around on his desk.

Taking the hint, the boys scrambled to their feet and silently hustled back to the locker room.

⚿⋎⊠⋎⍔⏐⏐⏐⏐⎍⊠⋎

Drills were extra brutal that afternoon and ran almost forty minutes longer than usual. By the time the final whistle blew the entire team was dripping sweat and dragging, but no one complained. They knew the importance of tomorrow's game. Even Jamal was on his best behavior through practice. But afterwards, he dashed for the door before the rest of the team had even broken huddle.

Like everyone else, Zach's limbs felt like rubber and it took every ounce of strength he had left to keep from collapsing on the floor. He gritted his teeth and stoically turned toward the locker room, hoping his knees would hold him up long enough to make it in.

He was halfway across the gym when without warning the lights went out. A rustling sound followed, then a rush of perfumed scents floated on the air toward him. His brain, just as exhausted as his body, didn't compute what was going on until the blinding lights came back on.

He lowered his head for a second to let his eyes readjust. When he looked up, there was a line of varsity and junior varsity cheerleaders in front of him, their gold pom-poms on the floor at their feet.

Liv, standing slightly in front of the line, gave him a wicked smile, clapped her hands together once, and yelled loudly, "All right, let's go!"

Eight of the girls were immediately lifted into the air by their teammates and all clapped their hands once in unison to signal the start of the cheer.

> "I don't know but I've been told," Liv shouted out the lines and the girls then echoed her words.
> "Someone here is getting old."
> "Want to be the first to say,"
> "Hope you have a happy day."

"Sound off," Liv yelled.

"*Happy,*" the girls replied.

"Sound off."

"*Birthday.*"

"Bring it on down."

"*Happy birthday … to you!*"

The eight jumped down, and they all grabbed up their poms and shook them as cheerleaders do as they rushed Zach.

He smiled graciously, but his eyes were glacial as they fell on Liv standing at the back. She had undoubtedly instigated this embarrassing little show to get back at him. He knew he was right when one of her eyebrows raised and the corner of her mouth turned up in an impish grin.

"Okay, okay, thank you. That was very nice, but …" Zach threw another stern glance at Liv, "unnecessary."

He held his hands up and tried to step back as the girls pressed in closer, but he was completely surrounded. "Come on, seriously, I need to get to the showers before Mabrey locks em up."

One of the girls seductively ran her fingertip down Zach's arm. "You want some company in the shower?"

The other girls giggled. Zach's teammates, standing in the doorway of the gym, howled and whistled their approval.

"That would be awesome, but ya know, with the big game coming up, it's probably not a good time for me to get kicked off the team." Zach joked, wanting to make light of the suggestion, although he knew the girl wasn't kidding.

"Look," he held his hands up, palms out as in surrendering. "I appreciate the surprise and the birthday wish. I do. But I'm tired and y'all need to be saving your energy for tomorrow's big game."

He gave a quick wave, broke through the circle of girls, and nearly ran out of the room, afraid of what else Liv might have planned.

But as he stepped through the door to the locker room, he came to an abrupt halt. His teammates were in a line with four of the guys standing on the bench behind the others.

"I don't know but I've been told," one of the forwards shouted. The others echoed him to mimic the girls.

"Someone here's about to get laid."
"Just want to be the first to say."
"Protect your schlong or you will pay."
"Sound off," the forward shouted.
*"Smash it,"* the boys replied.
"Sound off."
*"So good."*
"Bring it on down."
*"Smash it ... so good!"*

Zach pressed his lips together in a thin smile and bobbed his head up and down. "Funny. Very funny."

He cursed Liv silently as he shoved his way through the line. Before he even reached his locker, the door burst open on its own.

He loved his sister, but sometimes her unquenchable thirst for attention made him crazy. And since she was fully aware of how much he hated being drawn into her circus, there was no doubt in his mind that this little display of hers was payback for his earlier rejection.

A shudder ran through him at the thought of what else she might do to him to get revenge.

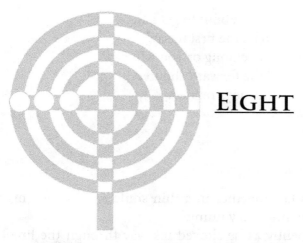

# EIGHT

There was a sea of green and gold at the Alamodome for the state championship semifinals, as both DeSoto and Cypress Falls High Schools had the same school colors. There was no confusion in which side was which, though, for the roar bounced back and forth each time a player from their respective team shot the ball through the hoop.

The third quarter had just begun. DeSoto was up 32-24, mostly due to Zach, who, as the game announcer kept exclaiming, was on fire. He was all over the court, popping up in the perfect spot on every play like a magician to either grab the rebound or to shoot. And every shot he attempted hit its mark. The DeSoto crowd was going wild, and the team, looking forward to securing the win, happily fed Zach the ball every chance they got.

Jamal was the only one who wasn't ecstatic about the situation. And his frustration was growing more noticeable as the game clock ticked down.

It had been announced in the locker room before the game that a recruiter from the Kansas Jayhawks was in the house looking for someone to fill a vacated spot on next year's squad. Jamal wanted that spot bad and everyone knew it, even Zach. But within the first minutes of the game, Zach had stolen the spotlight, and Coach's warning got lost in the roar of the crowd.

It was Cypress Falls' ball and one of their players took it down the court. Zach was two steps ahead of him, as he had been the whole game, and jumped for the rebound before the ball even left the player's hands—almost as if he knew the kid was going to shoot instead of pass and that the ball was going to bounce off the rim.

At the same moment, Jamal barreled into the mix, squeezed between two Cypress Falls guards, and pivoted his body into Zach.

All at once, the thunder of the crowd faded to a faint hum inside Zach's head and time began to move in slow motion. The players around him, except for Jamal, blurred out, and the crowd faded into the background. He could still see the lights of the jumbotron blazing brightly in the corner of his eye, though, burning the scores 34 and 24 into the back of his mind.

It seemed like he was floating on the air as he came down from his jump. Then, just as his feet were about to reconnect with the floor, Jamal extended his leg.

Zach opened his mouth to yell, but nothing came out. He landed on Jamal's foot and his body went one way, his knee the other and a white-hot pain exploded in his leg, jolting him back to real time. The screams of the crowd pierced his ears like knives, Liv's scream slicing through him the loudest.

Jamal jumped backward and pointed at a Cypress Falls' guard as soon as Zach hit the floor. No one was fooled, though. The referee had seen it all, as had almost everyone else in the auditorium.

Zach clutched his knee and rolled side to side in agony as the athletic trainer ran out onto the court. Coach was right behind him and pushed the players who were gathered around Zach into a wide circle. The entire DeSoto side went silent but for a few murmurs of shock. Liv leaned against one of the other cheerleaders for support and covered her mouth with her hand.

It took the trainer less than ten seconds to assess that it was a major injury and Coach motioned for his assistant to help carry Zach off the court. He was taken straight into the locker room to a standing ovation. Jamal was then escorted out of the auditorium to a barrage of boos.

After losing both star players, DeSoto's game went downhill. When the final buzzer sounded, the score was Cypress Falls 74, DeSoto 51.

ᘯᕁᛧ⸸�093ᛁᛁᛁᐃᛧ⸸

Zach laid on the bed in the ER with his eyes closed, pretending to be asleep so he didn't have to talk to anyone. He had torn his ACL and meniscus and badly sprained his ankle, and his whole leg ached and throbbed.

To add to his discomfort, his teammates had come straight over to the hospital after the loss and were rehashing the play over and over. Not a one of them stopped to think that the least of Zach's worries at the moment was the school losing out on the championship. Nor did they seem to realize whining about it wasn't going to change a thing.

When the nurse finally came in and shooed everyone out, except for his parents and Liv, Zach could have kissed her. There was no reprieve from the thoughts raging through his mind, though.

A short time later, after Mom and Dad stepped out of the room to confer with doctors about treatment options, Liv leaned over the bed and whispered into Zach's ear, "I know you're not asleep."

Zach inwardly cringed. Times like this he hated the connection they had.

"No," he said without opening his eyes, "but maybe I could be if everyone would just leave me alone."

Liv took his hand and squeezed. "It's going to be all right."

"No, it's not!" he exploded, glaring up at her, his electric blue eyes frostier than usual and the yellow circle around his pupils blazing. "You know how much I need that scholarship. Mom and Dad don't have the money to send us both to college at the same time." He turned his head away as a rush of emotion overtook him.

"Don't worry about that. I don't have to start school this fall. I've been thinking lately that it'd be kinda nice to take a break anyway," Liv said, but Zach knew she was lying through her teeth. "I can get a job and maybe take a couple online classes for a year or two so Mom and Dad will only have your schooling to pay for. We can make it work. It won't be a big deal."

Zach barked, "You're wrong. It *is* a big deal!"

Two of the "Get Well" balloons floating next to his bed popped. They both jumped.

Liv whirled around, then turned right back as Zach let out a moan.

A wave of pain turned Zach's world red for a moment, but that was nothing compared to the pain that stabbed his heart when he saw the anguish in Liv's eyes. He blew a breath out through his teeth.

"I won't let you give up your future because I made a stupid mistake."

"You didn't do—" Liv started.

"I did!" Zach cut in. "I knew Jamal wanted to impress the recruiter from KU, and I ..." Zach shook his head and looked away. "I don't know what came over me. Something weird happened. I don't know how to explain it.

A tic in his jaw began to pulse. "It started on the way down to the Dome. I fell asleep on the bus and had this bizarre dream that I was a little kid in the backseat of a SUV, and this weird looking dude who was driving ran the car off the road. When I woke up, I thought we had crashed for real, 'cause my head was splitting.

"You never get headaches," Liv said, her face etched with worry.

"I know I don't. But that's not even the weirdest part. The headache stayed with me until I started warm-ups. Then ..." He paused and looked up at the ceiling, searching for the right words. "A few minutes into the game, I started seeing these ... premonitions? I don't know how else to describe it. Dotted lines just started to show up all over the court."

Liv's brow was furrowed like she wasn't following what he was saying, but she nodded her head anyway.

"It was like someone was drawing out the plays in my head, but they weren't our plays. They were Cypress Falls'. Once I figured that out, it was easy to get in the right position at the right time 'cause I knew exactly what their players were going to do. I saw all their moves in advance. I could even see when a shot was going to miss and which way it would go, so I knew where to be for the rebounds."

Zach sighed. "I don't know where the info was coming from and I didn't know how to turn it off. But even if I could've turned it off, I don't know that I would've. So ..." he gestured to his knee, "this is what I get for cheating. It's my own fault, and if anyone doesn't go to college in the fall, it'll be me." His voice was hoarse with regret and pain.

He put his arm over his eyes to give her a not-so-subtle hint that he was done with the conversation, though he knew it was delusional to think she would give it up. She was as stubborn as he was, if not more so.

"Don't say that. Anyone in your place would've done the same thing. Jamal is the only one to blame for this mess." Her expression looked like she was in pain, too.

"But maybe there's a way we can both still go to college in the fall," Liv added. "Everyone's been talking about this new reality show that's just been announced. Rumor has it this billionaire dude is dying and since he doesn't have any children or family, he's doing this show that he's calling the Road to Riches to find an heir or heiress to give all his money to. It's all over social media and the news. And what's really cool is he's only letting eighteen-year-olds come one the show."

Liv paused and waited for Zach to say something, but all he did was shake his head and look away.

"I admit it's a long shot," she continued, "but he's gonna choose *someone*. And if we both send in an application, we'll have a double chance at it."

Zach blew a breath out through his nose. Liv had always been the dreamer. He was the realist.

"Sure, sounds good. Why don't you go ahead and send that in. And while you're at it, why don't you buy a bunch of lottery tickets, too."

He could feel Liv tense and knew his sarcasm had hurt her feelings, but he was in too much pain to care. Fortunately, Mom and Dad came back in at that moment and Liv swallowed whatever else she was going to say.

After talking with the doctors, the consensus was the fastest way to get him back on his feet was to do Arthroscopy surgery to repair his ACL once the swelling went down. But even with the surgery, there was no guarantee he'd ever be able to play basketball on a competitive level again.

Dad did his best to put a positive spin on the outcome, but Mom's tight smile didn't reach her eyes and Zach could read her well enough to know the real truth. He turned his head away and silently cursed Jamal.

Zach had never aspired to play basketball growing up. It was Dad, a former high school and college player himself, who had pushed Zach into trying out after discovering Zach's ability to jump higher than other boys. No one, though, not even Dad or Liv, knew how high Zach could actually jump or how fast he could run. He kept that and his other unexplainable abilities to himself in fear that people would shun him and think him a freak. But at the same time, he didn't want to disappoint Dad. So, he had tried out and put forth just enough effort to make the team.

But even holding back, Zach was better than most. Once colleges coaches and recruiters got wind of his skills, the pursuit began and his future was set. Dad, of course, was ecstatic with the thought of his son playing in the Big 12, and, as always, Zach went along with the ride because he couldn't bear the thought of letting his dad down. When he got the offer of a full ride to UT, though, he was glad he did.

Knowing that his parents would be free of the expense and burden of his college tuition is what got him through the last four years of the insufferable notoriety that comes with being a top athlete in Texas. But now that had all been for nothing.

An uncomfortable silence fell over the room. When midnight came and it still looked as if it would be a while before Zach was released, Dad took Liv to a hotel to get a few hours of sleep, so they'd be somewhat rested for the long drive home. Mom insisted on staying even though Zach vigorously protested. Fortunately, to his relief, she curled up in the recliner with a blanket and was softly snoring within fifteen minutes.

Zach couldn't keep his eyes open either, but his mind was too full to shut down. And each time he got close to drifting off, the number 03032003 would flash behind his eyelids and jerk him back.

Seeing numbers in his head was nothing new to Zach. He and Liv had both been diagnosed with synesthesia years earlier. But always before, numbers had appeared to him in a specific spot along a zig-zag path.

This number was not on that path. It was also in a spiral cone shape, the numbers growing smaller as they descended to the pointed end. Its shiny purple color was new, too, and the three number 3s were all blood red. The first 3 was also much larger and stood out from the others as if it were significant.

But it wasn't just that the number looked different. It was that even though it meant nothing to him, each time it reappeared, he got a stronger notion that it was somehow important.

Finally, in the early hours of the morning, he fell into a fitful sleep and dreamed of sitting in a lavish, wood-paneled office with shelves of books that went all the way up to the two-story ceiling. Liv and a girl with auburn hair down to the middle of her back and blue eyes that shone like crystals were there, too. The three of them together had won Road to Riches and were waiting to receive the promised reward.

However, instead of a prize, yellow-skinned lizards slithered in through the crack beneath the door. They scrambled on top of each other as fast as they came in to create a barrier that blocked anyone from getting in or out.

As soon as Zach realized what they were doing, he frantically grabbed handfuls of the reptiles and threw them off to the side. He yelled at Liv and the girl to come help, but there were too many of the scaly little creatures and they were coming in faster than the three could keep up.

Soon, the lizards had multiplied to the point they were crawling over their feet and up their legs.

Zach looked around for another exit or way out, but the office had transformed and was now windowless and empty. He sensed a presence in the dense shadows of the far corner, though, and opened his mouth to ask who was there. But his words stuck in his throat as a chilling laugh came out of the darkness.

The horrible sound got louder and louder and echoed off the walls, then all at once stopped, and a voice that sounded like metal scraping on metal growled, "I told you I would find you again."

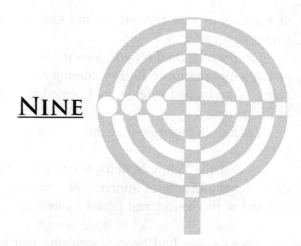

# NINE

The first four days after Zach's injury were pure torture. He couldn't do a thing with his leg hooked up to a cooling machine to keep the swelling down, so, Liv and Mom hovered over him non-stop and treated him like a complete invalid. The only time he had to himself to think things through was in the middle of the night when the pain woke him up.

The doctor had given him meds, but the pills made his head feel like he was swimming in the deep and he only took them when the pain became unbearable. The rest of the time he gritted his teeth and tried to occupy his mind with other things, such as what to do about college now that his basketball scholarship was doomed.

Mom and Dad kept insisting he would go to UT as originally planned, and nothing he could say made any difference. But no matter how hard they tried to pretend it wouldn't be that much of a financial burden on the family, he knew it would be. And that hurt almost as much as his leg did.

On the fifth day, Zach begged to go back to school just to get out of the house and away from Mom and Liv's constant coddling. But as it turned out, school wasn't a whole lot better. Liv somehow managed to appear at his side every time he turned around even though most of her classes were on the other side of campus. And every student in the school—at least it felt like that to him—came up to say how much what happened sucked and how Jamal was a total a-hole for doing what he did.

The only person who kept their distance was Jamal. But even

in a school of over three thousand kids, it was impossible to avoid someone forever.

On Zach's sixth day back, he was heading into the boy's restroom just as Jamal came out. Both of them jerked to a halt and Jamal's dark complexion turned pale. Jamal lowered his eyes but didn't move out of Zach's way.

Zach didn't move either other than to clench and unclench his fists.

Across the hall, a bulletin board overwhelmed with posters of club events and school information crashed to the floor. Both boys jumped at the sound and Jamal looked up, then looked right back down.

Zach's anger had been simmering just under the surface ever since the night of the game. When he wasn't thinking about his college future, he was envisioning what he would do the next time he faced Jamal. Not a one of the scenarios he imagined involved walking away and doing nothing. But the thought that Jamal might have regrets as well never entered his mind, either.

Now, though, standing just inches away from Jamal, Zach could not only see a gray aura of depression encircling his former teammate, he could feel the sorrow rolling off Jamal like ocean waves. That wasn't the kind of reaction he had anticipated, but he also never imagined he could ever feel pity for the guy who had caused him so much pain. But it was clear Jamal was suffering, too—just in a different way.

Out of the corner of his eye, Zach caught a glimpse of the assistant principal coming down the hall.

*Ah, fuck it!* He snorted in disgust and made a move to step around Jamal.

"Look bro, I'm sorry. I didna—" Jamal started as Zach reached to push the door open.

"Forget it," Zach snapped, his knuckles turning white on his fisted hand.

"I … I didn't mean for you to get hurt bad," Jamal added.

A fresh surge of rage swelled in Zach's chest and his eyes turned to cold steel as he turned back to face Jamal.

"Are you seriously going to stand there and fuckin' lie to my face, 'cause we both know that's not true. But I get it. I wasn't exactly being a team player that night. That doesn't excuse what you did, and I can't say I'm not glad to see you paying a price for your asinine actions."

Jamal blurted, "I am paying a price. My scholarship got pulled."

Zach paused and let the statement settle over him. It didn't help to make him feel any better, though. He balled his right hand into a fist and started to raise it, then noticed the assistant principal standing next to the fallen bulletin board watching them.

His gaze shifted back to Jamal, who had tensed in anticipation of getting punched in the face.

The assistant principal started toward them. "Is there a problem here, gentleman?"

For a nanosecond, Zach considered going ahead and fulfilling his dream by smashing in Jamal's nose. But then reason stopped him. Jamal had already cost him enough and a moment of satisfaction wasn't worth getting expelled for.

He locked eyes with Jamal as he replied to the assistant principal, "No, sir. No problem. We were just discussing how karma's a real bitch."

A small tic worked in Zach's jaw as he clenched his teeth and stared Jamal down for another second.

Then, he turned and proceeded into the restroom without another word.

# TEN

*May 1st*

I t was a gray, dreary day in DeSoto and the smell of rain hung heavy on the air. Prom had come and gone and a melancholy mood had settled over the seniors. Graduation, a short three weeks away, was all that was left of their high school experience. Those who were still living in the sheltered world of adolescence were looking forward to beginning their adult lives. They were the ones who still believed adulthood was all fun and games and would give them the freedom to do whatever they pleased. The others, those who had already learned the truth, were wishing their childhood would last a few more years.

Zach was one of the others and would have given anything to return things to the way they were before the semi-finals game. But no amount of wishing could bring back what was already gone. While his friends partied and enjoyed their last days of high school, he worked long hours at the local grocery store to earn money for college.

He was there at work, in the middle of sacking groceries from a full shopping cart, when Liv raced into the store, her cheeks rosy from excitement. Without saying a word, she thrust an envelope into his hand and bounced on the balls of her feet waiting for him to comment.

He set the envelope on the corner of the counter without giving it a glance. "I'm working, Livy. Can't this wait till I get home?"

"No, it can't. Open it."

"A little help here, Zach," the cashier said, pulling out a paper bag to start sacking items herself as there was no more room at the end of the conveyer belt.

"Yes, ma'am," he replied to the cashier. Then, to Liv, "I don't have time for this right now."

He turned his back on her and picked up a box of cereal to add to a bag. "I've gotta sack this stuff or I'll get in trouble."

Liv crossed her arms over her chest and stood her ground in front of a rack holding the compressed bundles of plastic bags.

Zach did his best to ignore her, but she was right in the way.

"You're going to get me fired," he hissed, reaching around her.

"I don't care. I need to know what that letter says."

"Yeah, well, you may not care, but I do." He blew out a frustrated sigh and raked his fingers through his hair. "Look, if it's that important, wait in the coffee shop. I'll try to take my break after this order."

Liv mirrored his sigh. "Okay, *finnne*. But don't be long. This *is* majorly important."

She grabbed the envelope and begrudgingly walked to the small grouping of tables in the corner of the store by the entrance.

Once Zach finished bagging the order, there were four others in line he had to do before he could take his break. It was well over thirty minutes later when he finally trudged toward the coffee shop. His leg ached and he was tired, and all he really wanted to do was go to the break room and lie on the couch. But he knew that if he didn't deal with Liv now, she'd make another scene and cause some real trouble.

Liv was sitting in the corner facing a window but turned the second Zach started walking her way, as if she could sense him coming.

He collapsed on a chair with a soft groan and propped his foot up on another to elevate his leg.

Liv was radiating with anticipation, but all she said as she pushed the envelope toward him was, "Open it."

Zach looked down at the envelope and focused on it for the first time. The return address said it was from a law firm by the name of Conway and Vik. He looked up at Liv, his eyebrows arched in question.

"I got one too," she said breathlessly. Then, unable to hold back any longer, added, "I told you it was going to be all right."

Zach's frown deepened as he tentatively tore open the envelope and pulled out the letter. His gaze brushed over the first-class airline ticket to Nice, France, and went straight to the symbol in the top left corner of the letter. It vaguely looked like the tattoo he had on his right bicep.

Liv leaned over, saw the ticket, and let out a small squeal. "Ohmigod, you made it in too! I just knew you were going to."

Her exclamation jolted Zach out of his reverie. He looked up at her smug smile, not sure what she was talking about.

"You didn't believe me when I told you not to worry about college. But I was right." She gave his shoulder a soft punch, then folded her arms on the table and leaned in closer. "I have a really good feeling about this. It's gonna be a new start for us. Big things are about to happen."

Zach quickly scanned the letter in its entirety. When he looked back up at her shining eyes, he shook his head.

"All this is is an invitation to the first challenge. It doesn't mean either of us will make it to the end and become someone's heir. I'm betting dozens, or probably more like hundreds, of these letters went out."

Liv gave a disgusted sigh. "Don't be like that. You really think this guy is going to fly hundreds of people to France?" She reached across the table and slipped her hand in his. "I'm telling ya, I have a good feeling about this. One of us is going to come out the winner of the whole thing. I just know it."

She pushed her chair back and picked up the keys to the car that were lying on the table. "I haven't told Mom and Dad yet and it's been absolutely killing me. I thought we should do it together, though, so … come on, let's go."

"I can't leave right now. My shift isn't over til six."

Liv tsked. "Well, then quit. You don't need to work anymore. Didn't you read the part that said you're guaranteed ten thousand dollars? That'll cover most of the next term of school."

"I can't just walk out and leave them hanging. I made a commitment."

"But you—"

"*No,*" Zach replied forcibly. "You're just gonna have to wait til my shift is over."

Liv shot darts at him with her eyes. "*Finnne.* I'll go over to Aria's and tell the girls, then."

Zach caught her wrist as she turned to leave. "The letter says we aren't to tell anyone other than our family members."

"Yes, I know. But I have to tell *someone,*" Liv whined. "I'll make them promise not to tell."

Zach let out a snort. "Are you fuckin' serious? Those girls keep a secret? It'll be all over social media before you get two steps out of her house."

Liv rolled her eyes. "Whatever."

"Seriously, Livy, I have a feeling about this too. I don't want to lose out because one of your friends let it slip."

Liv's face fell. She dropped back onto the chair. "I don't know that I can keep quiet about this for a whole month and a half."

"You can and you will. You'll do it for me. And for Mom and Dad. That ten thousand dollars is going to take a huge burden off them. And who knows, maybe …" One corner of Zach's mouth tilted up as he shrugged. "I guess we have as good a chance as anyone else to win." He put his hand on top of hers and squeezed.

She looked into his eyes for a long moment. "You really think so?"

"I do," he said sincerely.

Liv's face split into a wide smile. She enclosed his hand in both of hers. "I think so too! And the best part of it is that we get to do this together. Just you and me, like I've always told you it's destined to be."

THREE

# ELEVEN

*June 22nd*

S ofia's heart jumped into her throat when the pilot's voice came over the intercom announcing the flight's approach to the Nice Côte d'Azur Airport. She opened the window shade, put on her sunglasses to help with the glare, and pressed her nose to the window to witness the view. According to the internet, it was one of the most scenic approaches in the world. She had no way of knowing whether or not that was true. She'd never been out of Iowa, not that she could remember, anyway. She had to admit, though, that the view of the distant mountain peaks rising up through a low-hanging brown haze and the deep blue water sprinkled with white specs she assumed were yachts was quite impressive.

A sense of excitement pricked within her for the first time since she decided to come. But as soon as the plane dropped lower and more structures on the hillsides came into view, that excitement turned into an uneasy feeling and a sense of dread filled her.

Sofia's first-class seat was in the third row, which meant she was one of the first persons off the plane. She obediently followed the other passengers ahead of her down the jetway. As the light at the end drew closer, though, her steps began to drag.

She tentatively stepped out into Terminal Two and came to a dead stop in front of the exit tunnel. The passenger behind her mumbled something under his breath as he too came to an abrupt halt, then rudely bumped her shoulder as he went around her. But her brain was too overwhelmed to tell her feet to move, and she just stood there and gawked at the beautifully tanned people hustling to and fro as the remaining passengers flowed out and around her on both sides.

As the crowd began to thin, Sofia noticed a tall man, with auburn hair hanging down over his collar, leaning against a support column a short distance down the concourse. He was staring directly at her and didn't drop his eyes when she looked his way. But that wasn't what intrigued her about him. The man had a golden aura that literally glowed around him like a halo. She had never seen anyone with a golden aura before.

Then, as she was contemplating the uniqueness of that, a male voice entered her head. *"Mirari?"*

Sofia's breath caught in her throat.

"Madame Kaye?" a woman with a heavy French accent said, breaking into her thoughts.

Sofia flipped her head around to a stylish young woman in a slim navy suit and heels standing next to her, then quickly turned back to the man with the golden aura. He was gone.

Her hand automatically went to the stone pendant that hung around her neck as her gaze rapidly scanned the walkway, but he seemed to have vanished into thin air.

"You *are* Madame Kaye, yes?" the young woman said again, her practiced smile slipping a bit.

A strange sense of disappointment flooded Sofia. She reluctantly tore her gaze away from the concourse and looked back at the woman.

"Yes, I'm Sofia Kaye." She tried her best to sound as if she was in total control, but her voice cracked and betrayed her.

The woman's smile returned and her eyes sparkled. "Welcome to Nice, madame. I'm Celeste. I'm here to assist you avoid the hassle of entry and see you to your hotel without any delays," she added. "I have a cart ready to take you to your private lounge." She swung her arm toward a golf cart-type vehicle with a stout, olive-skinned man sitting at the wheel. "So, if you are ready, please follow me."

Sofia looked at the cart and shook her head. "No thank you. I think I can manage just fine on my own."

She turned away but stopped after taking only one step. People were walking both ways on the concourse and she had no idea which way she should go from here.

Sheepishly, she looked over her shoulder at Celeste. "I don't know how to get to the baggage area. Would you mind directing me, please?"

"Madame, you misunderstand," Celeste said, her eyes glistening with a hint of concern. "Monsieur Daher has made arrangements for me to take care of you and to see to your bags and passport control. I am at your service for whatever your needs may be. My only duty is to ensure your experience here at the airport is as painless and enjoyable as possible. Please let me be of assistance to you."

Sofia studied the woman for a moment. She'd always been leery of strangers, but if Daher had sent this woman as she said, it probably wasn't a good idea to refuse her.

She gave Celeste a curt nod and started toward the cart. "Thank you. Please forgive me. This is my first time traveling and it's all new to me."

Celeste wasn't just kidding about making Sofia's entry into France painless. She deposited Sofia in a large, bright lounge that offered free refreshments, a recharging table, and plenty of comfy hanging egg chairs to relax in, then left to collect Sofia's bag. When she returned, she had a customs agent with her. The man held Sofia's open passport up next to her face, gazed from one to the other, then gave a slight nod and stamped a page.

In less than fifteen minutes total, Sofia was out of the airport and in the back of a luxurious black Bentley headed into Nice.

The haze Sofia had seen from the plane still hung low over the city, but she was too busy looking at the azure water and the light-colored buildings with orange-tiled roofs on the rolling hills. The buildings were so tightly stacked, they almost looked as if they were sitting on top of each other.

As the car drove alongside the Bay of Angels, the crowds of tourist walking and biking grew substantially. But not even the look of delight on all of their faces could take away the uneasiness twisting in Sofia's stomach.

She closed her eyes and let her head fall against the cool glass as a sudden wave of nausea swept over her, another new experience for her. She never got sick. Not ever. Even when everyone else around her was sneezing and coughing all over the place.

But this wasn't that kind of sickness. It was more of a feeling that something was very wrong with this place. And no matter how bright the sun was shining, it still felt dark.

In no time at all, the car pulled up to a stately white, six-story building with a pink-domed roof that faced the Bay of Angels, and only the Promenade des Anglais between it and the shoreline. A fancy doorman wearing a top hat sporting a ridiculously huge, fuzzy, red feather and dressed in a royal-blue knee-length coat and short cape took her bag from the driver. He then led her up three steps and through the door of the Hotel Negresco.

The smell of the sea and coconut tanning lotion followed Sofia into the lobby. She stopped just inside the doors, feeling very much like a country bumpkin and knowing she probably looked like one, too. But she couldn't help herself and her mouth dropped open at the extravagance spread out before her.

The round, marble-tiled room sparkled under a crystal chandelier, and there was gold everywhere—on the crown molding, wall sconces, and even the curtains. The artwork adorning the walls and the marble sculptures sitting on pedestals looked to be straight out the Renaissance and would have felt right at home in any museum.

To another's eyes it might have been breathtakingly beautiful, but it just made Sofia feel more out of place than ever.

"You are all checked in, Madame Kaye," Celeste said, returning to Sofia's side with a man in a royal blue short coat, red trousers, and black knee-high boots. "This is André. He will show you to your room. Is there anything else I can do for you before we part ways?"

Sofia wanted nothing more than to follow Celeste back to the airport and go home. If it weren't for the fact she was in desperate need of the money, she would have done just that.

She swallowed hard and forced her mouth into a smile. "No, thank you, I'm fine. You were a really big help."

"You are most certainly welcome. It was a pleasure meeting you," Celeste replied.

A lump moved into Sofia's throat as she watched Celeste walk out the door. She took a big breath and turned back to André. He gave a slight bow, then led her down a short hall to the elevator.

Sofia's room on the fifth floor came with a magnificent view of the Mediterranean Sea, a gold and crystal chandelier and lavish antique furnishings, which included a canopy bed and a marble bust on a small round table next to an ornate armoire. Every square inch of the room screamed money and she was hesitant to even walk in on the cobalt-blue carpet speckled with little gold fleurs-de-lis. But André refused to enter until she did, and he was holding her bag, which she knew was extremely heavy with all the borrowed clothes Maddie had stuffed into it. So, she lifted her chin and entered the room, halting at the foot of the bed.

André set her bag on a small luggage rack inside a closet, pointed out the bathroom, the room service menu, and an envelope sitting on a small writing desk in a corner. He then poured her a glass of sparkling water from a bottle of Perrier on the desk and handed it to her.

"Monsieur Daher has asked us to inform his guests that though you may think the humidity is high here, you must drink lots of water and stay hydrated. Please heed his advice. It will make your stay more pleasant."

He turned to a sliding glass door next to the desk and opened it to let in the smell of the sea and the noise of the street below. He then bowed and left.

Sofia stood in the same spot for several minutes, holding the glass and staring at the envelope on the desk. She had no doubt it was a note from Daher. Her mouth filled with the taste of the rotten eggs again and she almost gagged on the bile that rose into her throat.

She lifted her eyes to the ceiling and took in three long breaths. *This money gets me where I want to go. I can do this.*

With her jaw set, she forced her feet to walk to the desk and set the glass down without taking a sip. She picked up the cream-colored envelope, which felt as soft as velvet, and stared at her name embossed in gold lettering on the front. Then, with the parasite that seemed to have taken up permanent residence inside her stomach twisting again, she read the invitation to a formal dinner tonight at Daher's villa.

Sofia dropped the invitation on the desk and walked out onto the petite balcony. The scents of fish, olive oil, garlic, and fresh bread drifted with the soft breeze that ruffled the fronds of the palm trees lining the Promenade des Anglais. White-tipped crested waves gently rolled onto a pebbly beach littered with umbrellas, towels, and sun worshipers in skimpy to almost non-existent swimwear. In the water, speedboats pulled paragliders and people on large inflatables.

Sofia moved to the end of the balcony and leaned over the railing, hoping to get a glimpse of Saint-Jean-Cap-Ferrat beyond the short peninsula that formed the Bay of Angels. All she could see was a small tip of land, but that was enough to send an icy shiver down her back.

*What am I doing here? This place isn't me.* She let out a sigh. *Please let me get the ten thousand dollars tonight at the dinner so I can go home. I showed up like the letter said, and that's all I had to do. To hell with the challenges!*

Weak and exhausted, Sofia turned back to the room. The flight had been a long one, and though the seats in first-class reclined almost flat, she'd been too hyped up to sleep. She longingly looked at the bed but didn't move toward it. If she did get the money tonight, this may be her only chance to shop and pick up the promised souvenirs for her friends.

Sofia pulled her phone from her pocket and blinked at the time. 11:09 a.m. *That can't be right.* It felt like she'd been up for more than twenty-four hours. She tapped the screen to bring up the weather and location. In bold, white letters it showed her location as Nice, France, where it was seventy-four degrees Fahrenheit and the time was 11:10 a.m. In smaller text next to the time it showed that in Iowa it was 4:10 a.m.

She rolled her eyes. *Ohmigod, the time difference! How stupid can I be? I totally forgot about it.*

Thank God she now had time to squeeze in both a short nap and shopping before the car arrived to pick her up for dinner at eight. Without hesitating another second, she hobbled across the room to the bed as fast as her legs would carry her.

With a kick, she removed her sandals and collapsed onto the striped, cream-colored bed covering. The mattress was softer than it looked, and the sheets were scented with lavender.

Within a minute, she drifted off and began dreaming of being chased through the woods by a man with wide-set hooded eyes, a short flat nose, and a wide mouth.

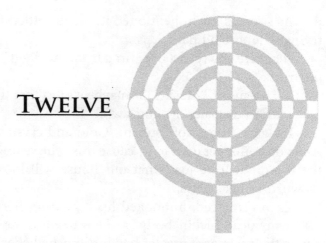

# TWELVE

Liv breathed out a long, *"Ohhh,"* as she stepped into the lobby of the Hotel Negresco. If she didn't know better, she would think someone had hijacked her dream and created a real-life version of it. The marble, crystal, gold, and art were just as she had pictured they would be in her future home—*exactly* how she pictured it. But, as she was so enthralled with the idea of being alone with Zach in the most romantic country in the world, that strange coincidence didn't even register in her brain. The warning bells ringing inside her head didn't break through the spell the city had cast over her, either.

She twirled in a circle, feeling as euphoric as the night she was crowned prom queen. "Isn't it gorgeous?"

She looped her arm through Zach's and tilted her head to the side to snap a selfie of the two of them. She then laid her cheek on his shoulder and batted her eyes up at him. To her surprise, his mouth was turned down in a scowl.

Liv straightened and pulled back a little to look into his full face. Along with his frown, there was a small tic just above his jawline that she knew only appeared when he was agitated or when something was bothering him.

"What? You don't like it?" she asked, genuinely shocked.

"God, no!" The words exploded from him. "Are you kidding?" He looked around the room. "This place has a creepy, weird kinda energy. Can't you feel it?"

As soon as Zach mentioned it, the unsettled feeling she'd been trying to ignore hit hard.

"I'm sure you're just over tired from the flight," she said, skirting the truth.

Zach paused. "Maybe. Or maybe it's just that this place is …" his lip curled in distaste, "it's god-awful."

Liv gave him a soft punch. "Gold and crystal are *never* awful! And you better get used to it, 'cause this," she swung her arm around the room, "will be just what our house will look like once we're crowned Daher's heirs."

Zach grimaced, unhooked his arm from hers, and mumbled, "Over my dead fuckin' body" as he walked to the registration desk where their personal greeter had just finished checking them in.

Liv's smile slipped, but it quickly returned when she caught a handsome bellboy standing against a wall checking her out. With a casual flip of her hair, she straightened her shoulders, pushed her chest out, and purposely moved her gaze around the room as if she hadn't noticed him.

A set of double glass doors at the end of the registration desk had the name Versailles stenciled in gold lettering above them. The doors were tinted so all she could see was darkness behind them, but she sensed a presence standing there, watching her from the shadows. A cold shiver coursed through her and the uneasy feeling churned in her stomach.

*Stop it! You're letting Z's paranoia get to you,* Liv scolded herself.

Although it wasn't just Zach's paranoia. Before they'd left Texas, she'd had an overpowering feeling that things were about to change between them.

It was just a feeling, not one of her real visions, so she didn't know what the change would be or when it would take place. That didn't make any difference, though. She would only allow herself one thought and that was that this trip was going to be a good turning point in their relationship, and she wasn't about to let some stupid paranoia or queasy feeling ruin it for her.

She pulled her gaze away from the door, smiled flirtatiously at the bellboy, and, with a renewed sense of purpose, flounced over to the counter to join Zach.

ᘿᚷᚱᚷᛈᛁᛁᛁᗡᛕᘿ

Zach didn't bother to take his shoes off before he flopped onto the bed. His brain was still on Texas time, and as far as it was concerned, it was 3:20 in the morning. He had managed to catch a few winks on the twelve-hour flight over, but he still felt as if he hadn't slept in two days. He really needed to grab a few hours of sleep, but ten minutes after he walked into his room, a knock sounded on the door.

He groaned out loud but didn't move.

The next knock was louder, and Liv's voice hissed through the door, "Come on, Z, I know you're in there. Open up!"

With a long, weary sigh, he heaved himself off the bed and let her in.

Liv, dressed in a crocheted lace cover up over a multi-colored monokini, stepped in and looked around the modestly decorated room.

"Wow, this is nothing like my room!" she exclaimed. "Mine is painted red and trimmed in gold and has this awesome giant armoire with mirrored doors." She shrugged. "I'm sure you wouldn't like it. Lucky for you they have drab and conventional rooms in just your style, too."

She turned around and saw him lying on the bed again. "What are you doing?" Her devilish grin evaporated. "You don't have your swimsuit on! Come on, we're wasting time. There are a ton of sexy, gorgeous French men down there on the beach waiting for me."

"Nooo," Zach moaned. "I just want to sleep."

Liv put her hands on her hips. "You can sleep when you get back home. This is the fuckin' French Riviera! When are we ever gonna get another chance to enjoy it on someone else's buck?" She stomped to the bed and pulled on his arm, dragging him to the edge. "Come on, you can sleep down on the beach."

Zach didn't have the strength to argue. He knew it wouldn't do any good anyway. She would continue to nag him and he'd have no peace until she got what she wanted.

He pushed off the bed and grabbed his swimsuit out of his bag on the way to the bathroom.

Closing the door, he leaned against the sink to keep from falling over and stared at his reflection in the mirror. Deep, dark circles ringed his eyes, accentuating his naturally pale complexion. All he had to do was add a couple long-pointed incisors and he'd be the perfect vision of a vampire.

Zach dropped his chin to his chest and tried to think back to the last time he'd felt this drained. He was up all night after prom just a month ago and had felt fine afterwards. There were plenty of other times, too, like all the nights he'd stayed up until dawn to study for a test, and he never felt this bad. And this was more than just feeling drained. He felt weird and unnatural, as if this place was literally sucking his energy out.

He splashed cold water on his face, telling himself over and over he was being stupid. It had to be what Liv said, he was just over tired.

After changing into his suit, he stopped in front of the mirror again and raked his fingers through his hair. "Ten thousand dollars," he whispered to his image. "That's what you came here for, so stop being a moron and get with the program."

He stared at his reflection, trying to psych himself up, but the uneasy feeling in the pit of his stomach refused to budge. After several long seconds, he gave up and staggered out of the bathroom.

At the sound of the door opening, Liv turned from the window holding a glass of water. "Here, drink this. The bellboy told me the reason I was feeling tired was because I was dehydrated. He said Perrier has the minerals your body needs to rejuvenate. So, drink up."

"And this bellboy is also a doctor?" Zach said sarcastically.

"I don't know. Maybe. All I know is I drank the glass he poured me and now I don't feel the least bit tired."

Zach shrugged. He couldn't imagine how a glass of water would make him feel any better, but it couldn't hurt either. He took the glass and chugged it down.

"Great! Let's go," Liv chirped, looping her arm through his.

By the time she dragged him the short distance down to the elevator, Zach was feeling more like his old self. The uneasy feeling in the pit of his stomach was even gone.

And when a long-legged girl in a thong bikini stepped into the elevator with them, everything else in his head completely vanished.

⎰⋇⯑⋌⎅⫶⫶⟑⋇⋰

Liv had never been a sun worshiper or a fan of lying out to tan. Zach wasn't either. Their complexions were too fair and they would just burn instead of tan. Their eyes were extra sensitive, too, and couldn't take the brightness, which meant they had to wear special dark tinted sunglasses.

But she didn't often get a chance like this to make Zach jealous and a little discomfort was a small price to pay.

As she hoped, the second she settled onto a deck chair shaded by a large umbrella, a stream of men began to parade in front of her making no attempt to hide their appraising glances. Several even stopped and tried to start up a conversation, but she brushed them off like irritating flies. There was only one guy that mattered, Zach, and he had abandoned her to sit with Claudette, the girl from the elevator.

Liv pressed her lips into a thin line and turned her head away as Zach applied sunscreen to Claudette's back.

At the water's edge, a group of pre-teen girls followed a wave as it retreated into the sea, then squealed with delight and ran back up the pebbly beach as the next wave came in. She used to be that young and carefree, though it seemed like that was decades ago, not just a few years. She and Zach had been inseparable then, and she had no fear of losing him.

How and when did that all change?

As memories of that more innocent time played in her mind, the hairs on the back of her neck suddenly stood on end and the sensation she was being watched swept over her. She scooted up in the chair and looked around.

Several hunky young men shifted their positions to make their muscles bulge when she turned her head in their direction. Normally, she would have seductively smiled back, but this time she was more interested in finding out the reason her skin was tingling.

Liv's gaze panned the fleet of boats anchored in the bay, stopping on a jet ski that bobbed up and down in the water beside one of the larger yachts. On it was a man holding a pair of binoculars that were pointed directly at her.

She lowered her dark tinted sunglasses to get a better look and to make sure she wasn't just imagining he was looking at her. The man lowered the binoculars at the same time.

A small "*ohhh*" slipped through Liv's parted lips as she saw the man had a golden aura. She blinked several times, thinking it had to be the brightness of the sun or a reflection. But when she looked again, the golden halo shining around him was still there. He was also, without a doubt, staring at her.

All at once a male voice entered her head. "*Alesandese?*"

She dropped her sunglasses and sat up straighter.

A waiter walking by at that moment stopped in front of her. "Did you wish to order something, madame?"

"No. No, thank you," Liv said, leaning to the side to see around him.

"Very well, madame." The waiter gave her a slight bow and moved on, but the damage was done. The man on the jet ski was gone, leaving only a wake in his place.

*Alesandese*, Liv repeated silently and felt a tug on her heart, as if it were the name of a person she'd lost. She wrapped her arms around her chest to stop her hands from trembling and collapsed against the back of the chair.

A shadow fell over her and Zach plopped down on the chair next to hers. "I'm starving. How about you?"

When she didn't answer, he looked over.

In one swift move, he swung his legs around and sat up on the edge of the chair to face her. "Are you okay?"

Liv turned her head toward him, then looked out over the water. She wasn't okay, but she didn't want to tell him that.

"I'm fine," she said, putting her sunglasses back on to hide her eyes.

Zach leaned over his elbows resting on his knees and took her hand. "You're not fine. I can see it on your face. Did one of these guys say something to you?" He glanced around at the men watching them.

Liv's gaze flew back to Zach and a spark of hope ignited within her. "Why? You jealous?"

He squeezed her hand. "That's not an answer. Something's wrong. You look ... kinda scared. If one of these guys has been harassing you, I—"

Liv cut him, "No, it's not that."

"Then what?"

She breathed a heavy sigh. "Have you ever heard the name Alesandese?"

Zach's brow furrowed. "Hmm … it does sorta have a familiar ring to it. It tastes like concord grapes. But … nah, I don't think so. Why?"

Liv closed her eyes and shook her head. "It just came into my head, and I … it feels like I've heard it before."

"Huh. Weird. I had a strange name pop into my head out of nowhere at the airport when we arrived." He shrugged. "You probably just heard someone say the name in passing once. But you're not upset because you remembered a name. There's something else. What is it?"

Liv winced. She could hardly tell him he had ruined her perfectly planned romantic afternoon by running off with another girl. "I don't know. I feel kinda lightheaded. It must be the jetlag."

Zach stood and gave Liv's hand a tug to pull her to her feet. "You know what it is? You need something to eat. Come on. Let's get some food. Then, we can rent a couple jet skis. Cause like you said, when are we going to have another chance to enjoy the French Riviera on someone else's dollar?"

Liv looked up at his sincere smile and couldn't help but smile back. "What about Claudette?" she asked, putting an over exaggerated French accent on the name.

He shrugged. "She's more interested in the guys who own those yachts out there then a poor lil' Texas boy like me."

Liv tried to give him a sympathetic look, but she was too happy to make it work. She did hide her satisfied smirk, though, as Zach helped her to her feet.

And as they walked arm in arm across the pebbly beach, all thoughts of the man with the golden aura vanished.

# THIRTEEN

S ofia awoke with a start to the sound of her phone rattling on a small table next to the bed. She blinked several times in confusion at the blood-red velvet upholstered chair that came into focus before she remembered where she was. With a soft moan, she rolled to her back and let her eyelids slowly drift close again.

When her phone rattled a second time, she yawned sleepily, reached for it, and pressed the home button. It took a second for her eyes to adjust, but as soon as the time 6:18 p.m. registered in her brain, she bolted straight up, wide awake.

"Ah shit," she muttered. "I've slept away the entire day!"

She scrambled off the bed and raced to the open door of the balcony. The sky was still bright but the sun was sinking toward the mountains, and only a few of the true die-hard sun worshipers were left on the beach, vying for the last rays.

"Shit!" Sofia repeated. This afternoon could very well have been her one and only chance to do some shopping and she'd blown it for nothing, because even after almost seven and a half hours of sleep, she still felt drained.

With a soft moan, she shuffled toward the bathroom and came to a stop in the doorway. The room was equipped with a bright gold bidet next to a gold toilet and gold clawfoot bathtub that had a hand-held sprayer in place of a shower head. It was dreadful and gaudy, but she didn't care. Bathrooms in a foster home were considered prime real estate. Rarely did she get five minutes to herself in the bathroom without someone knocking on the door.

Sofia ran her hand over the complimentary bathrobe and sniffed a bottle of chamomile bath salts and vanilla scented lotion sitting next to small bottles of shampoo and conditioner on the marble countertop as the tub filled with water. She let the water get almost to the brim before she threw in the bath salts, stepped in, and sank up to her chin. The steaming, apple-scented water went straight to work on the tension in her muscles, and all her troubling thoughts were replaced with the pure bliss of how good it felt.

The bathwater was completely cold by the time Sofia dragged herself out of the tub and dried off with the largest, fluffiest towel she'd ever touched. As she slipped on the sleeveless, navy lace skater dress Maddie had loaned her, she silently thanked her friend for insisting she bring it. She hadn't wanted to, but thank God Maddie had won that battle. Otherwise, she'd be wearing shorts and a t-shirt to the formal dinner tonight.

Once dressed, Sofia plaited her auburn hair into two loose braids, then twisted them into a fat bun at the nape of her neck. Back home she seldom wore makeup. There wasn't much point in trying to look attractive when everyone had already judged you to be insignificant and hardly gave you the time of day. But it was different here. No one knew her. She had a chance at a fresh start and this time she wasn't going to screw it up.

After applying a bit of mascara, blush, and lip gloss that Maddie had stuck in her bag, she stood in front of a full-length mirror and chewed on her lip as she turned left and right. The tall girl starring back at her didn't look all that different than the one she saw every day in the mirror, except for the makeup, which stood out like a neon sign to her. She hoped with all her heart, though, that the makeup and fancy dress would distract people enough they wouldn't notice her other flaws.

Sofia lifted the stone pendant to her neck, then stopped before slipping the chain over her head. It was the one and only piece she had from her former life. Her foster mother had returned it to her when she turned thirteen, and she had worn it non-stop ever since. But something inside her told her she shouldn't wear it tonight.

She dropped her arms and stared at the bluish-purple stone

lying in her palm. No one but her could see the small points of light twinkling within it or feel the energy that radiated from the stone, which was part of the reason she loved it so much. The other—the main reason she never took it off—was because it had once belonged to her real mom. No one had told her that, but in her visions her mom was wearing one just like it.

She brushed her thumb over the stone and watched the lights dance in response to her touch. Her neck felt naked without it, but the feeling she shouldn't wear it was too strong to ignore. But she couldn't leave it in the room either, it was too precious to her. And she'd heard too many stories of people's valuables going missing from hotel rooms.

With a sigh, she dropped the necklace into the mini purse she planned to take with her.

Twenty minutes early, Sofia took the stairs down to the Salon Royale, a domed ballroom that sparkled in the glow of an enormous crystal chandelier originally commissioned by Czar Nicholas II, according to the sign on the wall. As in the lobby, the salon had touches of gold everywhere: on the decorative motifs in the plaster between the stained-glass windows of the dome, at the tops of the Roman columns that circled the room, and in the gilded frames of the eighteen-century royal portraits that hung between the columns. The gold touches didn't impress her much, but the art did. She slowly wandered through the room to the sweet, soulful notes of a piano drifting from the Negresco Bar, stopping at each piece to read the plaque.

Lastly, Sofia made her way to the centerpiece of the room, a tall yellow contemporary sculpture of a dancing woman dressed in a multi-colored swimsuit and twirling on rotating platform. As she stood and watched it spin, the energy in the room suddenly turned dark and threatening and a strange sensation tickled the back of her neck. She tensed, and the hairs on her arms stood on end.

Without moving her head, she darted a glance to one side, then the other. Everything looked the same as it had a second ago, but it felt different. She held her breath and slowly turned around.

Hotel Negresco, famous for its diverse selection of antiques and art, brought people in from all walks of life. At the moment, it seemed they were all strolling through the salon, dressed in everything from shorts and halter-tops to formal evening wear. No one looked her way or paid particular attention to her. Still, she could feel a sense of danger closing in on her and her instincts told her to run.

She threw another furtive glance around the room and scurried across the marble-tiled floor, which seemed to have grown to the size of a football field. She ran down the short hall, across the lobby, and burst through the front doors as if a dozen demons were after her.

She bent at the waist and gulped in the night air.

"Is everything all right, madame?" the doorman asked.

Sofia looked up through her eyelashes. The tall man standing before her was dressed in the standard blue doorman uniform, but he had the face of a reptile instead of a man. She gasped and took a stumbling step backward.

"Madame?" the doorman repeated and reached out a hand to steady her.

Sofia blinked rapidly to dispel the image of the reptilian face, and the concerned look of the doorman, who was handsome enough to pass for a model, finally rematerialized in front of her. She blinked again until her brain fired up. Then her cheeks heated with embarrassment as she realized she had let her imagination get the best of her.

She looked down at her dress and brushed imaginary lint from the skirt as she tried to compose herself.

There was an awkward silence before she said, "I'm sorry. Um ... I'm fine." Her voice squeaked like a three-year-old's. She cringed and cleared her throat. "I'm just gonna wait down there for my car," she added and rushed down the steps toward the street before she embarrassed herself more.

The evening was balmy with an occasional breeze coming off the sea. It ruffled the skirt of Sofia's dress and cooled the moisture that had gathered on her forehead. The beauty of the red-tinted sky had drawn out a throng of vacationers, who strolled the walkway, talking and smiling serenely as only people on vacation can do.

But even with all the people surrounding her, Sofia never felt more alone and out of place. She craned her neck back and looked up at the sky. Only a few of the brightest stars shone through the lights of the Promenade des Anglais, but she knew the constellations well enough to picture them. Little by little her pulse and breath returned to normal, and the pounding of her heart in her ears was replaced with the boom of a bass turned up too high on one of the large yachts anchored in the bay.

Sofia wrapped her arms around herself and gazed out over the water. *You're being ridiculous. You've got to stop,* she silently chided herself. *There's nothing here to hurt you. Just stay calm. The money is almost yours.*

She inhaled a long breath, held it for the count of five and exhaled slowly.

At that moment, a slick black limousine pulled up to the curb. The driver jumped out, ran around the car and opened the back door. Four young people rushed up to the car and piled in.

Instead of closing the door, the driver stood stoically beside it, as if waiting for someone else. Sofia turned her head and looked back at the hotel, wondering who it would be.

"Madame Kaye?" the driver said.

Sofia started and jerked around, her eyebrows raised in question.

The driver swept his arm toward the door. "If you please," he added, bowing slightly at the waist.

"Oh," she replied weakly as it dawned on her this was the car she'd been waiting for. The one that would take her to the villa. Blushing to the tips of her toes, she stepped forward and bent her head to get in.

Just as Sofia lifted her foot, she heard a voice behind her say, "Hurry up, Livy! The car's here waiting."

Sofia's mouth suddenly filled with the taste of pickles.

At her hesitation, the driver took a firm hold of her elbow and practically lifted her into the car. Unable to do anything else, she plopped down on the first seat inside the door and leaned forward to look out the open door.

Standing at the top of the stairs was a harried looking young man with auburn hair beckoning to someone still inside the hotel. Several long seconds later, a girl with jet-black hair casually strolled through the hotel doors as if she were walking a red carpet.

Her strapless, emerald, mermaid-cut evening gown hugged her perfect curves down to her knees, causing more than one head to turn in her direction. The young man waiting for her didn't seem to notice or care. He grabbed hold of the girl's hand and nearly dragged her down the steps and didn't let go until they reached the car.

"Sorry we're late," the young man said to the driver as he helped the girl into the limo.

Sofia sucked in a sharp breath and pressed her back against the leather as the pair took their seats, their golden auras glowing in the dim lights just like the man she saw at the airport. In her whole life she'd never seen a gold aura before and now in one day she'd seen three. That couldn't just be a coincidence.

But it wasn't just their auras that Sofia took notice of. She had always been super sensitive to the vibrations of people's bodies. No two were alike, and once she felt a person's vibration, she never forgot it. Without a doubt she knew she'd been around these two before, though she couldn't recall ever meeting them, and that didn't seem logical. They were too striking of a couple to forget.

Stranger still, she felt an irresistible attraction to them, like that of a magnetic force.

The driver closed the door and hurried around the back of the limo, got into the driver's seat, and deftly performed a U-turn to the honks and yells of other drivers. As the limo traveled along the seacoast and headed out of the city, the six other occupants talked amongst themselves while Sofia tried to sort through a barrage of questions swirling inside her head.

"What about you?" a voice asked, jolting Sofia out of her reverie.

She looked up and saw that all eyes were turned on her. "Oh." She sat up straighter. "I'm sorry, what was the question?"

"Where are you from?" the girl to her left repeated.

"Iowa," she replied and internally cringed at the hoarseness of her voice.

A girl with a pierced eyebrow and nose and a henna-style tattoo covering the tops of her hands and going up to her elbows on both arms snickered. "Iowa? I went there once. Or I should say my boyfriend and I drove *through* there once on our way to Colorado to go skiing. I can't say there was much to see other than corn and cows." Her eyes suddenly went big and round. "*Ohhh*, all those poor little cows! Who's gonna milk them while you're here?"

A girl and a boy on either side of Henna Girl chuckled at the slam.

Sofia bristled. From the second she had stepped off the plane, she'd felt as if she had landed on an alien planet. Even the air smelled different here. But being bullied was the same wherever you went and she had enough experience to know exactly how to handle it.

Picking up a loose strand of her hair, Sofia made a show of curling it around her finger and smiled sweetly. "Yeah, I don't really have to worry about that," she replied. "You see, I, like sixty-four percent of all other Iowans, live in the city. I would love to live on a farm, though."

Henna Girl scoffed and gave the boy beside her a look that clearly said, *"What a loser."*

"But that's probably because I spend my time studying instead of in a tattoo parlor, so I know Iowa is second in the nation for food production," Sofia added with a satisfied smile. "In fact, it may interest you to know the whole world would have a hard time surviving if it weren't for Iowa farmers. Anyone with a brain would be thankful for the farmers' sacrifices instead of turning their noses up at them."

The boy next to Henna Girl snorted a loud guffaw. Henna Girl's upper lip curled, and she opened her mouth to fire back, but the girl sitting next to Sofia spoke up first.

"I'm Sophia, and this is Ethan," the girl said, pointing to the boy on her left side.

Sofia turned her head and gave the girl a genuine smile. "My name's Sofia too."

That started introductions going around the car. As it turned out, Henna Girl's name was also Sophia.

"Looks like I'm the odd girl out," Liv said with an exaggerated southern drawl. "Or maybe just the exceptional one." She flashed a smug smile. "I'm Olivia. This is my brother, Zach."

Sofia's mouth filled consecutively with the taste of pickles, then honey, as Liv said their names, and another jolt of recognition hit her. Her eyebrows drew together, and she stared harder at the couple.

They didn't appear to recognize her any more than she did them, but every ounce of her being told her she knew them. How was that possible, though? Olivia's accent was pure Texan and Sofia had never been to Texas.

The limo followed the road out of the city, around the bay, and proceeded into the hills of Saint-Jean-Cap-Ferrat, where mansions of the extremely rich and famous hid behind thick groves of trees. When the car finally stopped in front of a black and gold iron gate, Sofia's attention moved from Olivia and Zach to what was outside the window.

The villa was far from the lights of the city, but even taking that into consideration, the grounds seemed unnaturally dark. As they passed through the gate, the car's headlights reflected off a gold family crest medallion on the side of a concrete pillar. The crest depicted a shooting star flying over a large tree and a figure with the head of an eagle and the body of a lion, standing on its back legs clawing at the branches of the tree.

Sofia involuntarily shuddered and her already racing pulse accelerated a little more.

The limo continued up a twisty palm and cedar tree flanked driveway and came to a stop in front of a magnificent three-story mansion. Like everything else in Nice, the house, with its double staircase leading up to a front porch lined with Greek columns, conveyed money.

Sofia shifted in the seat and pressed her nose to the glass for a better view. The central section of the house was bathed in the glow of spotlights, as was a bronze statue of Athena draped in a marble tunic standing to the side of the stairs. Every tree and brush twinkled with thousands of tiny faerie lights, but just beyond the glimmer an ominous darkness pushed against the barrier of light to break through.

Sofia remained in her seat as the others exited. When it was just her and Zach left, he rose and moved toward the door, then stopped and lifted his hand.

"After you." The timbre of his voice flowed over her like a sweet melody and a rainbow of colors exploded in her head like fireworks.

She leapt to her feet so fast she stumbled backward. Zach reached out and took hold of her hand to keep her from falling, and the second their skin touched, a shock wave equivalent to that of a sonic boom blasted through Sofia.

She and Zach both flinched simultaneously, but instead of letting go, their fingers curled around each other's as if neither wanted to lose the connection.

The nape of Sofia's neck began to prickle with a soft ache and a vision of three giggling toddlers playing on a playground in a park sped through her mind in lightning speed.

At that same moment, the blue LED mood lights on the ceiling and the rope lights around the bar and base of the seats flickered and went out. That didn't prevent her from seeing the yellow rings around the pupils of his eyes spark like flames, though.

"*I know you,*" Zach's voice spoke inside her head.

"I know you too," she whispered back out loud.

Zach's eyebrows shot up in question and they stared into each other's eyes with the same confused look on their faces.

"Come on, Z," Liv called out, shattering the moment. "We're going to be late."

Sofia let go of Zach's hand with a jerk, but her eyes stayed locked with his even though she could feel heat moving up her neck.

"You better go. Your sister's anxious to get to the party."

"She's not my sister. Not by blood anyway," Zach replied.

Sofia's mouth formed a soundless O. He didn't have to tell her that; she already knew. But how was that possible?

The vision of the three toddlers flashed behind her eyes again. This time they were sitting in a circle holding hands. Her heart moved into her throat and she drew back.

Zach hesitated, looking as if he wanted to say something more. But instead, he just sighed, turned, and bent nearly in half and stepped out the door.

Sofia felt like her heart was being ripped from her chest as she watched Zach walk away with Olivia. When he reached the corner of the house and looked back over his shoulder, the tightness in her chest swelled. She collapsed back onto the seat, confused and more than a little scared. Something very weird was going on, and for the first time in her life she didn't know how to deal with it.

She rested her elbows on her knees and buried her face in her hands. From the time she'd been old enough to think for herself, she'd figured out what she wanted and how to get it. But now, all of a sudden, everything seemed blurred, and she wasn't certain of anything anymore.

To make matters worse, she had a sinking feeling she had crossed a threshold and was headed down a new path that she wasn't at all prepared to deal with.

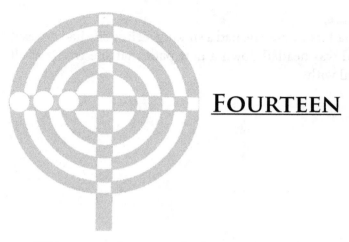

# FOURTEEN

L iv stood next to the limo and gazed up at the flat-roofed, sand-colored mansion. The house and manicured grounds looked every bit as expensive as she knew they were. She had spent hours researching the mansion on the internet before leaving Texas and had counted the minutes until she could see it up close and in person. But now that she was standing in front of what she thought would be her dream home, her skin crawled and a small voice in her head whispered she should get back in the car and leave before it was too late.

She pulled out her pendant that she had tucked in the bodice of her dress, shut her eyes, and closed her fist around the smooth bluish-purple stone. The energy of the stone always had a way of calming her, but the sense of tranquility it brought her only lasted until she opened her eyes and found herself standing amid knee-high vegetation, surrounded by trees and the overpowering scent of cedar and pine.

Liv inhaled sharply and looked around in wonder. On her left, the lights of the villa shone through the trees. The limo was parked in the driveway just as it had been when she got out of it.

*What the hell?* She had just been wishing she was away from the house, and now she was in the woods with no recollection of how she got there.

The muted sounds of string instruments coming from behind the villa where the party was already in progress drifted through the trees. Liv turned in the direction of the music, but there was a jungle of foliage in between and it was too dense for her to see anything more than a soft glow from the lights through it.

She sensed a dark and malevolent presence lurking in the shadows, though, and every cell in her brain screamed to run back to the light. But her feet seemed to be glued to the ground and refused to move. She held her breath as she slowly scanned the landscape, looking for the source of the malignant energy.

She'd always been able to see extremely well in the dark, but this darkness seemed almost opaque, and the only things she could clearly make out were the larger shapes of trees and cactuses. But on her second pass through, she picked up a movement at the edge of the trees about fifty feet away.

Liv narrowed her eyes and stared hard at the spot until an outline of a tall, broad-shouldered man came into focus. He was standing with his back to her between two trees. She couldn't see his face, but there was no denying the ominous energy she had felt was radiating from him.

She shivered as an icy chill ran up her spine, then squinted to try to make out more details. Instead, a distant memory of a man with reptile-like features popped into her head. She let out a small gasp.

The sound was little more than a sigh, but the man visibly squared his shoulders and raised his head as if he'd heard her.

She took a step backward onto a brittle twig. The loud snap pierced the night air like a gunshot. Her hand came up to her mouth to hold back a scream.

For a moment, she  forgot to breath as the man started to turn toward her. But,  just as she was about to get a full view of his face, a bright light shined in her eyes and blinded her. She brought her arm up to shield her face and stumbled backward into cold, hard metal. It took another moment for her eyes to refocus before she could see anything more than a white circle. She looked around and found she was back on the driveway standing next to the limo.

Liv whipped her head around toward the woods, which had closed in again and were as dark as if a black curtain had been drawn shut in front of them. She put her hand on the rear fender of the car to steady herself. *What the hell's going on?*

She'd had visions before, many times, but they had only ever shown her things to come, or occasionally a flashback from her past. Never before had they presented things as they were happening in real time. They also only showed her things that pertained to her or to Zach. A man standing in the woods watching a party had nothing to do with either of them.

Or did he?

She shook her head to clear the thoughts that were making her heart race. "This is ridiculous. I'm just spooked from all of Z's talk. That's all," she whispered, hoping and praying she was right.

But in her gut she knew that wasn't the case.

### ∠ҲʀϒⅢ⊿Ҟㅈ

Ukani, dressed in a black leather jacket and black slacks, stood so still it was nearly impossible to tell him apart from the trunks of the trees. He didn't need to be there watching the selected ones come in. He couldn't tell a Pleiadian from a human just by looking at them any better than anyone else could. That's why they'd gone to the trouble of designing the maze—to sort the Guardians out of the crowd.

This was the third and final group, though, and they still needed to find one more Guardian. The second group had produced the other two, the boy and one of the girls. If the last girl wasn't here tonight, the redemption he was desperately counting on wouldn't happen, and he'd die in disgrace.

He gnashed his teeth together at the thought of his name being spoken with contempt on his home planet for all the centuries to come and refocused his attention on the group gathering on the lawn.

Just as with the first two groups, it was apparent these young people, laughing and drinking the free-flowing booze they weren't allowed to have in the States, had some Pleiadian blood in them. But none stood out as Ukani had hoped. And as more candidates strolled in, an inkling of doubt began to nag at the back of his mind. He tried to ignore it, but it was persistent and wouldn't go away.

When the headlights of the last limo flashed through the trees, Ukani balled his hands into fists and let out a soft growl. He had waited fifteen years for this moment—far beyond his limit of patience. It wasn't just that he was ready for this to end, he needed it to end. The mines had taken more of a toll on him than he let on, and he could feel a little more of his life essence drain away every day.

There was still time for him to get his revenge, though, and that is what kept him going. Once he delivered the three Guardians to Daher and proved he was and always would be the best enforcer in the universe, he would kill the Three so Daher would have no chance of reclaiming Earth.

Ukani felt a rush of joy at that thought and wished he could live long enough to witness the Anunnaki Elite strip Daher of his rank. But he knew that was highly unlikely. Daher would have him killed as soon as the Guardians fell. The knowledge that Daher would be stuck on Earth for the rest of his life and would have to live with the humans and the shame of his failure would just have to be good enough.

The sound of a barely audible gasp jolted Ukani out of his thoughts. He lifted his chin and focused his third eye on the trees behind him. His third eye, located on the back of his head, couldn't see clear images, but could distinguish the differences in light and dark, which was useful when someone tried to sneak up on him.

The snap of a twig confirmed what his eye had already told him—someone was there.

Ukani turned but only got a glimpse of a girl with pale skin and long, dark hair before she vanished before his eyes. He stared at the spot where the girl had been standing, then moved a few paces to the right so he could see the limo parked in the driveway.

The same girl was now standing next to the car staring into the woods.

Ukani's lipless mouth stretched into a wide, thin smile, the only true smile he could produce. He'd always considered himself superior to the other enforcers, and now this reaffirmed that fact. He'd found the three Guardians just like he assured Daher he would.

Ukani pushed back the temptation to run, grab the girl, and take her straight to Daher. He knew the Anunnaki would want solid proof and the maze was what could give him that. And after all these years, a few more hours wait was nothing.

"I've got you," he sneered under his breath.

With a great deal of effort, he tore his gaze away from the girl and made his way to the house to break the news to Daher.

ᘯᚷᚱ᛭ᛈᛁᛁᛁᐃᚴᛋ

Liv shuddered as she gave one last look at the woods and turned back to the mansion. Two well-built men in suits stood along the path that ran down the side of the house. She did a double take. Had they been there all along?

"Ohmigod," she groaned, letting her head fall back so she was looking up at the night sky. *How stupid can I be? Of course, a guy like Daher would have security stationed around the grounds of his villa.*

She felt like a paranoid fool, but still jumped when a voice came over a loudspeaker from the back of the house announcing dinner would be served in fifteen minutes.

She swallowed back her heart, which had leapt into her throat and hissed, "Damn you, Zach!"

She took a deep breath, dropped her stone pendant back into the bodice of her dress, and turned to the open limo door. "Come on, Z," she called, her voice dripping with acid. "We're going to be late."

A minute later, Zach stepped out of the limo.

Liv slipped her hand into his and closed her eyes as a familiar tingle and rush of strength coursed through her.

"I'm so glad you're here with me. I don't know if I could do this without you," she said, and meant it.

She snuggled up against him as close as she could get without crawling inside his suit jacket and breathed in his scent. It didn't give her as much relief as she hoped for, though, as a chill remained wrapped around her spine and an ominous feeling had a firm grip on her stomach.

And for the first time in her life, she actually felt a little scared.

# FIFTEEN

**Z**ach stepped out of the limo into the still night air and tugged on his bow tie that was all of a sudden too tight around his neck.

The tops of the tall palm trees surrounding the villa rustled in the breeze coming off the sea, but none of the coolness made it through the thick vegetation to the ground. And the air felt extra stifling with the fire Sofia had lit burning bright inside him.

He barely noticed Liv slip her hand into his and snuggle up against him as the sensation of Sofia's touch replayed in his mind. He hadn't felt an energy like Sofia's since … actually, he couldn't remember ever feeling anything like that before. It was like he'd been renewed. Like he was finally whole again, and even his mind seemed clearer.

But now with his brain fully functioning again, the sense of danger he'd felt earlier was back stronger than ever.

Zach still wasn't sure where the danger was coming from. But he did know one thing—it wasn't coming from Sofia. He was as sure of that as he was they were somehow connected. Just like he and Liv were connected. Though that was confusing and made no sense whatsoever. He'd only just met Sofia.

In those few minutes he held her hand, though, the hole in his heart that had been there forever had filled in. And now, the thought that when this was over she'd return to Iowa and he to Texas, and he'd never see her again, frightened him more than any thought of danger.

Liv practically dragged Zach down the path alongside the house and through a miniature replica of the Arc de Triomphe. On the other side of the Arc, a double staircase took them down to an enormous yard interspersed with lavish gardens and exotic plants.

They stopped at a white event tent set up at the base of the stairs, where a young woman signed them in, collected their passports, and handed them two of the three remaining nametags. They then followed a crushed rock walkway lined with flaming torches, marble benches, and pedestals holding pots overflowing with every imaginable color of flower through manicured lawns that any golf course would envy.

The walkway wound around a rectangular pond filled with water lilies and ended at a temporary bar set up in front of a row of open French doors that led into the house. The majority of guests were congregated in small groups around the bar and doors, paying little attention to a string quartet playing on a raised terrace above a concrete wall that bordered the yard and kept the woods at bay.

Someone had gone to a lot of trouble and had spent a ton of money to transform the area into an enchanted garden with globe lights hanging on wires overhead and faerie lights sparkling everywhere. But the darkness pulsed like a living being just beyond the lights.

Liv hugged Zach's arm tighter and purposely kept her eyes away from the trees, focusing instead on the guests, who were also their competitors. There seemed to be an equal mix of male and female contestants in the crowd, but that was where the diversity ended. Everyone was tall, thin, and white. Even their facial features were similar, right down to their blue eyes.

"This is really weird," Liv whispered, more to herself than to Zach.

"What is?" he asked, without turning his attention away from the top of the stairs.

"Everyone here, the guests anyway, look like they're related. I mean, look at 'em. They all kinda look ... like us."

"Hmm," Zach replied distractedly.

Liv turned to him, then followed his gaze to where Sofia was standing at the top of the stairs.

"Seriously?" she hissed, giving him a soft push away.

Zach started and looked around at her. "What?"

She had put up with the girls Zach dated in high school because she didn't consider them worthy rivals. But Sofia was different. Liv had felt something shift inside Zach the second Sofia had introduced herself in the limo. It was written all over his face now, too.

"You haven't heard a single thing I've said, have you?"

Zach had the decency to blush. But before he could reply, she went on.

"You're a fuckin' moron, you know that? Why are you doing this? Why her?" Liv turned her head away so he couldn't see her nose turn red. "I can't fuckin' believe this."

She started to walk away, but Zach caught her hand and pulled her back.

"Hey, I'm sorry. What did I do?"

"Are you seriously asking me that?" Liv snapped. "You haven't looked away from that girl since you got in the limo!" Her throat suddenly tightened. "How can you do this to me?"

Zach's eyes widened, as if a light bulb had clicked on in his head. He put an arm around Liv's shoulders and pulled her into a hug even though she tried to push away.

"I'm not doing anything. And it's not what you think. There's just ..." He paused as if searching for the right words. "To tell the truth, I don't know what the fuck's going on. I feel ... something about Sofia feels familiar. Like I've known her my whole life. I just can't figure out when or where we could've met, though."

"That's because you've never met her before. Hello ... she's from Iowa. We've never been to Iowa."

"Yeah, I know. That's what's so weird. I can't explain it, but I'm one hundred percent positive I know her." Zach pulled back so he could look Liv in the eye. "You're super-sensitive to people. Do you feel anything special about her? Anything familiar?"

Liv buried her face in his shoulder. The last thing she wanted him to know was that she too had felt something familiar about Sofia.

"She's just another girl who wants to get into your pants like all the others. Or maybe it's this place ... I don't like it here. *Everything* feels off. I'm starting to think maybe we shouldn't have come."

"That's what I've been tryin' to tell ya ever since we got here! There *is* something weird about this place." Zach paused. "But we've come a long way. We can't leave yet."

Liv's spine went rigid. "Why? Because of *her*?"

Zach stepped back, took hold of her chin and forced her to look up at him. "Yes … partly, anyway."

She clenched her fists, wishing for once he'd lie to her.

"But not just her," he went on. "We came to get the twenty thousand dollars. That's not just for us. It's for Mom and Dad, and we can't leave until we get it."

A shudder ran up Liv's back. "But what if this weird something we're both feeling is something bad?"

Zach's eyebrows rose. "Is it? Have you had a vision?"

For two seconds she considered telling him about the man in the woods. But she wasn't a hundred percent sure the man was a threat. It could turn out that he was just part of the security team and then she'd feel like the biggest fool ever.

A server in a short white jacket and gloves walked up behind Zach and cleared his throat.

Liv hastily turned her attention to the man, thankful for the intrusion.

The server gave a bow as he swept his arm toward the house. "Madame, monsieur, if you would please make your way into the dining room now."

"Yes, we were just going in," Liv replied without looking back at the concern on Zach's face.

The band around Liv's heart tightened as she slipped her hand through Zach's offered arm. She'd had such big plans for this trip, but so far, the only thing that had gone the way it was supposed to was Zach was still at her side. For the moment, anyway.

And if Sofia thought she could waltz in here and steal him away, she'd better think again. Liv was totally prepared to fight like hell if she had to to keep her man.

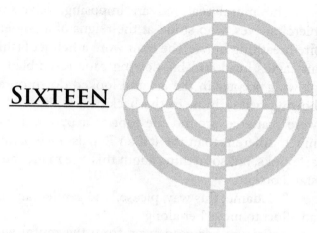

# Sixteen

S ofia stepped out of the registration tent just as Zach and Liv reached the threshold of the door into the house. She stopped to watch them, thinking again what a stunning couple they made.

*I wish it was me, not Olivia, on Zach's arm.* She winced at the thought. *What am I saying?*

"Madame, dinner is about to be served," a young server said interrupting her thoughts. "If you please, you need to get seated."

"Oh," Sofia looked around. Other than the few servers cleaning up, she was the only one left in the yard. "I'm so sorry. Yes, I'm going."

A member of the house staff was waiting for her at the doors and led her through a sitting room with a baby grand piano and walls covered with renaissance-style paintings from waist high to the ceiling. The next room was even larger and more ornate, with larges vases of flowers everywhere and two massive chandeliers over a long mahogany dining table with eighteen high-backed, padded chairs.

Neither room, however, compared to the third—the ballroom. Thanks to the free drinks supplied in the garden, the conversation was loud and punctuated with bursts of laughter at the six round tables arranged in a cluster that didn't even take up half the room. A rectangular head table holding five unoccupied place-settings faced the others.

Sofia paid no attention to the attendees and instead focused her sights on the colorful mural painted on the ceiling.

The mural featured an imposing, olive-skinned man with piercing eyes, who stood at the reigns of a golden chariot led by a fire breathing horse. The man wore a helmet fashioned to look like an eagle's head and his flowing cape resembled wings. He held a glowing scepter in the air and looked down on a horde of people bowing before him. In the background, burned, bleeding corpses were scattered around the foot of a pyramid. The scene was not much different than the Italian Renaissance paintings she'd seen in art books, but something about this one made the hairs on her arms stand on end.

"Madame, this way, please," the gentleman guiding her said, in an effort to move her along.

Sofia tore her gaze away from the mural with great difficulty but continued to look up every few paces as she followed the server around the back of the tables. She happened to be looking up at the exact moment he came to halt behind the last empty chair and ran smack into him.

"Oh! Sorry," she mumbled, doing a quick check out of the corner of her eye to see if anyone had noticed.

Three of her tablemates were talking and paying no attention. The other two, Zach and Olivia, were staring at her. And from the sympathetic look on Zach's face and the smirk on Olivia's, they had witnessed her clumsiness.

Blushing to her toes, Sofia hastily took the chair the gentleman had pulled out for her. The minute she sat down, a flurry of waiters carrying trays laden with bowls converged on the tables.

Sofia had had nothing to eat all day other than a bit of fruit and cheese in the lounge at the airport, but the thought of eating now was no more appealing than the thought of participating in this ridiculous game show. But as she didn't want to get drawn into the conversation around her, she leaned over the bowl and took minuscule sips of the onion soup.

All at once, the chatter in the room faded and the clinking sound of spoons being dropped into china bowls rang through the room. Sofia looked up and noticed every eye in the room was focused on something behind her. She turned in her chair and watched several people walk from the back of the room to the head table: a boy and a girl who both looked to be around her age, and two distinguished older gentlemen in expensive-looking suits.

The shorter, older looking of the two gentlemen stopped behind the chair directly left of the center place setting. The other man stood behind the chair to the left of him. The young people took the seats on the right end of the table. The middle seat was left empty.

"On behalf of your host, Monsieur Daher," the older man said, "I would like to welcome you and congratulate you on your achievement of making it to the first challenge of Road to Riches." He showed his bleached white teeth in a welcoming smile as applause rang through the room, but his dark eyes were as cold as a viper's.

"My name is Jared Conway." He lifted his left hand toward the man on his left. "This gentleman is my partner, Evan Vik. We have the honor of being legal counsel for the show. These two young people," he gestured with his right hand, "are Nicholas Holt and Hannah Perry. They have the honor of being the only contestants from the first two groups to have made it through the maze in the allotted time."

Nicholas gave his fist a pump in the air above his head as soft murmurs erupted around the room. Hannah looked doe-eyed at him and smiled shyly.

A boy at Sofia's table who had introduced himself as Aidan said, "A maze? Sweeeet! I'm a wiz at mazes."

Emily, a girl sitting next to Liv replied, "If only two people out of seventy-two were able to finish, I'm gonna say this isn't your everyday kind of maze."

"Who said there were seventy-two other people?" Aidan fired back.

Emily gave him a condescending pfft. "No one, asshat. But assuming the other two groups were approximately the same size as this one, it's simple math."

"Yeah, but—"

Zach shushed Aidan mid-sentence and gestured toward Conway, who had raised his hand to silence the room.

"Monsieur Daher had hoped to join us this evening," Conway continued, "but unfortunately, a business matter arose that needed his attention, and … well, he didn't become the man he is by ignoring his responsibilities."

A twitter of laughter rose from the crowd.

"Thus, is the real life of a billionaire." Conway's tone turned more serious. "It's not all sailing yachts and attending red carpet events as some may think. Whomever is chosen as his apprentice will be expected to accept and mimic this kind of work ethic and lifestyle. But trust me, there'll be plenty of time to enjoy the benefits that come with being one of the richest in the world."

He went on, talking over the smatterings of chatter that sprung up around the room. "As you already know, since I let the cat out of the bag earlier, your first task is a maze. That may not be the kind of contest you were expecting, but Nicholas and Hannah are here to attest that this maze, designed by Monsieur Daher himself, will challenge you in ways you cannot imagine."

Nicholas nodded his head in confirmation.

"For the purposes of logistics," Conway continued, "you'll be divided into two groups. The first group of eighteen will run the maze tonight. The remainder will go tomorrow night. But first, to give you a small glimpse into what your future could be like if you're lucky and talented enough to make it to the center of the maze, we've flown in world-renown Chef Aaron from Paris to prepare you a magnificent meal, the likes of which you've never tasted before. I've personally been waiting for this moment all day, so, without further ado," he spread his hands out in front of him, "please eat and enjoy."

A short round of applause followed as Conway and Vik sat. The servers reappeared with bottles of Perrier, and an excited but more subdued chatter filled the room as glasses were refilled with sparkling water and dishes were collected.

"Geez, they must have made the maze ridiculously tricky if only two people have made it through," Liv said to Zach.

"Were you really expecting the challenges to be easy?" Emily answered her. "Not all of us here can be put on the show, you know. Actually, a maze is an ingenious idea to start off with if you think about it. It takes cognitive and mathematical skills to solve. It'd be a sure bet if you were wanting to eliminate a ton of, let's say, not-so-smart people real fast." She looked pointedly at Liv.

Sofia picked up her glass and took a quick drink to hide her smile as Liv threw a hard glare back at Emily.

Abby, the girl sitting next to Sofia, spoke up in a squeaky voice,

"Does anyone else think it's weird they'd send us into a maze at night? I mean, even if the thing is lighted, there'll be lots of shadows. Me and my friends did a corn maze at night a couple years ago. It was outrageously hard to find the way out. And it was *sooo* creepy, too." Her eyes rounded. "Oh my gosh, you don't think they'd have scary people jump out to trip us up, do you?"

"They could, I suppose," Emily replied. "Stuff like that would get a lot more people watching the show for sure. It *is* all about ratings, you know."

Abby turned a pale shade of green as everyone else at the table threw out theories of what might happen inside the maze.

Sofia shot a glance at Zach, then looked right back down at her hands in her lap.

Going into the maze in the dark didn't worry her. She had exceptional night vision and could see almost as well at night as in the daylight. She could also see UV light waves and colors. But she had learned from experience to keep both of those secrets to herself. People didn't like or accept those who were different from them. And she couldn't be more different.

It still made her cringe every time she thought of the torture she went through when she showed a girl, who was supposedly her best friend at the time, her ability to see in the dark. She was in elementary school then and still naïve to the repercussions of letting others know she had uique abilities.

But she learned a quick, hard lesson the next day when she walked into the school and everyone shrunk away from her as if she was some kind of ghoul. Whispers behind her back followed her all the way to her classroom where she discovered her classmates had moved their seats away from hers, leaving her desk with the word FREAK scribbled across the top, an island by itself in the middle of the room.

She hadn't yet built a wall around her emotions and that betrayal nearly destroyed her. Her nose started to run like a river like it always did when she got upset. It then turned bright red. By the end of the day, everyone in the school was calling her Rudolph the Red-Nosed Freak. And to her horror, that nickname stuck and somehow followed her to every school she went to after that.

Right then and there, Sofia pledged to herself she'd never tell anyone her secrets again. She'd kept that vow ever since and hadn't once been tempted to break it.

Until now.

She folded and unfolded the napkin in her lap. It seemed important to Zach that he get through the maze and she knew she was equipped to help him. But what would it cost her if she revealed she was a true freak of nature? And what would he do when he found out that she was a mutant?

As she tried to come up with a way to help him without exposing herself, one question kept coming to the forefront. Why did she care so much about what Zach thought of her? It wasn't as if they were friends or anything. She'd probably never even see him again once this was over.

Through the next four courses of almond-crusted duck breast with small potatoes and carrots, sorbet, a cheese platter, and a fresh fruit tart, Sofia tried to pull her thoughts out of the fog that had moved in and was clouding her brain.

She had yet to come up with a solution when Conway's voice broke through her reverie.

"I hope you enjoyed this stupendous dinner as much as I did."

The group responded with applause and hoots.

"I also hope you didn't stuff yourself too much, and you can still move, because this is the time you've all been waiting for." Conway paused, letting the tension and excitement build. "What do you say … are you ready to tackle the maze?"

A loud explosion of "Yes!" echoed through the room.

Conway held up a hand to quiet the crowd. "If you would now please look at your nametags. If yours has a small star in the bottom corner—"

A thin, ferret-looking young man appeared at Conway's elbow and handed him a folded note. The counselor frowned as he took the slip of paper and ran his thumb under the wax seal. The crease between his eyebrows deepened as he read it, but when he looked back up at the participants, his face was as smooth as his silk tie.

"It seems our benefactor wishes to be present for the running of the maze. He is the producer of the show, so that, of course, is his prerogative. It *is* after all his money paying for this event.

Unfortunately, he's still tied up in his meeting and has asked us to postpone the maze for this evening."

A host of exclamations and groans rose from the tables.

Conway held up his hand to silence the crowd. "Have no fear, you'll all get your chance at the maze. We'll notify you at your hotel of the new date and time as soon as we determine Monsieur Daher's availability.

"Until then, you're free to enjoy the beaches and explore the lovely city of Nice and its plentiful attractions … at the expense of the show, of course, due to the delay." He smiled broadly, again showing his impeccable set of pearly whites.

The crowd's disappointment instantly flipped to one of delight. The sound of chairs scraping the floor followed, as the candidates got to their feet for a standing ovation.

Sofia and Zach were the only ones who remained silent and seated.

Conway let their enthusiasm go on for several seconds too long before he silenced them a second time. "On behalf of Monsieur Daher and Road to Riches, we thank you for your understanding and patience. You are now free to go and enjoy the rest of the evening. Your drivers have brought your cars up front and are ready to take you back to your hotels. Please follow these servers to your cars."

*I can't frickin' believe this! Who does he think he is?* Sofia thought as the other contestants noisily gathered their things and headed to the door. She had hoped she could collect the money this evening and be done with this. But now it looked as if if could go on for days if not weeks if Daher so deemed.

Her breathing accelerated as a spark of rage lit inside her, pushing aside the uneasy feeling that had been nagging at her. And if someone were to look close enough, they might have seen steam come out of her ears.

# SEVENTEEN

The two attorneys stayed at their places, smiling plastic smiles and nodding to the crowd as the young people shuffled out. When the group had dwindled down to half, the counselors abandoned their posts and retreated to huddle with the Ferret Man, who'd been waiting at the other end of the room.

Zach stood beside his chair, leaving Sofia the only one still sitting. She stared intently at the counselors as they put their heads together and engaged in what looked like a deep conversation.

As the number in the room continued to shrink, Liv tugged on Zach's sleeve and whispered, "What are we waiting for? Let's go."

Zach shifted his weight from one foot to the other. "We should probably head out to our car," he said loudly, looking at Sofia.

She didn't move a muscle.

Liv let out a disgusted snort, took hold of Zach's elbow, and attempted to pull him toward the door.

He resisted, then pulled his arm out of her grip and walked around the table. "Sofia?" He softly touched her shoulder.

She flinched as an electric shock shot through her.

Zach repeated, "Our car's waiting for us. We need to go."

Sofia turned and looked up at him as if she'd forgotten he was there. Then, she whipped back around in her seat and glared at the counselors' backs.

"They seriously expect us to just sit around and wait until that self-centered billionaire decides to bless us with his presence?" she hissed through her teeth. "What about *our* time? *Our* lives? I have a job too. And if I don't get back to it, I'm gonna lose it."

She rose so swiftly her chair flipped over backward. Zach caught it before it hit the ground.

The yellow ring around Sofia's pupils danced like a flame. "The only reason I'm here is because the letter said I'd get ten thousand dollars if I showed up. I couldn't care less about being on the show or going through some stupid maze. I want my money, so I can go home. I'm done with this charade."

She threw her napkin on the table and stomped off toward the counselors.

"What's she doing?" Liv asked incredulously. "Is she out of her mind?"

"Shit," Zach said under his breath and hurried after Sofia.

Liv groaned out loud but followed.

Ferret Man's eyebrows lifted at the sight of Sofia coming toward them. He tilted his head in her direction to alert Conway and Vik, who both turned just as Sofia came to a stop.

"I'm sorry to interrupt," she said before either of the men had a chance to open their mouths. "The letter I received from your office promised me ten thousand dollars if I came to Nice."

Conway arched one eyebrow.

Sofia went on, "No other obligation was mentioned in terms of receiving the money. It for sure didn't say we'd have to sit around and wait, for God knows how long, until Mr. Daher can fit us into his schedule."

Liv stepped up next to Sofia. "The letter didn't say we *had* to compete in your competition to get the money, either. So, technically, you owe us the money right now, and we could sue you for breach of contract if you don't give it to us."

Sofia blinked at Liv in shock, then looked back at Conway. To the outside world, the counselor might have appeared calm, but she could see murky red spikes in his aura that told her he was struggling to contain his anger.

"I'm sorry," Sofia hurriedly said to defuse the tension. "We're not meaning to be disrespectful." She threw a quick side-glance at Liv hoping that was the case for her, too. "Personally, I don't plan to sue you. It's just that I have a job and I need to get back to it. Every minute I'm here are minutes I don't get paid. Mr. ... I mean, Monsieur Daher has been more than generous. I truly appreciate his hospitality, but honestly this whole reality show thing is a waste of my time. He's not gonna choose someone like me to be his heir."

She took a breath. "So, if you don't mind, I'd like to collect the money you promised me so I can go home and get back to my life."

Conway's mouth turned up in a strained smile that was about as warm as liquid nitrogen. "I understand your position, madame. It would be a shame, though, if you two were to miss out on the maze and the opportunity it could afford you. It's clear you both have strong spirits as well as no fear of speaking your mind ... two qualities Monsieur Daher is looking for in an apprentice."

He looked at Vik, who gave a slight nod of his head. He turned back to the girls.

"Could you give me and my associates a moment to discuss this matter? Maybe we can come up with an amenable solution that will get everyone what they want." Conway waited for Sofia and Liv to nod their consent, then turned and walked to the side of the room. Vik and Ferret Man followed.

"What the hell was that, Liv?" Zach whispered harshly as soon as the counselors were out of hearing range. "Threatening to sue these guys? Are you fuckin' outta your mind?"

The fiery gold ring around his pupils had expanded leaving only a thin band of blue visible.

Liv's bravado crumbled under his glare and she suddenly looked like a little girl. "I don't know what came over me. I think it's this place. It's affected my mind. But Sofia's right in that they do owe us the money." She reached for his hand. "As soon as we get it, I think we should go home, too, and forget about the rest of this."

A small tic pulsed in and out above Zach's rigid jawline. "I'm not ready to leave yet," he said, pulling his hand free.

An image came into Sofia's mind of a young red-headed boy putting himself between her and a bully on a playground. It vanished just as quickly as it came. The young boy looked a lot like a younger version of Zach, though. But how she knew what Zach looked like when he was little she didn't know.

"There's something weird going on here," Zach went on. He raked his fingers through his hair and blew out a sigh. "I know this is going to sound crazy, but I think we were brought here for a reason other than the show. A reason that involves all three of us."

Liv's eyes flashed and her chest inflated.

"Yes, the *three* of us," Zach added before she could object. "I don't know how or why, but we're all connected somehow. I feel it. And I'm not leaving here til I find out what the hell's going on."

Liv bristled and lifted her chin. "You're wrong. You don't kno—"

"They're coming back," Zach interrupted.

Sofia and Liv both turned as Conway and Vik came to a stop in front of them.

"You're in luck," Conway said, flashing his white teeth. "We were able to get in touch with Monsieur Daher. He was disappointed to hear you want to leave, but as I suspected, he was impressed with your courage to stand up and speak your mind." He turned to Sofia. "He appreciates your dedication to your job and understands the predicament you're in. He's instructed his assistant, Tabari, here," he lifted his hand toward Ferret Man who was standing a little behind Vik, "to wire ten thousand dollars to your account and Madame Schultze's, too. We'll just need your bank information. But ..."

Sofia held her breath.

"... Monsieur Daher wanted me to ask if there was any way you two would reconsider and stay?"

Sofia stared at Conway. That was not what she had expected him to say.

Receiving no response from the girls, Conway went on. "He has authorized me to offer you an incentive to help you make the right decision. Would perhaps ... let's say a fifteen-thousand-dollar bonus offset the sacrifice you'd be making if you stayed? This, of course, is on top of what's already been placed in your account, bringing the grand total to twenty-five thousand dollars if you stayed and participated in the maze."

The number $25,000 popped into the air in front of Sofia. She swallowed hard. Thank God, Conway blathered on and didn't wait for her to answer, for her mouth was as dry as a desert and she couldn't have answered even if she had known what to say.

"Monsieur Daher also asked me to extend you both an invitation to spend the night here at the villa in hopes that a little taste of the luxury you'd get if you perchance won the competition will aide in changing your mind. The next flight out of Nice is not until tomorrow afternoon, anyway, so that will give you time to enjoy the Olympic-sized swimming pool, the stables, and of course, the villa's gardens, which are unrivaled in their variety of rare and exotic plants."

Conway paused, but Sofia and Liv both remained too tongue-tied to speak.

"I understand you have little knowledge of Monsieur Daher, and thus cannot appreciate the magnitude of this offer," Conway said, his tone carrying a hint of impatience. "But let me assure you, it's significant. He's a *very* private man. Only a few select friends have ever been invited to stay here. This unique opportunity he's offering is a testament of how impressed he is with you. I highly recommend you take it seriously. Monsieur Daher is accustomed to getting what he wants. At the moment, it seems he wants you to stay and participate in the competition."

A sudden chill swept over Sofia and her breath froze in her chest. She took a step back and bumped into Zach. She opened her mouth, then closed it, still unsure what to say.

"Um ..." she finally stammered after a sidelong glance at Liv. "I ... don't have my pajamas with me. They're back at the hotel." The minute she said it out loud, she realized how lame the excuse sounded, but it was the only thing that had come to mind.

The corners of Conway's mouth twitched, as if he wanted to laugh. "Not an issue. The villa is fully stocked with an assortment of nightwear, casual clothing, and more toiletries and personal items than you even knew existed. I'm sure there'll be something to your liking."

"I won't stay unless Zach can stay, too, and also gets the bonus," Liv said brazenly, taking a couple steps backward to stand beside her brother.

Vik leaned in and whispered something in Conway's ear.

Conway's gaze traveled down the length of Zach and back up. "I'm sure that can be arranged. The villa has more than enough bedrooms to accommodate all of you."

"I, um ..." Sofia flipped a quick looked over her shoulder at Zach and Liv, who both appeared to be as dumbfounded as she was. "Would you give us a moment to talk about this?" she asked, turning back to Conway.

"Take as much time as you need."

Sofia's instincts told her to run out of there as fast as she could, but she led Zach and Liv a few feet away. "I don't like this. It doesn't feel right. Why does this guy want us to stay so bad? He doesn't even know us."

"Well, he's invested a lot into this," Liv replied. "And maybe he's sicker than what everyone thought. I don't think the news ever said what he's dying of. It could be that he doesn't have that much time left. And since we've shown we have some of the qualities he's looking for, it makes perfect sense he'd want us to hang around."

Zach gave her an open-mouthed 'what the hell' look. "Weren't you the one who just wanted to go home?"

Liv tucked her arm in his and batted her puppy dog eyes at him. "I overreacted. Besides, that was before he offered us an additional fifteen thousand freakin' dollars! Come on, Z, we're talking about taking home fifty thousand dollars between the two of us. Maybe even more, if one of us ends up winning the whole thing. Think of Mom and Dad and how this is going to take away their worries. They won't have to dig into their 401Ks now."

Though Liv was talking directly to Zach, her words hit home with Sofia. The siblings' back and forth quickly faded into white noise as her own thoughts turned to the twenty-five thousand dollars. That money, along with the scholarships she'd already been awarded, would get her through the first year at MIT with some left over for her second year.

"Sofia?"

She started and looked up. Zach and Liv were both staring questioningly at her.

"I'm sorry, um … what were you saying?"

"We've decided to stay. Don't screw this up for us," Liv stated bluntly.

Sofia's stomach clenched tighter as she looked from Liv to Zach.

He shrugged. "It's too good of a deal to turn down. Our parents aren't rich and don't have the money to send two kids to college at once. This money will take a huge burden off our family. "

Sofia had hoped he'd give her more of a reason to stay than just the money.

"I get that you're not keen on staying. I don't blame ya," Zach added. "Like I said, I've got a weird feeling about this place, too. But Livy and I will both be here, so it's not like you'll be alone." He reached out like he was going to take Sofia's hand, then hesitated and let his arm drop to his side.

Sofia's defenses crumbled a little under Zach's sweet, hopeful smile. She really would like to spend more time with him. The extra money would be great too. But the mere thought of staying overnight in the villa turned her stomach. And her gut was usually right.

She closed her eyes and gritted her teeth. The number $25,000 floated in the darkness behind her eyelids.

*You came here to get money for your future. It's the only way you can make your dream come true,* she told herself. *You're already here and it's only one night. What could happen in one night?*

Sofia took in a deep breath and opened her eyes. Zach was watching her. As their eyes locked, a calm washed over her and the turbulence in her mind quieted. No one had ever looked at her the way he did or had an effect on her that he had. She could almost picture herself falling into those fathomless blue eyes of his and getting lost in them forever.

"*I don't want you to leave,*" Zach's voice said inside Sofia's head. Her breath caught in her throat. "*You and I belong together. I think you know that too.*"

She internally winced and tried to look away, but his tender gaze held her captive.

"Are we just going to stand here all night?" Liv asked curtly.

Sofia blinked and swiveled her head around. Liv's piercing glare, sharp as a knife, killed the spell Zach had placed over her. She lifted her chin and crossed her fingers that she wouldn't end up regretting this decision.

Her stomach was tied in knots as she walked stiff-legged back to the counselors. "We accept the invitation. Please thank Monsieur Daher for his hospitality."

"Excellent," Conway replied and gave a genuine smile for a change. "We've just heard back from Monsieur Daher. He has finished his meeting and is on the way back as we speak. And, knowing how anxious you are to move on, he's agreed to let you to go through the maze this evening—if you don't mind the late hour."

Sofia's stomach twisted tighter, but before she could object Liv spoke up.

"That'd be freakin' awesome!" Liv tucked her arm through Zach's in a possessive manner. "We can't wait to show Monsieur Daher that we're absolutely the ones he's looking for."

Conway snapped his fingers in the air. A man in a black steward jacket with gold-braided epaulettes on the shoulders materialized from a side door. "Our guests will be spending the night. Please escort them to the east wing and see that they have whatever they require."

He turned back to the three. "Monsieur Daher should arrive within the hour. You can use that time to get settled into your rooms. Someone will come for you when we're ready. Until then, is there anything specific you need?"

Liv again spoke up for them all. "No, sir. Thank you."

"Very good, then. If you think of anything, please let Pierre here know." Conway gestured toward the man in the black jacket.

Pierre gave a slight bow in reply. "This way, if you please." He started toward the door the other contenders had exited through.

Liv took Zach's hand and followed. Sofia gave Conway a wary smile and trailed after Zach, keeping her gaze locked on his back so she wouldn't have to look at Tabari, whose wide creepy grin reminded her of the Joker's.

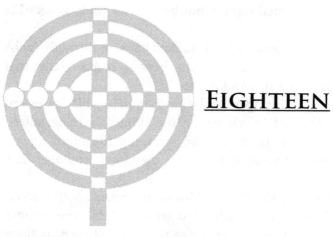

# EIGHTEEN

S ofia, Zach, and Liv followed Pierre up the stairs to the third floor where a woman from the house staff was waiting. The woman dipped a curtsy as she was introduced, then in a stiff, formal manner escorted Sofia and Liv to the women's guest closet. Pierre and Zach continued down the hall to the men's area.

The women's closet was really more of a boutique than a closet and was bigger than all five bedrooms in the Miller's foster home put together. Rows of clothing racks and shelving were stacked high with the latest styles from the most expensive luxury brands, sorted by color and occasion. Liv squealed with delight and pushed past Sofia, who stood in the doorway and gawked.

"Ohmigod, look at these dresses!" Liv gushed going from one rack to the next. "All the famous designers are here: Oscar de la Renta, Dior, Saint Laurent." She reverently ran her fingers over a red taffeta evening gown.

"This is ... crazy," Sofia said more to herself than to Liv. "Who keeps stuff like this on hand? And why?"

"Billionaires, that's who. And if you can afford it, why not?" Liv sighed. "God, what I wouldn't give to have a quarter of this stuff."

Sofia skimmed the nearest racks, all of which held a variety of formal evening attire, which included dresses, skirts, blouses, and jackets. "We're here to pick out pajamas and something to wear and in the maze, not walk the red carpet. Where's the everyday stuff? Or something that's not covered in sequins?"

The staff woman snapped to attention as if someone had flipped on her switch. "This way, madam."

Sofia followed her to the back of the closet, where she was shown a selection of casual clothes, though Sofia's idea of casual was *way* different than Daher's. Even the t-shirts had designer labels.

It took a bit of digging, but she finally managed to find a short-sleeved shirt and shorts pajama set made of pink satin with tiny black hearts all over it. They were finer than the clothes she wore out in public, let alone to bed. For the maze she picked a simple running shirt, shorts, and tennis shoes that no doubt cost more than her whole wardrobe put together.

Liv, however, was the complete opposite. She loved everything and couldn't make up her mind what to choose. By the time they finally made it to their individual rooms, Sofia was exhausted and more than ready to get out of her high heels and lace dress. She changed into the shorts and t-shirt she'd chosen for the maze and sat down on the edge of a huge four-poster bed to wait.

The room was bigger than her hotel room and had a small sitting area with two high-backed padded chairs and a large velvet-tufted ottoman arranged in front of a fireplace. She had no doubt Liv was probably loving this, but she felt completely out of her realm.

Too anxious to sit still, Sofia got up and walked to the open window. She leaned against the sill, pulled her pendant out of her t-shirt, and unconsciously ran her thumb over the stone.

Off in the distance, the hillside was ablaze with a yellow glow from the clusters of hotels and shops that crowded the Bay of Villefranche's coastline. She breathed in deeply and tried her best to focus on the mixture of floral scents from the gardens, but no matter how beautiful and peaceful the night seemed, she could sense something dark and shady hovering in the air.

The rattle of the doorknob startled her out of her musing. She dropped the pendant back inside her shirt and spun around, wishing she were anywhere else but here.

The doorknob rattled again.

Sofia held her breath and watched with trepidation as the knob then turned ever so slowly.

*Oh God, I don't wanna do this.*

The door inched open. She covered her mouth with her hand,

then swallowed back her heart that had jumped into her throat as Liv's head peeked around the edge.

Sofia sagged against the sill. "Oh my God, Olivia, what are you doing in here?" She frowned and stood up straight. "Wait … how'd you get in? The door was locked."

Liv shrugged and closed the door behind her. "Let's just say I'm resourceful."

She strolled to the bed, lifted Sofia's pajama top with two fingers, and scoffed, "Seriously?"

Sofia marched around the bed and yanked the top out of Liv's clutch. "Did you break into my room just to make fun of my pajamas?"

Liv *tsked*. "Hardly. They aren't worth my time."

"So why are you here, then?"

Liv sat down cross-legged on the bed and gave her hair a flip. "I know what you're doing, and I'm here to tell ya it ain't gonna work. Zach is a true Texan. That means he can't help but be sweet to everyone he meets. But don't mistake his good manners for interest, because you see, Texas men like their women strong and fearless. So your poor little lost girl act is gonna get you exactly nowhere with him."

Sofia crossed her arms. "Is that right? So, how's the bitchy prima donna working for you? I admit I don't know him very well, but he really doesn't seem like the type who would put up with that kind of neediness and bullshit for long."

The smirk on Liv's face vanished and her eyes narrowed malevolently at the same moment a knock sounded at the door. Several bulbs in the chandelier exploded with a loud pop and hundreds of tiny glass daggers rained down on Sofia.

"Sofia!" Zach called out in surprise from the doorway.

Sofia recoiled and lowered her arms, which she'd raised to cover her head. Glass shards littered the carpet all around her except in a perfect circle where she stood, as if she'd been holding an umbrella. *Ah shit, not again!*

Zach rushed to her. "Are you okay? What happened?"

She looked up and scuffed her toe through the glass to spread it around as inconspicuously as she could. "I'm fine." She turned, dragging her feet through the shards to scatter more of them, then walked to the one of the chairs.

Zach glowered at Liv, who stood beside the bed with a purely innocent look on her face. He crossed to the ottoman and sat down facing Sofia.

"You sure you're okay? You didn't get cut or anything?"

Sofia crossed her arms and rubbed her hands up and down them. "I'm good, really. It was, um … you know how these old homes are; bad wiring." She lowered her eyes and pretended to brush fragments from her t-shirt so he couldn't see she was hiding something.

A housemaid cleared her throat from the doorway. "Excuse me, mesdames and monsieur—" Her words trailed off as she noticed the glass on the floor. She looked up at the chandelier. "Oh, my." She quickly looked around at each of them. "Was anyone injured?"

"No," Sofia replied hastily. "We're all fine. A couple lightbulbs just blew out. I think it might have been a power surge."

The maid looked up at the light fixture again. "Nothing like that has ever happened before," she said, sounding very doubtful of Sofia's explanation.

Liv, her face a little pinker than it had been a minute ago, asked, "Did you need something?"

The maid lowered her eyes. "The master has returned and has asked me to inform you the maze is ready whenever you are."

"Great! We're absolutely ready," Liv answered for all three of them. "Come on, Zach." She walked to the door and looked over her shoulder.

Zach hadn't moved.

"You don't keep someone like Mr. Daher waiting. Let's go," she said more firmly.

Zach stood and reached out his hand to Sofia. "I guess it's time … shall we?"

Sofia turned away from his hand, got to her feet on her own, and grabbed her mini purse on the way out the door.

At the bottom of the stairs, the maid handed them off to Pierre, who then escorted them into a large library with volumes of books on shelves that went all the way up to the two-story-high ceiling. A man with thin shoulders, slicked-back black hair, and an abnormally large head was seated at an antique desk, tapping away on a laptop.

He looked up and pushed his chair back as the three entered the room.

"You must be my guests," he said, his voice carrying harsh undertones and an unrecognizable accent.

Sofia unconsciously shuddered and took a step back as he rose and rounded the desk. Everything about the man was larger than life, from his height to his huge beak-like nose and his heavy brow that hooded his piercing, yellow eyes, which seemed to look right through her.

But it was the dark energy exuding from him that made her the most wary.

"I'm Makin Daher," he said, walking straight up to Liv. "And you are?"

"Olivia Schultze, sir" she said in a small voice.

"Ah, yes, Olivia. It's so nice to meet you." He took her hand in his, bent over it and kissed it, then looked into her eyes for an uncomfortably long moment before he moved on to Sofia.

A wave of nausea swept over Sofia as Daher took her hand. His skin felt hot and scaly and it was all she could do to not yank her hand back and wipe it on her shorts when his lips touched her skin.

After moving on and shaking hands with Zach, Daher stood back.

"I apologize for any inconvenience you may have suffered on my behalf. But I'm delighted you agreed to stay so I could make it up to you."

Daher addressed all three of them, but Sofia got the distinct impression he was really only speaking to Liv.

"Twenty-five thousand dollars has been deposited into each of your accounts. But I want you to keep in mind that is a mere pittance to what you could receive if you successfully complete the maze." Daher rubbed his hands together, a gleeful glint in his eye. "And speaking of mazes … I'm ready if you are."

Sofia looked at Liv, expecting her to answer, but for once Liv seemed to have lost her voice.

"Yeah, sure," Zach said in his sister's stead.

"Excellent. Now, if you would please hand your phones over to Pierre." Daher nodded to his manservant who stepped up and held out his hand. "Phones are not allowed in the maze, I'm afraid. You'll get them back when you return."

The look on Liv's face said she would rather give up her arm than her phone, but after Sofia and Zach both relinquished theirs, she reluctantly gave hers up too.

Daher nodded. "Please go with Pierre now and he'll take you to the car that will transport you to the maze."

Sofia started. "You mean the maze isn't here?"

Daher snorted in disgust. "You think I would relinquish my sacred gardens for such a thing?"

Sofia cringed and moved closer to Zach.

In response to her reaction, Daher softened his tone and added, "My gardens are my sanctuary. I couldn't bear to forfeit so much as an inch of them. There's not enough land on this property to build a full-size maze like what we needed anyway. And needless to say, the neighbors wouldn't have been pleased."

Daher went on as he ushered the three to the door. "I understand your eagerness to prove yourselves, but don't worry, it's just in the hills outside Nice and only a thirty-minute drive away."

His gaze moved up and down Liv. "I'm anxious myself to see how you fare. You've already shown great fortitude, so my expectations are high. In fact, if I were a betting man, I'd place my bet on you making it to the tower in record time."

Daher's mouth pulled back into what Sofia assumed was supposed to be a smile, but there was nothing pleasant or reassuring about it. She shuddered and hesitantly followed Pierre down the hall. It was a relief to get away from Daher, but at the same time, she had a feeling she was trading one unbearable situation for another.

The strangest looking vehicle Sofia had ever seen was waiting for them in the driveway. The car, or whatever it was, sort of looked like an alien spaceship on wheels or an armored vehicle whose body had been cut into sharp angles and triangular facets by a diamond cutter.

Pierre opened both the front and rear doors on the passenger side. Sofia moved toward the back, but Liv pushed past her, climbed in, then patted the seat next to her. "Sit here, Z."

Zach raised his eyebrows at Sofia.

Her cheeks warmed, but she shook her head. "No, that's okay. You go ahead."

Sofia took Pierre's offered hand and climbed into the front passenger seat before Zach could say anything. Resting her elbow on the window ledge, she put her fist in front of her mouth to hold back the onion soup that threatened to come up. She had never vomited in her life, but the way her stomach was roiling she feared her first experience might be right here in this ridiculously luxurious car and humiliate her in front of Zach.

But luck seemed to be with her for a change, and the sick feeling subsided as soon as the car drove out the gate of the property.

Sofia let her head fall back against the snakeskin-covered headrest, closed her eyes, and pondered whether being in Daher's presence is what had made her feel sick. She winced at the thought.

*Stop it! You're being a wuss. He's just a man who happens to have a lot of money. After tonight, you won't ever have to see him again. You can hold it together for a few more hours for twenty-five thousand dollars.*

She pressed her fingernails into the palms of her hand and mentally repeated the mantra, *it'll all be over soon.*

But no matter how hard she tried to convince herself of that, she couldn't get rid of the nagging feeling she was losing control and getting in over her head.

# NINETEEN

Mountains had always intrigued Sofia, though she'd never been anywhere close to one before. The highest point in Iowa was in a parking lot in Osceola County. She'd always thought of mountains as being magical, but it wasn't magic she felt as the car drove through the rolling landscape, littered with scrub brush and white boulders in varying sizes. It was dread.

And the whispering sounds coming from the back seat didn't help.

It was well past eleven when the driver finally turned off the paved road and the car bounced across the rocky terrain of a plateau for a short distance more. The lights of the city were a glimmer in the distance. Beyond them, the water glistened blue and purple in the light of the moon. It was a scene straight off a picture postcard, but Sofia barely gave it a glance, as the sky in all its splendor grabbed her full attention from the moment she stepped out of the car.

Sofia had never seen the universe alight with such color that had nothing to do with the sweet sounds of Rachmaninoff that instantly started up in her head. In the city, where she'd lived her entire life, only the brightest stars were able to make it through the light pollution. But here, in the middle of nowhere, there was nothing to block the sky's brilliance, and she felt as if she'd been reunited with a long, lost part of her soul.

She opened her arms wide and twirled slowly in a circle as a strange energy seeped in from the ground and moved up her legs and into her body, melting away the tension in her shoulders.

God, how she missed spending time under the stars. Whenever she stood beneath them, space and time seemed to shift and she would be transported away into another dimension—one that was filled with serenity and where she could be herself. Her mind would clear, and she'd be able to think through all her problems. Best of all, there was no one there in her own little imaginary dimension that could hurt her.

But ever since she moved out of the Miller's on her birthday, she hadn't had time for the stars or anything else except for work and study. As a result, her whole system had gotten out of whack, her emotions had been all over the place, and she hadn't been herself.

The driver's voice broke through her trance. "These UTVs will take you from here."

She started and looked around. She'd gotten so lost in the stars she forgot for a moment the real reason she was there.

Zach and Liv were standing by the front of the car where three utility task vehicles were parked. The driver stood next to them, pointing into the darkness.

"The maze is approximately four kilometers in that direction." He turned to Zach. "May I see one of your arms, please."

Zach held out his arm, and the driver snapped a rubber bracelet around his wrist. He then did the same to Liv.

"These bands need to stay on your person while you're in the maze. They'll help us find you if you get lost. Your UTV driver will drop you off at one of four entrances. When you hear a horn blast, enter. If you try to enter before the horn, your bracelet sensors will pick it up, and you'll be disqualified. You have fifty minutes to get to the tower in the center of the maze where Monsieur Daher will be waiting. Any questions?"

Zach and Liv both shook their heads.

Zach looked back over his shoulder at Sofia. "You ready?"

Liv's spine visibly straightened. She shifted her position to put herself between Zach and Sofia and answered, "Yup, I'm ready to leave all the losers behind."

Without looking to see if Sofia was coming, Liv took Zach's hand and pulled him toward the UTVs.

Sofia's right eyebrow raised. *Really? Well, let's just see who the loser is.*

She hadn't planned on trying super hard to get to the center of the maze, but oh, how she would love to show Liv up. Just to see the look on Liv's face at the end when she saw Sofia standing next to Daher in the tower might be worth it.

But then the thought of being close to Daher made Sofia feel sick again. She blew out a breath and looked up at the stars.

"Is this a mistake?" she asked under her breath.

"Madame," the driver said as he approached her with her band. "It is time to go. May I see your arm, please."

Sofia didn't move. *If I'm supposed to try and win this thing, give me a sign.* She scanned the sky in hopes it would somehow show her what to do, but the stars had no answers for her. She blew out a long sigh, turned to the driver, and held out her arm.

As soon as he snapped the rubber bracelet around her wrist, her stone pendant began to buzz against her skin. But she didn't have time to think about it. Zach and Liv were already settled into the passenger seat of their UTVs and the driver was urging her to get into the last one.

As soon as Sofia fastened her helmet strap under her chin, the driver gave a signal and all three UTVs roared to life and took off, kicking up a cloud of dust in their wake.

Aside from the magnificent views of the coastline to her left, and the just as impressive surrounding mountains to her right, the plateau was barren and uninspiring. Under different circumstances, though, she might have found it stunning.

She might also have enjoyed the ride if it weren't for the sudden dips and jarring bumps of the vehicle bouncing over the rocks. The driver swerved back and forth to avoid as many as he could, but there were too many of them. And each time the UTV hit a rock, Sofia was nearly launched off the seat. She had to concentrate hard and keep a steel grip on the roll bar to keep from being tossed about, which, other than the excruciating jolts, wasn't a bad thing, as it kept her mind away from the maze and Daher.

From a distance the maze looked like a dark stain on the land with a tall, lighted tower sticking out of the middle. But as they sped toward it, it began to take shape and she could make out a line of evergreens in large containers standing side by side that made up the outer wall.

About twenty yards from the maze, Zach's UTV veered off to the left and Liv's went to the right. Sofia's vehicle continued straight and stopped in front of an entrance lit by three flaming torches on each side.

The driver walked around and helped her out. Her hands shook as she removed her helmet and handed it to him. He threw the helmet into the back without saying a word, then climbed back into the driver's seat, and drove away, leaving her standing there by herself.

Sofia's knees felt weak as she turned toward the maze and stared up at the towering wall of evergreens. She hadn't expected the maze to be this elaborate or this massive. It made her feel very small, as the evergreens themselves were at least six-feet tall, not counting the three-foot-high containers they were planted in.

From where she stood, the only visible part of the tower was the very top, which had a wrought iron fence encircling a giant, intimidating statue of an eagle illuminated by a spotlight. The eagle was posed with its wings pointed straight up and its talons outstretched as if it were swooping down to snatch up its prey.

The strange energy she'd felt when she stepped out of the car earlier was stronger here and sent goose bumps up her arms. But that didn't bother her as much as the fact that there was no camera crew or officials around. She had seen plenty of behind-the-scenes episodes of reality TV and knew there were always crew members and assistants all over the place, even though they never appeared on camera.

Sofia hesitantly moved to the break in the wall that served as the entrance, being extra careful not to cross the imaginary line that would set off her sensors. She bent at the waist and turned her head to the right to peek inside. All she could see was an empty pathway that led off into the darkness between two rows of the tall evergreens.

She turned her head to the left and sucked in a sharp breath.

On the ground, a line of small stones shining a brilliant fluorescent green made a trail halfway down the path to an evergreen with a sparkling white lollipop symbol on its front side.

*Holy shit!* Sofia jumped back.

Seeing fluorescent-colored stones was nothing out of the ordinary for her. Many rocks absorbed UV light, which made them glow in the dark. But the symbol was another thing.

She lifted her face to the stars. "Is this a sign?" she whispered in wonder. "Are you trying to tell me I should do this?"

At that moment, the loud blast of a horn shattered the silence.

Sofia closed her eyes and swallowed back her racing heart, which had leapt into her throat. She wasn't usually this jittery, but ever since she had arrived in Nice, her nerves had been as tight as a bowstring.

The moon was almost full and the sky was alight with stars, but still, the night seemed darker than usual and she was more aware than ever that she was alone. She nervously shifted her weight from one foot to the other.

The driver had said she had fifty minutes to make it to the center. That wasn't much time for a maze this size, though nothing said she had to do it. She could just sit out here and enjoy the stars and wait for someone to come and get her.

As if on cue, a wolf howl sounded from off in the distance, followed by a louder, much closer howl. She gulped and looked around.

There was definitely no camera crew present and the UTV had left. She was on her own and had nothing to use to fend off the wolves if they did draw nearer. And she had read enough about wolves to know that wouldn't end well.

"Crap," Sofia mumbled under her breath, fixing her gaze on the entrance of the maze.

Both of her options, of either running the maze or possibly being attacked by wolves, sucked.

"Oh, what the hell," she sighed and reluctantly walked into the maze.

Sofia took the path to the left and came to a stop in front of the symbol, which was an exact replica of the one on the letter she had gotten from the law firm. It was as clean and perfect as on the paper too, which was strange, since it seemed to have been painted on the surface of an evergreen.

She cocked her head to one side, then the other, and reached out her hand. It went straight through the image. She yanked her hand back and frowned.

Then it hit her.

"Omigod, it's a hologram!" she exclaimed, reaching through the symbol again. "How on earth did they do this?"

As far as she knew, hologram technology had not yet been developed. She leaned closer and studied the trees on both sides to see if she could tell where the image was coming from. But wherever source was producing it was well hidden.

She stepped through the 3-D image and looked back. The symbol and the tree both looked exactly the same, and she still couldn't see what was producing the illusion.

*Wow, I guess if you have enough money, you can do anything.*

Sofia turned her back on the symbol and focused her attention on the new pathway. Like the other one, there was no artificial lighting, and the trees blocked a good portion of the moonlight, which made it exceptionally dark. That wasn't an issue for her, but not knowing what was real and what was another hologram could present a huge problem.

An uncomfortable feeling replaced her awe.

She gazed down the path to the right and noticed a trail of the phosphorescent pebbles. The other path had them too, but she had been so enthralled with the symbol she hadn't given them much thought. But it now suddenly dawned on her that the two trails of stones had only gone one way.

A tightness filled her chest as she looked left and then back to the right. It was too farfetched to think that the pebbles were a part of the natural landscape. The only other possible explanation then was that they had been intentionally placed to guide someone through the maze.

Her brow puckered in confusion. People like her who could see UV light were extremely rare. And the majority of those who could, were older people who had had cataracts removed. For the show to assume they would get eighteen-year-olds who could follow a trail of UV light didn't seem reasonable.

So what was the point of the stones then?

"Ohmigod!" Sofia gasped out loud. If someone had UV glasses, they would be able to see the trail. Did that mean that Daher was giving certain people the glasses so they would have an advantage over the others?

Sofia bristled as a sense of righteous anger surged through her.

Zach and every other contestant had come here thinking they had a chance to win. But in actuality, the whole thing was a sham, just as she had told Maddie it was. Knowing she had been right all along didn't make her feel any better, though.

"Ughhh!" she cried out and looked around for something to hit. Several pebbles flew into the trees without her touching them. *This is so not right!*

She looked up at the top of the trees where she assumed the cameras filming her were placed and raised her middle finger.

"Let Daher know I'm onto him, and he's not gonna get away with this!" Sofia yelled, still staring up. She pressed her lips together and then grumbled to herself, "This is so messed up."

With her jaw clenched and her hands balled into fists, she stomped off, wondering if Liv or Zach had been given a pair of the special UV glasses.

The stones led her around curves and twisted her back and forth between the walls of evergreens. With each new turn, her anger burned a little hotter, and it spiked when she went through a second hologram that would have looked like a dead end to someone who couldn't see the pebbles. Those unfortunate ones would have had to retrace their steps, which would have cost them no telling how much time, and probably would have cost them the game, too.

As Sofia huffed on, her thoughts turned to the way Daher had practically drooled over Liv back at the villa. *I bet anything he gave her a pair of the glasses. Poor Zach. He really wanted to win this.*

Preoccupied with feeling bad for Zach, she didn't pay attention to where she was going until she was suddenly standing on the lip of a pit that was at least eight-feet deep and took up the entire width of the pathway. There didn't look to be any way around it, and she couldn't tell if it was short enough to jump over because of a mist rolling down into the pit, obscuring the other side.

*Great! So where am I supposed to go now?*

She looked back the way she had come to see if she had missed any stones going off in the other direction. There was only the one marked trail and it led right up to the edge of the pit.

*Why would they ...* A startling thought hit her all at once. What if the pebbles hadn't been set out to help people get through the maze at all? She had assumed that, but they could have just as easily been placed to keep people from reaching the center. And all this time she could have been following the wrong path.

Sofia closed her eyes and heaved a weary sigh. *Omigod, how could I be so stupid? I should've listened to my gut and walked away.* She shook her head. *This is so wrong!*

She felt like a fool, but she was also furious. Whether the stones were meant to help or hinder made no difference. Either way they would affect the outcome and Daher had to know that. He never had any intention of it being a fair race.

She ground her teeth together, wishing she could out him and let the world know what a fraud he was. But who would believe a nobody from Iowa over the richest man in the world?

Sofia stared down into the pit, tired of the stress and tired of her insides feeling like they were tied up in knots. A trail of the shiny stones led across the bottom and disappeared into the mist. Her eyebrows drew together. *Why would they—*

"Oh, no ... you've got to be kidding me! You expect me to jump down there? Then what? Climb up the wall on the other side?" Sofia snorted and let her head fall back. "I can't freakin' believe this!"

All of a sudden, a musty, rotten scent drifted to her on the air. It was something she had smelled before, but she couldn't place where or when that was. Still, it made the hairs on the back of her neck stand on end.

Sofia turned very slowly. Not five feet from her stood a towering man with broad shoulders, wide-set hooded eyes, short flat nose, and a wide mouth. She flinched, and, without thinking, took a step backward.

For a nanosecond, she teetered on the edge of the pit, flailing her arms to regain her balance, but the ground beneath her feet crumbled and there was nothing she could do.

Her scream was cut short by her loud *oomph* when she hit the dirt at the bottom. Fortunately, whatever had been used to dig the hole had left enough loose dirt on the bottom to pad her landing a bit. Still, it was quite a jolt. She winced in pain and moaned out loud as she rolled to her side. But she wasted no time worrying about her aches. That man was up there somewhere. She didn't know who he was or why he was there, but every instinct in her body told her to get as far away from him as possible.

Sofia gritted her teeth, pushed herself onto her hands and knees, and crawled toward the fog. The dense air quickly swallowed her up as she had hoped it would. But it also created a whole new problem. She couldn't see anything other than the glowing pebbles directly beneath her, which she was no longer certain were set out to guide her to the tower. But they were leading away from the man, and that was what she wanted at the moment.

Her knees were caked with dirt by the time she reached the vertical wall at the other end of the pit. She quickly sat down, pressed her back against the cool, hard surface, and barely noticed the sharp point of a rock poking through her t-shirt.

She wrapped her arms around her knees to stop them from trembling and tried to convince herself the man was not a threat. He had just been standing there. For all she knew, there could be a perfectly innocent reason as to why he was there—like, he'd come to show her the way back. She knew that was a more logical explanation than the one thrumming in her head, but the man reminded her of one from an old nightmare—one she used to have when she was a little girl—and, no matter how hard she tried, she couldn't shake the feeling he meant her harm.

Sofia's racing heart beat a steady cadence inside her head, but she was still able to hear a muffled thump as if someone had jumped into the pit. *Oh no, he's coming after me!*

She dug in her heels and pushed backward, but there was no place to go. Her back was already up against the wall.

Scrambling to her feet, she pressed her palms against the dirt and rocks that made up the wall and felt her way along for a handhold to climb up. Just as she was losing hope, her fingers touched something smooth and cold. She leaned in closer, then recoiled as a pale face with eyes as round as saucers appeared right in front of her.

It took her a moment to see through her panic and realize the startled face was her own, reflecting off a solid piece of steel that was polished to a sheen. The metal was set a couple inches inside the wall, like an elevator door, and for the blink of an eye, she thought she had found a way out. In the next blink, though, she realized how ridiculous it was to think someone would go to the trouble and expense of putting an elevator in a temporary maze.

Her hopes plummeted right back down to her toes.

It really did look like an elevator door, except it had no button or keypad on the wall. She ran her hand along the smooth edge and gave it a push to see if it would move. Nothing happened.

As she looked closer, she noticed a slight discoloration right in the center. It was barely noticeable, but as she leaned in, a familiar shape took form—the lollipop symbol.

Sofia hesitantly placed her palm flat over the symbol. A green light instantly outlined her hand. Then, the whole symbol glowed brightly, and the door silently slid into the wall, exposing a long tunnel.

For a half second, she forgot to breathe as a dozen different thoughts raced through her head, all leading to the same conclusion —she was being played for a fool. The maze had obviously been rigged to allow Daher to hand-pick who made it to the tower and moved on to the next challenge and who did not. The stones, the pit, the holograms were all his manipulation tools. But he hadn't counted on her being able to see the stones without glasses or help.

All at once, it dawned on her that the man above the pit was probably just a hologram, too. "Oh, you son of a bitch!" Sofia snarled to the air as she glared down the long, narrow tunnel. It had been carved through the same white rock that was scattered all over the ground above. There was no light other than at the far end, which was obviously coming from the tower since nothing else in the vicinity was illuminated.

She began to tremble again—this time with rage. *Boy, are you ever gonna be surprised when I walk in.*

The corners of Sofia's mouth turned up in a wicked smile, picturing the look on Daher's face, and Liv's too, as she was more convinced than ever that Liv was one of his chosen ones. Too bad they had taken away her phone. Capturing the moment in a picture would have been priceless.

Her smile grew wider, and she purposely stepped through the doorway. But the second the door slid shut behind her with a soft whoosh, a sense of panic took over and her smile faded. She froze in her tracks. Had she just walked into a trap?

She shook her head. *Stop it! Why would they go to all the trouble and expense to lead someone here just to trap them?*

She blew out a disgusted sigh and started down the corridor. Her steps were a little more hesitant than before, though, and her heart jumped into her throat when a black metal support beam lit up with a click as she passed it. She jumped again as the other support beams blinked on one by one all the way down the corridor.

A low rumble sounded in her throat and she squeezed her hands into fists.

*Aghh, I'm SO ready to be done with this!*

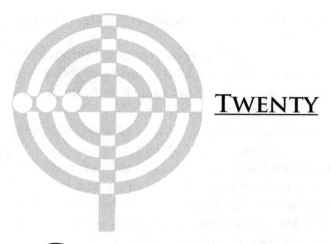

# TWENTY

Sofia burst out of the tunnel into a circular cavern and came to an abrupt halt. Spaced around the wall were openings to three other tunnels like the one she had just come through. In the center of the room a spiral staircase rose up and disappeared into a circular opening in the ceiling. The light was coming out of that same opening.

She stared at the hole, knowing Daher was up there. A wave of nausea struck her, and her feet suddenly wouldn't move.

*He didn't choose you, 'cause he didn't think you were good enough to go on to the next challenge,* she told herself to rally her anger. *You have to prove him wrong. Prove them all wrong. You're not a worthless piece of crap as everyone has treated you your whole life.* She took in a big breath and squared her shoulders. *You've got this.*

Before Sofia could take a step, Liv rushed out of the opening to her right.

Liv's eyes went big and round, then narrowed when she saw Sofia. "How did you get here so fast?"

Sofia wasn't surprised by Liv's arrival. She was, however, shocked to see Liv wasn't wearing glasses.

"Where are your glasses?"

Liv scoffed. "What are you talking about? I don't wear glasses."

"But ..." Sofia's brow furrowed. "How did you see the trail, then?"

Liv's eyebrows rose and her eyes went wide again.

*Ohmigod.* Sofia's mouth dropped open and her voice carried a hint of awe when she asked the obvious, "You don't need special glasses to see the stones, do you?"

Instead of answering, Liv let out a squeal as Zach emerged from the opening on the left.

"Z! Oh, thank God you made it." Liv started around the staircase toward him.

At that moment, the rubber bracelets on all three of their wrists lit up simultaneously. A weird tingling sensation moved up Sofia's arm, then a sharp pain pierced the nape of her neck. She winced and pressed her hand to the back of her head. The air around her all of a sudden became heavy and felt like a wall pressing in on her from all sides. Then her body went numb.

Liv screamed and dropped to her knees. Zach was hunched over, his hand on the back of his head, too.

"What's happening?" Sofia asked weakly. "I ... I can't breathe."

Several rocks the size of golf balls dropped to the ground around Sofia. One bounced off the hard-packed dirt and struck her on the shin. She struggled to lift her arms to cover her head as she looked up at the ceiling, sure that it was collapsing in on them, but there wasn't so much as a crack in it. The rocks were just materializing and falling from thin air.

"Liv, stop!" Zach rasped. "What are you doing?"

"I'm not doing anything. It's not me!" Liv screamed back.

The rocks were falling now throughout the whole cavern, except in the tunnels.

Sofia forced her feet to move toward the closest opening, dodging the rocks the best she could. But they had begun to drop faster and avoiding them was near impossible. And it seemed like the tunnel was getting farther away instead of closer.

She opened her mouth to call for help. At the same moment, she was pelted with a whole cluster of rocks. Intense pain exploded on the top of her head and her knees buckled. Then everything went black.

ᒪᚷᛉᛌᚠ|||ᚪᚷᛌ

"Get into the tunnel," Zach yelled to Liv. "You'll be safe from the rocks there."

He turned toward Sofia to make sure she had heard too and saw her lying on the ground a few feet from the tunnel opening.

"Sofia! Are you okay? Can you make it into the tunnel?"

She didn't move.

"Ah, shit," he said under his breath and started toward her, though each step was an effort, as if a strong current was pushing against him.

The noise of the rocks pounding into each other and bouncing off the spiral staircase was deafening. Still, Liv's piercing scream rose above it all.

Zack looked over to the tunnel that was closest to Liv, but she wasn't there. "Livy!"

He frantically looked around until he caught sight of her cowering beneath the curve of the stairs. He ducked a rock, then yelled, "What the fuck are you doing? Get back to the tunnel!"

"No! We have to get up to the tower!"

"For Christ's sake, it's raining rocks. Forget the tower. Sofia's hurt and needs help. Get in the tunnel before you get hurt, too."

Liv raised up, glanced at Sofia lying on the ground, then glowered at Zach. A rock whizzed by and missed her head by a mere millimeter.

She squatted down. "No, you forget *her!*" Her exasperation made her voice shrill. "Time's almost up. We gotta go *now.*"

Zach ignored Liv and pressed on, struggling to place one foot in front of the other. When he finally reached Sofia, he knelt down and gently placed two fingers on her neck. She had a faint pulse, but her skin was cold and blood was oozing from a nasty cut at her hairline.

As quickly as they started, the rocks stopped falling as if an invisible dome had closed over the ceiling. An eerie silence filled the room.

"Thank God! Come on, let's go before they start up again," Liv yelled as she scrambled around the staircase to the steps.

"I can't leave Sofia like this. She's unconscious and bleeding."

The glare Liv threw him held a combination of anger and misery.

He opened his mouth to say he was sorry, but Sofia moaned and his attention snapped back to her.

"Come on, Z," Liv whined. "We said we'd do this together. Remember? You can send one of Daher's people down to help her after we get up there."

The tic above Zach's jaw line pulsed. He had never let Liv down before and he hated to do so now, but what if the rocks started falling again? Sofia could be seriously hurt.

He shook his head. "I can't. I'm sorry. I don't—" He stopped short as Sofia stirred. He leaned over her and tenderly pushed a stray strand of hair off her cheek. "Shhh, it's okay. I'm here."

A choking sob came from the staircase, followed by the sound of rapid footsteps on metal.

He jerked around just as Liv's legs disappeared through the hole. *Fuck!*

Sofia's eyelids fluttered, then opened.

"Hey." He gave her what he hoped was a reassuring smile, though he wasn't sure they were at all safe.

"What happened?" A line creased Sofia's forehead and her eyes darted side to side. She struggled to push herself up.

Zach slid his arm under her shoulders to help. "Take it easy," he whispered as he pulled her in and held her against his chest.

He craned his head back to the staircase, hoping Liv had changed her mind. She hadn't.

*Dammit Liv, why couldn't you just listen to me for once?*

She had always been strong-willed and stubborn. And though he knew she could take care of herself, this time it felt like she was walking into something way over her head.

They were all in over their heads.

# TWENTY-ONE

L iv climbed to the top of the stairs, where a platform extended to a door. Outside was a short landing that led to another set of stairs, spiraling upward around the outer wall of the tower.

She stepped out into the night air breathing heavily, but not because of her hurried race up the stairs. Because half of her heart was still down in the cavern below. She pressed her back against the outer wall, bent forward, and covered her face with her hands to hold back the scream building at the back of her throat. Nothing could stop the ache in her chest, though.

*This was supposed to be my and Zach's time. He was going to see how much he needed me and how much better we are together.*

Liv angrily swiped her hand under her drippy nose, pushed away from the wall, and stomped to the steps. But instead of heading up, she spun around and paced back.

*Ugh, God, why? It's so not fair! Zach was just starting to come around. Then* she *had to come along and ruin everything.*

She stood at the bottom of the stairs and looked up. The upper part of the tower was bathed in a light as brilliant as the sun, making it impossible to tell how much farther up she had to go. She stared into the light for a long moment, hoping to burn away the image of Zach leaning over Sofia, but all it did was put a big white spot in the center of her vision.

She dropped her head and sniffed back the drip from her nose.

*Damn you, Sofia. You didn't even want to do the maze. You wanted to leave…*

Liv's back went rigid as a sudden thought came to her. "Ohmigod, that's it!" She couldn't believe she hadn't thought of it earlier.

*They'll send her home when she doesn't make it to the tower!* Her head swam with the thought of new possibilities.

*She won't get in the way anymore if she's not around. This can still work. All I have to do is talk Daher into letting Zach stay with me. That shouldn't be hard.*

Excitement bubbled up her throat and gushed out in a giggle. She checked the time on her fitness tracker. Two minutes and twenty-eight seconds were left on the timer.

"Shit!" She turned back to the steps and scurried up, taking them two at a time.

The light became more intense the higher up Liv went. She used her arm to shield her eyes, but that didn't help much. She knew she had to be getting close, but she could barely even see the next step to put her foot down.

When she finally reached a landing, her heart was racing. She still couldn't see a thing, but she knew Daher was close. His dark energy was palpable, and her stone pendant had become hot against her skin, the same as it had in the library when she first met him. That was the only other time it had ever done that.

"Ahh, it's good to see my expectations were right on the mark," Daher's disembodied voice said from within the white blur of light in front of her. "You have no idea how pleased you've made me, my dear."

He sounded so close, but the damn light was impossible to see through.

Liv started as her hand was suddenly lifted and hot lips pressed against her skin. A wave of nausea swept over her and she jerked her hand back without thinking.

"Oh … sorry, sir," she quickly uttered to cover her faux pas. "I, um … the light is so bright I didn't see you there."

With the snap of a finger, the light went out. She blinked, but it took several seconds for the white circle in her eyes to fade. When

Daher, who was standing just inches in front of her, came into focus, she unconsciously jumped back.

Luckily, Daher's reaction was quick, and he caught her arm before she fell backwards down the stairs. He smirked in amusement. "My apologies, my dear. I sometimes forget that light is an unnecessary commodity to some."

Liv's stomach dropped. What did he mean by that? How could he possibly know she could see in the dark? Her parents didn't even know.

The corners of Daher's mouth curved up as he rubbed his hands together like a little kid about to reach into a candy jar. But his eyes remained cold. "I guess there's no reason for us to delay any longer. Let's go meet your fellow Guardians, shall we?" He presented his elbow for her to take.

"Guardians?"

Daher dismissed the question with a wave of his hand. "It's a catch-word we've coined for the show. Sounds more majestic than saying champion or victor, don't you think?"

He took her hand and tucked it into his arm.

The sick feeling Liv had been trying to hold back since he kissed her hand moved into her throat.

"Oh, wait, sir ... my brother—"

"Is of no concern to you anymore," Daher interjected. "You are the Guardian. He is nothing. My people will locate him and the girl using their wristbands," he pointed to the one on Liv's arm, "and they'll be transported back to their hotel."

He started up the stairs. Her hand was still tucked in his arm and she was forced to go along with him. But she wasn't about to give up that easily.

Liv yanked her hand free and said in a voice that was squeaky with panic, "No, sir, you don't understand! He's not in the maze. He's right below us in the cavern." She looked down at her tracker. "And time isn't up yet. He could still make it. You have to wait."

Daher's piercing eyes darkened. "You're mistaken. I don't *have* to do anything. Besides, he will not be coming—"

"You don't know that, sir."

Daher's nostrils flared and his chest expanded. "I *do* know." His voice boomed. "As I've already told you, he'll be taken care of. I've spent far too long searching for you Guardians. I don't want to waste another minute."

Liv shrunk back. At that moment, a horn blasted through the silence, signaling time was up.

The glint in Daher's eyes made Liv shudder. "You see, I'm always right. You'll find it in your best interest to remember that."

He silenced Liv's protest with another snap of his fingers. A muffled clunk sounded behind the wall and the hum of a motor started up. A few feet above them the giant eagle statue shuddered, then began to descend into the tower.

As the statue sank out of sight, two green lights appeared in the sky above it. The lights were lined up horizontally about two car lengths apart and blinked on and off. They hovered over the tower, dropping lower in the sky at the same rate of speed as the eagle descended.

Within a few seconds, the green orbs were close enough that Liv could make out a small football-shaped craft between them. The craft had wings like a plane situated near its rear. Each time the lights on the wingtips blinked on, she could see a row of what looked like teeth hanging down on the undersides of the wings. Another set of short wings at the nose had the same teeth-like looking appendages.

The craft was descending vertically, like a helicopter, but that wasn't the strangest thing about it. The strangest thing was that it made absolutely no sound.

Liv was so fascinated she was barely conscious of Daher leading her up the last few steps to the short wrought-iron fence around the top of the tower, now ringed in yellow lights. She craned her neck all the way back to watch the craft silently rotate forty-five degrees above her head and land on the pad where the eagle had previously sat. As soon as the wheels touched down, a side panel lifted and exposed four seats, two of which were occupied.

Daher's left hand closed over Liv's, as if he feared she would pull free and get away, and walked her up to the craft.

"After you, my dear." He released her hand at the same time he placed his other on the small of her back and gently pushed her toward the seats.

Liv looked inside. The two previous winners Conway had introduced at the dinner were sitting in a row behind two empty seats. She raised her eyebrows in question at Daher.

"But ... where's Zach going sit?"

Instead of replying, he gripped her around the waist and started to lift her into the craft.

Though she was startled, her reaction was automatic. She placed her palm against the side of the craft and pushed back. "Get your hands off of me! I'm not getting in there. I'm not going without Zach."

The pilot in the cockpit swiveled in his chair and started to rise to help, but with a sharp command from Daher that Liv couldn't understand, he sat back down.

Daher dropped his hands but remained right behind her, blocking her from getting away. "I'm disappointed to hear that, my dear. I was thinking you might be the one I've been searching for. But if you're no longer interested in becoming my heir, please tell me now and I won't waste any more of my time."

*Ah, shit!* Liv twirled around. Daher was standing so close she could smell a scent of melon on his breath. She took an involuntary step backward.

"No, sir. I mean, yes, sir, I'm still interested," she blurted. "I, um ... it's just that Zach and I have never really been apart." It was hard to look him in the eyes, but she forced herself to do so, hoping he would be moved by the sincerity he saw on her face. "I was actually going to ask if you'd allow him to stay with me even though he didn't make it to the top of the tower in time. Because, you see, he would have if he hadn't stopped to help Sofia. That's the kind of guy he is. Super sweet and always thinking of others. Please, sir, I'll be forever grateful if you let him stay with me." She clasped her hands together to keep them still and waited for his answer.

His face remained a brooding mask for what seemed like an eternity. Then his jaw visibly relaxed.

"Foolish girl, you have no idea how your life is about to change or how insignificant that boy will soon become. But as I'm feeling rather magnanimous tonight, I'll allow you two to stay together, *but* ..." He held up his index finger. "... only if you agree to travel with me now on the jet."

Liv released the breath she'd been holding. But her sense of relief was cut short by Daher's next words.

"You should also know there are consequences to pay for those who defy me. Keep that in mind before you decide to test my patience again."

Liv's mouth had gone dry, but she did her best to sound sincere. "Thank you, sir. I truly do appreciate your generosity." She turned toward the craft. As she lifted her foot to climb in, she added, "You're wrong about Zach. He'll never be insignificant to me."

She sat down in her seat and put her hand over her pendant. Holding it usually made her feel better, but instead of taking away her growing unease, it made it worse. She could feel its heat through the material of her top, like a warning sign that she shouldn't trust Daher. She pushed the feeling away and turned her thoughts to Zach.

As soon as Daher climbed into the seat beside her, the side door lowered and latched in place with a click.

"Please buckle your seatbelts," the pilot said in a strange, unfamiliar accent. "We're about to take off."

From the back row, Nicholas added, "Hang on, you're about to experience the most radical ride of your life."

Liv gave him a half-hearted smile and turned her head toward the tinted shield that served as the window as well as the ceiling of the craft. It felt like a mistake leaving Zach behind, and not just because of Sofia. She closed her eyes. *Dammit, Zach, why aren't you sitting here beside me?*

A pop and a girlish giggle broke her concentration. She looked around to see that Daher had swiveled his seat to face the two behind and was filling champagne flutes for Nicholas and Hannah from a bottle of Dom Perignon. He filled two more and handed one to Liv, then took the last one and raised it in the air for a toast.

"To the end of a long search and the prospects of a glorious new future."

Daher tapped the rim of his flute to each of the others. The sweet ring of the finest crystal filled the cabin as the other three followed suit.

Liv had never been a fan of champagne, but she raised the glass to her mouth and took a sip. The fizz tickled her nose, and to her surprise, the fruity taste and explosion of the bubbles against her palate was kind of seductive. She suppressed her own giggle and took another sip.

"Wow, this is really, *really* good," she said, and giggled again at hearing her words slur a bit.

"Yes … I've always considered it one of the small tastes of wealth. So, drink up, my dears. There's plenty more where this came from." Daher sat back, his glass still full, and watched as the three hastily drained theirs.

Feeling suddenly lightheaded, Liv let her head fall back against the headrest. The empty flute in her hand was getting heavier by the second, and even though she had it resting on her thigh, she could hardly hold onto it. She closed her eyes and sighed contently, though she didn't know why. Something had been troubling her just minutes ago, she was sure of it. She scrunched up her nose and strained to recall what it was, but it remained just out of reach.

*What was in that champagne?* Before that question could register in her brain, it too was swallowed up by the abyss that was rapidly closing in.

Just as she was about to surrender to the darkness, a familiar voice spoke in her head.

*"Livy! Where's he taking you?"*

The voice was faint and sounded very far away, but it stirred something in her chest. She tried to latch onto it, but the pull of the abyss was too strong.

*"Livy!"* the voice called again, from even farther away.

"Zach?" she murmured groggily.

The darkness then overcame her and her mind went blank.

# TWENTY-TWO

Sofia leaned against Zach's chest and blinked the room into focus. Her body felt like it had been used as a punching bag, and the slightest movement of her head made the throbbing inside her skull worse. But she had to move. She had to get up to the tower before time ran out.

"Easy now ... take it slow," Zach said tenderly as he helped her up to a sitting position.

She put her hand to her forehead to stop the spinning and felt something wet. She pulled her hand back and stared at her red fingertips.

"You've got a nice little cut at your hairline, but I don't think you'll need stitches," Zach answered before she could ask.

She wiped her fingers on her shorts, not caring that the blood might stain, and very carefully turned her head to look around the room. "Where's Liv?"

Zach lowered his eyes. "She went on ahead."

Sofia reared back. Another wave of dizziness washed over her. "She went on without you?" she stammered, thinking her lightheadedness must have affected her hearing.

A streak of pain crossed Zach's face. "Yeah. I couldn't go and leave you behind. You were bleeding and unconscious."

*Liv had no trouble going without me,* Sofia thought and immediately cringed. That was mean and unfair. Liv didn't owe her a thing. But then neither did Zach, and he'd given up his one chance at becoming a billionaire to stay with her.

As the heat of shame moved up her neck, she lowered her eyes and stared at the face of her watch. *Oh!* She jerked up.

"There's still a minute and a half left before time is up!" She lifted her arm so he could see. "You could still make it if you hurry."

Zach shook his head. "I can't—"

"Yes, you can. I'm fine. Seriously. Go and catch up to Liv."

Without warning, the light from above went out, throwing the cavern into darkness. Sofia and Zach both jumped and looked toward the stairs, then back at each other.

"Hurry! You can do it."

The desire on Zach's face was evident even in the darkness, but he still hesitated. "Come with me."

"No, I'll just slow you down." Sofia forced her mouth into a smile to reassure him.

He still didn't move. "You sure you'll be okay?"

"Yes ... definitely. Now go!"

Zach jumped to his feet. "As soon as I check in, I'll come back for you."

"Great."

Sofia's smile slipped as he hurried to the staircase, but she quickly put it back in place when he paused at the bottom and looked back.

"You're sure?"

"Yes, just go!" she croaked, and bit down on her tongue to keep from calling him back.

ᘯᚷᚱᚾᛈ|||ᐃᚴᘯ

Zach raced up the spiral staircase and bolted through the door. Just as he was about to place his foot on the first step of the outside stairs, the horn blew. He jerked to a stop.

*What the ...* He frowned. No way had it taken him a minute and a half to climb the spiral stairs.

His mind went back to when he had entered the maze and seen the fluorescent trail. He wondered then if it was a fluke or if someone had purposely put them there to cheat. Now he knew the truth. The challenges were all a hoax set up to appease the TV audience and make the producers lots of money. And he and Liv had bought into it one hundred percent.

He moved away from the wall and looked up. The only thing he could see at the top of the tower were yellow lights. In the sky above, however, was an odd-looking plane descending straight down.

His mouth dropped open in awe as it rotated, then landed. The second it touched down, it dawned on him what was happening. *Nooo!*

Zach rushed up the stairs, but the craft had already taken off and was rising vertically by the time he got to the top. It rose to about one hundred feet above the tower, then shot off like a bullet parallel to the ground, heading west—away from Nice.

*"Livy! Where's he taking you?"*

He repeated those same words out loud as he looked around, but there was no one to give him an answer. *"Livy!"*

"Fuck!" He raked his fingers through his hair and looked up at the sky. What the hell had he been thinking, letting Liv go on by herself? He had known the second he stepped off the plane that something was off about this place. And the attention Daher had given her back at the villa was creepy. Daher had acted like she was the only one in the room and had barely even noticed him or Sofia…

His stomach dropped. *Sofia!*

## ᒍᚷᛝ᚜ᚅᛚᛁᛁᛚᚴ᚜

Sofia's smile vanished the second Zach's head disappeared through the hole in the ceiling. She rubbed her hands up and down her goosebump-covered arms, wincing each time she touched a bruised spot where a rock had hit.

She was used to weird things happening to her or around her. But never before in her life had she gotten hurt, even though there were plenty of times when she should have been. That was because of her invisible dome that had always protected her, like at the villa when the lightbulbs exploded over her head.

No one else knew about her dome. In fact, she herself didn't know for certain that it was a dome or exactly what it was. That's just how she thought of it—an invisible dome that came down over her and kept her from all harm. Though she actually didn't like to think about it at all. It was another reminder of how different she was from everyone else.

But now that it seemed as if her dome was no longer functioning, she realized how she had taken it for granted and wished she had done more to figure out what it was. Then maybe she could have kept it working when the rocks began to fall.

Sofia closed her eyes and massaged her temples. Trying to make sense of everything that had happened over the last twenty-four hours was exhausting and made her headache pound harder.

*I knew I shouldn't have come. God, I'm so gonna kill Maddie when I get home!*

A blast of a horn interrupted her thoughts. She reared up, then looked down at her watch and frowned.

"It's too early! They blew the horn too early!"

A loud clunk echoed through the opening in the ceiling, followed by the sound of gears grinding. She twisted toward the spiral staircase, her muscles tense and ready to spring in case the rocks started to drop again.

Everything remained still, but she knew that could change in a heartbeat. And without her dome, the chances of her getting seriously hurt were way too high for her liking.

With a groan, she pushed herself to her feet and limped into the tunnel, wishing again for the tenth time that she had listened to her gut earlier.

# TWENTY-THREE

Zach flew back down the stairs circling the outside of the tower, slowing only when he got to the spiral staircase, which was too narrow to take at a high speed. But as soon he got below the ceiling, he jumped over the railing and landed on the floor of the cavern, as effortlessly as if the distance was only four feet instead of ten. Without hesitating, he flipped around to where he'd left Sofia.

She wasn't there.

The guilt of having failed Liv that was already weighing heavily upon him doubled. "Sofia!" he called out, his voice cracking with fear.

The pause that followed seemed to last an eternity, but he didn't take another breath until he heard a small voice come from within the tunnel.

"I'm here."

He dashed across the room. "Are you okay?" His voice was husky with emotion. "Why did you come in here? Did the rocks start falling again?"

"No." Sofia sat up. "I just didn't think it was smart to stay out in the open. But what happened? They blew the horn early."

Zach took a slow, deep breath and sank to the ground beside her so she couldn't see his knees shaking. He'd been afraid Daher had taken her, too.

He let out a long sigh. "I know. I didn't get a chance to get to the top."

Sofia shifted uncomfortably. "I'm so sorry. You would have made it if it weren't for me." She looked down at her hands.

"You have nothing to be sorry about," he snapped, a sudden rage filling him and pushing the guilt aside. "It wasn't your fault. It's that bastard Daher's! I think he rigged the maze so he could take Liv."

Sofia perked up. "What do you mean, so he could take Liv? Where is she?" She looked past him to the stairs.

Zack had been trying to convince himself he was wrong about the maze being set up in Liv's favor, but after saying the words out loud, he knew without a doubt it was true. He balled his hands into fists. A rock lying near the opening of the tunnel flew into the spiral staircase with a resounding clank.

Sofia recoiled, her eyes wide.

"Daher took her." Zack got to his feet, paced to the entrance and back.

"Where did they go?"

"I don't know. I didn't get to talk to her. They'd already taken off in a plane by the time I got to the top of the tower." He wheeled around to face her, the tic in his jaw showing his agitation. "They flew off in the opposite direction of Nice."

He glared into space as a half dozen scenarios sped through his mind. He turned and paced back to the tunnel opening. "This doesn't feel right. I've got to find her and get her back."

Sofia quietly digested what he'd told her, trying to make sense of it. "How could Daher have known Liv would be able to see the trail he'd laid through the maze and not know we could too?"

Zack jerked around. "You can see UV light?

"Well, yeah. How do you think I got this far?"

A voice behind Zack startled them both.

"Seeing ultraviolent light is a trait of our people."

Zack whirled around as Sofia leaned to the side to see around him.

Standing just outside the entrance to the tunnel was the man she'd seen at the airport, his golden aura gleaming like a light in the darkness. Her mouth dropped open and she scrambled unsteadily to her feet.

"What do you mean by *our* people?" Zack asked.

"I'll be happy to explain everything once we get you out of here," the man answered. "We need to be gone before Daher's people arrive to pick you up."

He stepped to the side and swung his arm out, inviting Zach and Sofia to go first.

Zach moved backward to stand in front of Sofia, shielding her from the stranger. "You really think we're stupid enough that we'd just blindly go with you? Who the hell are you?"

The man smiled and lifted his hand. With a flick of a finger, the rubber bands on both Zach and Sofia's wrists dropped to the ground, and Sofia's pendant stopped buzzing.

"My birth name is Gilamu, but I go by Will here in this world," the man said. "I'm a friend. The only one you have here, actually. And like I said, I'll explain everything once we're away from this place. If you wish to get Olivia back, you'll come with me now."

Zach's back went rigid. "What are you saying? Do you know where they've taken Liv?"

"That hasn't yet been confirmed, but if I were to guess, I'd say Egypt," Will replied.

Zach's eyes narrowed. "Egypt? Come on, man—" The rest of his words dissolved on his tongue as a voice that sounded just like Will's spoke inside his head.

*"This isn't the time or place for your skepticism, Garaile."*

Will went on as if he hadn't just spoken to Zach telepathically, "You have no idea who or what you're dealing with, but I'm willing to bet you've already detected the danger Daher presents to you three. Am I right?"

Zach tensed. It was true he had felt a sense of danger right from the start, but he wasn't sure it was wise to admit that to Will.

ᘇᚷᛉᛦᚲᛈᛁᛁᛁᚨᛉᛌ

Will's golden aura and the strong energy he emitted intrigued Sofia. She stepped around Zach and asked, "Were you the one I saw at the airport?"

Will bowed his head slightly in acknowledgement. "You always were the more astute one of you three. Yes, it was I."

"Did you put a name in my head?"

"I did … Mirari," Will replied without hesitation.

The name felt like a hug, and Sofia's mouth filled with the sweet, salty taste of saltwater taffy. "Who's Mirari?" she breathed, her heart in her throat.

Will opened his mouth to answer, then snapped it shut and tilted his head to the side as if listening. He looked back at Sofia, his smile gone and a yellow ring around his pupils sparking like fire.

"They're coming. We have to go." His words were a command, and his tone left no room for discussion.

He swiftly moved toward the tunnel Liv had emerged from earlier. "This way. Hurry."

Sofia started after Will, but Zach caught her arm after two steps. "You aren't seriously going to go with him, are you?"

"Yes," Sofia answered, surprising herself by that admission.

"But you don't know him or where he wants to take you."

Sofia looked into his eyes, which mirrored the uncertainty she felt. She shrugged. "Well, technically, we didn't know Daher, either, but we followed him here."

"Yeah, and look what happened. He's now got Liv."

She pulled her arm free and entwined her fingers in his. "I feel I can trust this guy. I don't why but I do. Besides, we're going to need help to find Liv and he's our only option."

Will shouted from the mouth of the tunnel, "Sofia, Zach, we're running out of time!"

Sofia squeezed Zach's hand. "Come on, he's not a bad guy. I know you can feel it too. And aren't you a little bit curious to know what he meant by 'our people?'"

Zach's jaw turned hard and the tic appeared in his right cheek. "I don't know. This kind of feels like we're being played."

Sofia could almost see the wheels turning in Zach's head, but she didn't know what else to say to convince him.

After a moment, he let out a sigh. "I guess you're right, though … we don't have a lot of options."

ᘈᚷᚱᚾᚢᛁᛁᛁᗄᚴᛋ

Zach and Sofia walked into the tunnel where Will was waiting next to the metal door at the far end. Will placed his hand in the center of the polished surface and the door immediately slid open.

"We need to go quickly now." He urgently waved his hand to hurry them forward.

Zach followed Sofia through the door and into a pit that had fluorescent stones scattered across the floor, just like the one he had entered earlier. Only here there was no mist obstructing the view.

He put his hand on the small of Sofia's back and urged her forward, assuming they would follow the trail of stones back to the start of the maze.

"No, this way," Will whispered loudly.

Zach turned around.

Will was facing the earthen wall to the left of the door. And without saying another word, he bent his knees and jumped to the top of the pit, clearing it by a good half a foot.

Zach reared back. He knew he could have easily made that jump, even now after his knee surgery, but he'd never seen anyone else jump that high.

Will called down, "Come on, no time to lose. They're almost to the pit." When neither Zach nor Sofia moved, he added, "Do you want to be taken like Liv was?"

Zach jolted out of his stupor and looked over at Sofia. "Can you jump?"

Sofia snorted. "Yeah, I can jump—like a normal human being. But I'm not a total freak of nature who can jump *that* high!"

Zach winced. This was the exact reason why he'd always kept his athletic abilities a secret. But, like it or not, he didn't have any choice. There was no way he could make the jump without her seeing how big of a freak he really was.

He turned to the wall and called up to Will. "I'm going to lift Sofia. Grab hold of her and pull her up."

Without giving Sofia a warning, he wrapped his arm around her thighs just above the knees and lifted her. She gasped and held onto his head for support as he walked the few paces to the wall.

As he raised her higher, Zach said through his teeth, "Reach up and take Will's hand."

Will gripped her hand as soon as she was in range and effortlessly pulled her up, setting her on the ground next to him as if she weighed no more than a bubble.

A second later, Zach joined them.

The look on Sofia's face was a mixture of shock and apprehension as her gaze moved from Zach to Will and back. "How did you ... you just..."

"Follow me." Will jogged off down the pathway without looking back.

Zach reached out for Sofia's hand. She shrunk back and shook her head slowly side to side.

"You can see UV light *and* jump eight feet. What else can you do?"

His stomach clenched as if she had punched him in the gut. *Fuck!* If his ability to jump high wigged her out this much, what would she think if she knew everything?

He lowered his eyes and picked at imaginary dirt under his nails. "Look, I'm a basketball player." He glanced up through his eyelashes. "I've been training since I was thirteen to jump for rebounds, and I've gotten pretty good with all that practice."

Sofia put her hands on her hips and raised her eyebrows skeptically. "Seriously? I'm not stupid or that naïve. Wilt Chamberlain holds the record for the highest vertical jump by any basketball player, and it was four feet."

"How do you—" Zach started, but Will ran up behind them.

"What are you doing?" Will asked, clearly agitated. "Daher's men are almost here. You can't let them see you!"

Sofia rounded on him, her hands still on her hips. "I'm done with being told what I have to do. I'm not going anywhere until I know what's going on."

Will's face remained a mask of calm, though his voice turned hard. "There isn't time to explain the situation to you at this moment. You're just going to have to trust me and believe me when I say you're putting all our lives at risk. And every minute of delay makes it less likely you'll ever see Olivia again."

Zach brushed Sofia aside and stepped forward. "What do you mean? Is Liv in danger? And don't tell me you don't have time to explain."

Will's eyes sparked dangerously. "I was hoping not to have to do this." He reached into his pocket.

A searing pain, as if someone had stabbed him with a knife,

pierced the nape of Zach's neck.

He doubled over and grabbed at the back of his head. Out of the corner of his eye, he saw Sofia fall to her knees, clutching the back of her neck as well.

Then his vision turned white with pain, and he felt himself falling in slow motion.

# Twenty-Four

Liv reared up and gasped for breath as if she'd just swum up from the depths of the ocean. Her head still felt like it was under water, though, and a dark energy pressed in on her from all sides, making her feel queasy. She covered her face with her hands and leaned over her knees.

*What the hell happened?*

She tried to recall where she was and how she got there, but her memory was a blank slate from the time she'd left Zach and Sofia in the cavern.

*Zach!*

Liv closed his eyes and focused her mind to connect with him, but there was nothing there but an empty void—like he no longer existed. That had never happened before. Even when he was all the way across town from her, she could still feel him in her heart.

*Ohmigod, Zach! Where are you?* The air around her suddenly seemed too thin and there was no oxygen to breathe.

She lifted her head, her eyes wild and panicked. A few feet in front of her a partition partially concealed a man sitting in front of an instrument panel. *What the...* Her brow furrowed as she stared at what looked like navigation images on three different screens on the panel.

She turned her head to the side and jerked back. Daher was sitting in the seat next to her. All at once it hit her—she was on the strange-looking plane from the tower.

"You've woken up just in time, my dear. We're about to reach our destination," Daher said casually, as if nothing out of the ordinary had happened. "I hope you had a restful flight."

More of the pieces of what had happened snapped into place. Liv shrunk back until the side of the craft stopped her. "Did you drug me?"

Daher flipped his hand in the air. "I don't care for that phrase. It has a bad connotation. I prefer to think of it as being a good host and ensuring my guests don't suffer the monotony of a long, tedious journey."

"But you *did* drug me ... without my permission," Liv fired back.

Daher's penetrating eyes turned even harder.

At that precise moment, Nicholas stirred in the seats behind them. Hannah rustled as well and looked around groggily.

"What happened?" Nick mumbled, rubbing his fists into his eyes.

Daher swiveled his seat around, his demeanor instantly reverting back to that of the gracious host.

"Perfect timing. I was just telling Olivia we've almost reached our journey's end. Are you hungry?" He went on, answering his own question. "Of course you are. No worries. I've had Chef Aaron prepare another magnificent spread, which is waiting for you in your suite."

"You keep alluding to our destination," Liv said in a biting tone, "but you haven't said where that is."

Outside the tinted plexiglass window, the black of night was fading fast and dawn was lighting up the horizon, silhouetting clusters of skyscrapers sticking up through a polluted sky. She waved her hand toward the view. "That's *not* Nice."

Daher turned his head toward Liv and smiled, though it appeared forced. "You're very astute ... and right, my dear. That's Cairo."

Liv jerked up straighter in the seat. "Cairo! Like in Egypt?"

Daher nodded.

Her heart leapt into her throat. She flipped back to the window. *Ohmigod, this can't be happening!*

Every single warning bell inside her went off and she could barely hear herself think. This for sure was not what she had expected. And where was Zach?

She whirled back to Daher. "Sir, you said Zach could stay with me. Are you bringing him here, too?"

Daher patted her on the leg. "I told you he was the least of your worries now."

Liv involuntarily flinched. "But you said—"

He held up his hand and cut her off. "I'm well aware of what I said. I told you not to worry. Your friend is being taken care of. You can't expect to book a last-minute seat on a commercial flight at Côte d'Azur in the height of high season."

The craft suddenly dropped several feet. Hannah screamed.

Liv went stiff and held her breath, thinking her panic had caused the plunge. *No, no, it's going to be okay. Calm down.*

"Sorry about that, sir," the pilot said. "We hit a small air pocket. Everything is under control now."

Liv took a deep breath and pictured Zach to help calm her mind. *It's okay. It's okay. I can call him as soon as we land and tell him to get here ASAP.* Another thought hit her. She cringed. *Ah, shit, Daher took my phone!*

The craft shuddered again.

She tensed. *It's okay. I can sill make this work. I just have to hold it together. Someone gonna have a phone I can use. I'm not going to let Daher keep me and Zach apart. I'll drop out of the competition if I have to.*

A sudden longing gripped her. She dropped her chin to her chest. She really didn't want to have to give up on all that money.

*Please, God, don't make me choose between Zach and the show. I need both.*

# TWENTY-FIVE

The first thing Sofia became conscious of was the pungent smell of rotting garbage mixed in with the sweet smell of cinnamon and cloves. The second thing was that she was lying on a lumpy mattress on her side with a warm body pressed up against her back and an arm draped over hers so she couldn't move. A dream of being held in her mother's arms lingered on the fringes of her mind. She smiled and nestled closer to the warmth.

But a nagging voice in her brain told her something wasn't right. The body pressed up against her wasn't soft like her mother's. It was rock hard and muscular. As was the arm. She also had a dull ache in the back of her head, and she couldn't recall where she was or how she got there.

Sofia forced her eyelids open, though they felt as heavy as lead. A small room with purple walls came into focus. A few feet from the bed, a glass door led out to a small, narrow balcony. Through the dirty, streaked glass she could see a flat roof of another building, which didn't appear to be much more than ten feet away. The roof was littered with piles of trash, and there were multiple bricks missing from the side of the building and more were crumbling away.

She crunched up her nose in disgust. *Oh man, this has got to be a dream, 'cause that's definitely* not *Nice.*

The hand lying on her stomach suddenly moved. She tensed and held her breath as it traveled down her arm and curled its fingers around hers. The touch sent a familiar charge through her and the remaining fog of sleep dissolved.

Sofia rolled to her back and turned her head to look into Zach's eyes. He was lying on his side staring back at her. His dilated pupils completely concealed the yellow ring around their outer edge, leaving only a thin strip of blue iris showing. The blue was a deeper shade than what she remembered, but she'd never been this up close to him before, so it could just be that she hadn't noticed. Or it could be that she was still dreaming.

If this was only a dream, then she could do things she'd never do if awake. Like reach up and push back the lock of hair hanging down over his forehead. To test her theory, she lifted her hand. His hair was so soft she couldn't resist running her fingers through it.

A fleeting thought that dreams don't have the sensation of touch passed through her head, but his enticing mouth distracted her before it stuck.

Other people might say Zach had thin lips, but to Sofia they were super sexy, especially when they were slightly parted, the way they were now. A perfect, thin line of stubble decorated his top lip, which was odd as there was no stubble on his jaw or anywhere else on his face. Just there in that one spot, as if it had been painted on to accentuate how symmetrical and kissable his mouth was. She couldn't look away.

She moved her hand to his chest. His heart was racing almost as fast as hers was. Still, she hesitated. She'd kissed boys before, but she'd never been the instigator of the kiss. She ran the tip of her tongue over her bottom lip.

*It's just a dream, so it doesn't matter,* she told herself, and before she could talk herself out of it, she closed her eyes and leaned in.

The world, or maybe just her heart, came to a stop. At the same time, every cell in her body came alive. But just as their lips were about to touch, an arc of electricity jumped between them. Her eyes shot open and she jerked back, as the heat of mortification moved up her neck.

*Ohmigod, this isn't a dream!*

In one swift move, Sofia twisted around and threw her legs over the side of the bed. *God, how could I have been so stupid?*

She sniffed back a drip from her nose and started to rise, but Zach reached out and caught hold of her arm so she couldn't get away. She was burning with embarrassment, but his touch still sent a shiver through her.

Zach kept a hold of her as he scooted around and sat up on the bed next to her. She turned her head away, too humiliated to face him. To her horror, he reached up, gently took hold of her chin, and turned her face back to him. She quickly lowered her gaze to avoid looking him in the eyes.

"It's okay," he said simply.

His voice was husky with desire, which made her cheeks burn even hotter. She wanted to run away and find a hole to hide in, but her muscles all seemed to have frozen in place.

She cringed as he reached up and brushed her hair away from her face. He then tensed and pulled back.

Sofia's heart stalled.

"What happened to the cut on your forehead?" he asked.

*I'm dying of embarrassment and you're worried about my cut?*

She reached up to her hairline and felt around. The skin was as smooth as the rest of her forehead. At that same moment, she realized her head wasn't throbbing anymore, either. She held out her arms. All the bruises from the rock shower were gone.

Forgetting her embarrassment, Sofia looked up at Zach. Surprisingly, he didn't look disgusted or mad. He just looked as shocked as she felt.

"What the heck's going on?" she whispered. The last thing she remembered was standing by the pit in the maze.

She moved her gaze around the tiny nondescript room. Its sparse furnishings consisted of a small table next to the bed, which was bigger than a twin but not big enough to be called a double. And now that she was sitting up, she could see more of the view through the glass door.

Down the street from the building with the trashed roof, two well-kept structures with large domes and tall spires topped with what looked like onions stood out. It was the same kind of architecture as the Islamic Center in Des Moines. Beyond those two buildings was a solid mass of structures tightly packed together, many with the same domes and spires with onion tops rising through a hazy brown sky.

A new sense of panic filled her. "Where are we?"

"You're in Cairo … or to be more exact, the Gamaliya District."

Will stood in the doorway, holding a gold tray with an intricately etched gold and silver teapot and two crystal cups trimmed in gold. He walked around the bed, set the tray on the table, and proceeded to pour tea into the cups as if it were just another ordinary day.

"As I suspected," Will continued, "Essol—or I should say, Makin Daher, since that's the name you know him by—brought Olivia straight here. His persistence is nothing if not predictable, which is good for us."

Will handed Sofia a cup of tea. She accepted it robotically as her brain tried to digest the thought of being in Egypt.

"Hold on … did you say we're in Cairo. Like in Egypt?" Zach asked.

Will nodded.

"How did we get to Cairo? I don't remember—" Zach frowned, then reached up to the back of his neck. "What did you do to us?"

Sofia's memory fired up just then and her hand went to the back of her neck, too. "Why is the back of my head so sore?"

"I apologize for that," Will said. He turned and called out something in a language that sounded remarkably similar to the song Sofia's biological mother sang in her memories.

There was a rustle on the other side of the door, then a tall, pale man wearing sunglasses came in carrying a wooden chair. He set the chair down at the end of the bed. Will said something else to the man, who nodded and left.

Will pulled the chair around to face Zach and Sofia and sat down.

"I did promise you an explanation once we got away from the maze and I always keep my word. But let me warn you, it's a long story, and there's a lot to absorb. I'll try to condense it the best I can, but certain things can't be cut out."

He paused, as if looking for the right words. "Several hundred thousand years ago, the Anunnaki and the Pleiadians, two races from different planets, battled for control of this world."

Zach snorted loudly and rolled his eyes to the ceiling.

Will remained composed. "I understand you were raised in a society that refuses to believe there are other intelligent species in the universe, but you asked me for an explanation. It may not be the one you want to hear, but I don't lie. Lying is strictly a human trait. All I ask is that you listen to my words and open your mind to hear the truth. Can you do that?"

Sofia, her chest tight with expectation, gave a quick nod.

Zach begrudgingly nodded as well.

"Good. So ... as I was saying, the Anunnaki and the Pleiadians. The Anunnaki were the first to arrive on Earth, preceding the Pleiadians by several years. They were desperate to find gold to repair their deteriorating atmosphere and had been scouring the galaxy for planets with an abundance of the natural resources they could plunder.

"When the Pleiadians arrived to document the species of Earth, they discovered the Anunnaki had already enslaved the native inhabitants and created a whole new crossbred species, using a combination of their own genes and the genes of Earth's primitive species, to do the backbreaking work in the mines. Those crossbred slaves they created are the origin of the modern-day Homo sapiens— the so-called missing link that humans have searched for to explain their evolution."

Zach held his palms up and scoffed, "Okay, that's enough. If I want to hear this kind of bullshit, I'll watch an episode of Ancient Aliens on TV."

Sofia didn't know what to think. Will's story was pretty far out there, but at the same time, his words triggered something in her brain. Not a memory per se, but something that felt familiar.

Will studied Zach for a moment. "I see human influence has had a stronger grip on you than I had hoped. Maybe a demonstration will help."

The bedside table suddenly rose several inches off the ground and smoothly moved to the foot of the bed, setting down next to Will's chair.

Zach shifted his gaze from the table to Will's face. "How'd you do that? ... Who are you?"

"I am a Pleiadian from the planet Pleiades," Will replied. "The birthplace of your parents."

A small sound came from Sofia's mouth as she sucked in a breath. *Pleiades? That's my constellation!*

Zach said something under his breath, then louder, "You have no idea who my parents are. And whatever game you're playing here, count me out."

"You're wrong. I knew both your parents well. Your biological parents that is," Will said. "You, in fact, are just like your father."

"Do you know my parents, too?" Sofia could hardly contain her excitement. "Are they here? Will you take me to them?"

Will's cool demeanor slipped and the yellow ring around his pupils flashed. "I'm sorry, Sofia."

She deflated as fast as a ballon that had been pricked with a pin.

"The Anunnaki are a race of savage, cruel warmongers, and we Pleiadians have always been their nemesis. When our ancestors arrived and discovered the Anunnaki were here, they couldn't stand by and allow them to decimate Earth as they had so many other planets. A terrible war broke out. In the end, our people were victors and drove the Anunnaki out. But the Anunnaki vowed to return and reclaim Earth, which they believe to this day is rightfully theirs. To prevent that from happening, the original Pleiadians constructed a power grid around the planet and left behind a small group of their people to keep the grid up and running and to watch over mankind's development."

Will shifted uncomfortably in his chair and took a deep breath before he continued. "The power grid has kept Earth safe from invaders for hundreds of thousands of years now. But in 2001, a monster solar flare knocked it offline. It took us longer than expected to get it back up and running, and during that time, five Anunnaki battle cruisers, commanded by Daher and carrying a number of Dracuzian enforcers, got through. The Dracuzians are known throughout the galaxy as being exceptional hunters and assassins. Daher had brought them along to track down and kill all of us remaining Pleiadians. I and a few others managed to evade them, but your parents and Zach and Olivia's were not so lucky."

Sofia sucked in a sharp breath as she bent forward and wrapped her arms around her stomach as if she'd been punched.

Zach sat stone faced, the tic in his jaw pulsing.

Will's nose was redder as he pressed on. "Daher believes he has killed off every Pleiadian on Earth except for you three."

A look of horror streaked across Zach's face. "Wait ... are you wanting us to believe we're some kind of alien?"

"I'm giving you the facts. You were born on Earth, but yes, you're full-blooded Pleiadian."

Sofia stared blankly at the gold thread that was woven through the black bed covering. *I'm an alien, and my parents are dead.* It sounded too bizarre to be true, but she knew in her heart it was.

Drips from her nose splattered on the back of her hand as a pang of sadness stabbed at her heart. "I didn't even remember my parents until a couple years ago," she muttered out loud to herself. "How could I forget my own mom and dad?"

Will leaned forward and started to reach out to her, then seemed to change his mind and sat back. "You couldn't help it. After you were rescued from the attempted Dracuzian kidnapping when you were three years old, I inserted a chip on your brain stem to block the memory of that experience and the first three years of your lives."

Zach touched the back of his neck. "You ... " His eyes went round. "Fuck! That's how you knocked us out, isn't it? You had no right to do that. Take it out ... *now*!"

Will's shoulders slumped as if his burden had just doubled. "It was put there for your own good. Your parents and others sacrificed their lives to keep you hidden. If you had started using your powers as children, Daher would have found you and you wouldn't have had a chance. I couldn't let that happen.

"And yes, my disabling the blocker in the maze is what knocked you out. The block was only intended to last until you turned eighteen, anyway. You've probably had a few memories already start seeping into your brain. More will be coming soon. Then all that I've told you will make sense."

"No," Zach spit through his teeth. "I don't believe you. I'm not some alien freak. I want this thing out of my head."

Sofia could feel the panic and fear roll off of Zach and she understood. She'd been ostracized most of her life and was used to being an outcast. She guessed, though, that he had lived a normal life with a loving family and had probably never been taunted or bullied for being different. To someone like that, the thought of not fitting in would be scary.

Zach stood, balled his hands into fists, and took a step toward Will.

Sofia reached out and grabbed hold of his arm. An explosion of energy surged through her, but she didn't let go. "Don't. Getting in a fight isn't going to help anything."

Zach's glare moved from Will to her. "This guy knocked us out and kidnapped us!"

"If I hadn't, Daher's men would've taken you," Will interjected. "And you'd never see Olivia again."

In one quick move, Zach yanked free of Sofia's grip, stepped around her, and grabbed a fistful of Will's shirt, pulling the older man in so they were face to face. "Where is she? Tell me, or so help me God—"

In the blink of an eye, Zach flew backward across the room and slammed into the wall.

"Zach!" Sofia screamed, as he slid down to the floor, gasping for a breath.

"Why'd you do that?" She glared at Will.

"Because he needed to see I'm who I said I was." Will sounded dejected. "If he doesn't accept the truth, there's no hope of rescuing Olivia or saving this planet."

He smoothed the front of his shirt. "I can see in your eyes that you know what I told you is true. So, please ... talk some sense into him and get him onboard. One way or another, he *is* going to have cooperate and do his part. It'll be a whole lot easier on all of us if he does so willingly."

Sofia waited until Will closed the door behind him before she turned back to Zach. His eyes were closed, but his breathing was normal.

"He's gone," she whispered.

Zach's eyes shot open. Without saying a word, he jumped to his feet, rushed to the glass door, and slid it open. "We've got to find a way out of here."

Sofia sat back on her heels as a blast of heat from the outside rolled into the room. "Where're we going to go? We don't know anyone here. And we don't speak the language."

Zach walked out on the narrow balcony and leaned over the railing. "Fuck, there's no fire escape."

She let out a sigh, got to her feet, and joined him.

Spread out below was a bustling street packed wall to wall with pedestrians. Cats and skinny dogs ran unhindered through the melee of donkey carts and food and merchandise stands. Vendors shouted in Arabic, each trying to be heard above the other, and scents of roasting meat, baking bread, and potent spices floated on the overheated air. But not even those strong tantalizing smells could mask the stench of rotting garbage.

Zach stared intently at the flat rooftop of the building across from them. "I think we might be able to jump to that roof and go down their stairs. Or maybe—"

"Zack." Sofia laid a hand on his arm. "Please just listen to me for a moment. Say we get out of here, then what? Where will we go?"

"To the American Embassy. They've got to have one here in the city somewhere."

Sofia looked out warily over the mass of people. "But we don't have our passports. They collected them when we arrived, remember? … And what about Liv? Don't you want to find her?"

Zach went still.

"Will said he would help us get her back. If you just give him—"

"I don't trust Will." Zach barked. "That story about us being aliens …" He shook his head. "The guy's a total nutjob."

"But what if we are aliens?" Sofia replied.

A pile of rubbish on the roof of the building across from them exploded, sending bits of paper and other scraps into the air.

"That's ridiculous," Zach said between clenched teeth, "We're *not* aliens."

Sofia bit down on her lip.

"Once we make it to the Embassy, they will help us find Liv." He strode into the room, went straight to the door, then looked back at Sofia and pressed a finger to his lips as he slowly turned the knob and opened the door a crack.

She hurried over and looked past his shoulder. Their room was at the end of a short hallway. Across from them was another door, painted bright yellow. At the opposite end of the hallway was a pointed archway leading into another room, from which muffled voices were coming.

"It sounds like they're all in a room down the hall," Zach whispered. "Maybe they'll be distracted enough that we can get by without being seen."

Before Sofia could get a word out, he slipped out the door.

*Oh crap!* The thought of trying to find the way to the American Embassy on their own was about as appealing as returning to Daher's villa. But the thought of staying here by herself wasn't much better.

*Crap, crap, crap,* she repeated. *Why do some people have to be so stubborn?* She shook her head, then blew out a long sigh and followed him into the hall, praying she wasn't making a huge mistake.

Sofia crept up beside Zach, who was pressed against the wall next to the archway. Two distinct male voices could be heard coming from the room beyond. One was definitely Will, speaking in the same strange language he'd used with the man who brought him the chair. The second voice she didn't recognize. She sensed a third person, but they were farther away, as if in a room beyond this one.

Zach pointed to a heavy looking door down an entry hall across from them.

Will's speech from inside the room suddenly became a little louder and changed to English. "Kemen, I want you to head over to the pyramid and make sure everything is set up for tonight."

"I already did—"

The sound of footsteps and the rustling of strings of beads being knocked together cut the rest of Kemen's words off.

"And you'll check it again as you were told." Will's words were muffled as if he had moved farther away into another room. "You swore an oath on your life to protect those three Guardians and they need us now more than ever before. We can't afford to leave anything to chance.

"Now, get over to Khufu and see that the sentries are set, and the area's been cleared. I don't expect Essol will show up with the three much before midnight, but now that he has Olivia and believes we're all dead, he may think he's invulnerable. But you can bet that he'll still be prepared for every possibility. We must be, too. The future of this planet and the human race are riding on us getting the Guardians safely away from him."

Zach looked around at Sofia and whispered, "Did you hear that? Daher's taking Liv to the pyramids. That's where we need to go. C'mon, let's do it."

Sofia's mind raced as he dashed to the door. *Why would Daher be taking Liv to the pyramids at midnight?*

Zach's voice leapt into her head. *"C'mon!"*

She looked up at the door where a little redheaded boy, maybe three years old, stood, gesturing excitingly for her to come. She blinked and the vision dissolved, and it was Zach now at the door urgently beckoning her to come in the exact same way the little boy had. The two looked remarkably alike, the main difference, other than age, was the hint of fear in Zach's eyes.

A sudden overwhelming desire to protect him hit Sofia like a brick. She darted a glance into the room to make sure no one was watching. Then, before she could chicken out, she streaked to the door and slipped out behind him.

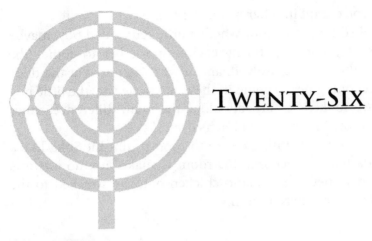

# TWENTY-SIX

The Four Seasons Hotel sat on the east bank of the Nile and offered a stunning view of the river as well as the tall, modern skyscrapers that crowded the opposite bank. The city of Cairo beyond was shrouded in a thick brown smog and only the faintest shapes of a few buildings could be detected.

Liv couldn't have cared less about the amazing view from the three-bedroom penthouse suite, though. She barely even took note when she walked into the lush suite that it was like stepping back in time to a pharaoh's palace. Gold, alabaster, and precious gem artifacts that looked like the real things, not replicas, were displayed in glass cases throughout the rooms, giving it more of the feel of a museum than a private apartment.

Nicholas and Hannah sat side-by-side on a velvet tufted sofa, completely absorbed in killing the zombies that staggered across the seventy-seven-inch TV screen, as Liv paced before a wall of windows and fumed.

With a huff, Liv came to an abrupt halt, flipped around, and asked for the third time, "You guys really didn't know Daher was bringing us to Egypt?"

Instead of answering, Hannah let out an ear-piercing squeal. "You did it! Ohmigod, you're so brilliant." She threw her arms around Nick in a smooth, calculated move that even a five-year-old could have seen through.

Liv blew out a disgusted breath, stomped over to the pair, and yanked the controller out of Nick's hands.

"Hey!" Nick barked.

"Look, you morons, this is serious. We've been drugged, brought to a foreign country in the dead of night, and are now locked in a room with some roided-out dude guarding the door. And we have no phones, no internet, or any way to contact anyone. That doesn't bother you?"

A canopic jar with a jackal-headed stopper crashed to the floor next to the sofa without anyone touching it.

Nick looked over, then shrugged, got to his feet, and walked to the bar where trays of food had been laid out. He stuffed a whole dolma into his mouth and mumbled as he chewed, "I'm not complaining. As long as I'm still in the game, I'm good."

Hannah sprang to her feet and rushed to the bar as if she were tethered to Nick. "Why don't you just chill out," she said with a haughty look.

"Yeah. Chill," Nick added, putting an arm around Hannah's shoulders. "And take advantage of these perks while you can. Cause, once I win, you'll be sent home and all this will just be a fond memory."

Hannah giggled and snuggled closer to Nick.

"Ughh," Liv groaned and turned back to the windows. "I'm stuck here with a couple complete idiots!" she muttered under her breath.

She leaned against the glass.

*Oh, Z, I need you. I don't think I can get out of this mess without you. Where are you?*

Liv closed her eyes and reached out with her mind again, though she didn't really expect to feel anything. To her surprise, a small familiar feeling flickered in her chest.

Her eyes flew open. She held her breath.

*"Z, is that you?"*

# TWENTY-SEVEN

Zach glanced over his shoulder several times to make sure no one was following, as he and Sofia raced down the two flights of stairs. They burst out into the open and came to a halt.

Handcarts and makeshift stands lined both sides of the narrow, brick-paved street, their merchandise spilling into the thoroughfare, leaving no room for cars. Even scooters had a hard time navigating through the congestion, and the constant blaring of their horns combined with dogs barking and vendors yelling over each other was ear splitting.

Zach looked right, then left. "This way, I think."

He took hold of Sofia's hand and cringed as her anxiety charged through him like a bolt of lightning. He looked into her round eyes and opened his mouth to tell her everything was going to be all right. At that exact moment a voice came into his head: *"Z, is that you?"* His mouth snapped shut and he went still.

The voice sounded just like Liv, but was it or had he imagined it? With the cacophony of noise around them, he wasn't sure.

*"Livy?"*

*"Zach? ... Oh, thank God. Are you here in Cairo?"*

*"Yes, I'm here. Where are you?"* He stared blankly at the building across the street, waiting for her reply. Nothing came. *"Livy! ... Are you there? Talk to me!"*

∠⋋Ꞃ⋋ⅮⅠⅠⅠ◿⋋⋋

Liv sagged against the windowpane and pressed her forehead to the cool glass, trying to get control of her emotions. She hadn't thought Daher was going to let Zach come, but he must have had a change of heart. She wiped a drip from her nose and breathed a sigh of relief, sure that everything was going to be all right now that Zach was here in Cairo, too.

As she pictured their reunion, a cold, malevolent energy swept over her and took her breath away. She turned just as Daher walked in, then her stomach dropped as the room blurred out and a vision of a man with yellowish green skin, wide-set hooded eyes, short flat nose, and wide mouth filled her head. She recognized him as the reptile man from her nightmares when she was little, but he hadn't haunted her dreams for years.

She blinked rapidly to get the image out of her mind, but it wouldn't go away. *Ohmigod!* Her hand went to her chest as she realized she wasn't having a vision at all. The man was real and was standing right behind Daher.

Liv took a step backward and bumped into the window as a voice from the past ran through her head: *"I found you once, I'll find you again."*

A blinding pain suddenly stabbed the back of her head. She doubled over as everything in her vision turned red. Someone called out her name, but they sounded very far away, and she was in too much pain to answer. Her knees buckled and she started to fall, but blackness moved in before she hit the floor.

ᘔᚷᚱᛏᛈᛁᛁᛁᘔᚷᛉᘔ

Sofia watched Zach's blank stare turn to a look of panic.

"What is it?" she croaked through a tight throat.

He looked around frantically. "We've got to get to the pyramids." Without further explanation, he started to elbow his way into the mob of people.

The biggest crowd Sofia had ever been in was the one time she had gone to the Iowa State Fair. The vibrations of so many people at once had overwhelmed her then. This horde was ten times worse, but she jostled her way through the crowd the best she could behind Zach.

Sofia had always considered herself street smart, but Iowa

street smart was like dipping your toes in a wading pool compared to being here in Cairo where it was more like jumping off a high cliff into the ocean. The air was also sweltering hot, and they could hardly go a foot without a vendor thrusting something in front of their faces: a blue glass evil eye trinket, a bright-colored scarf, a piece of gold jewelry. And the farther away from Will they got, the more vulnerable she felt. By the time they finally broke through the crowd, she was literally shaking in her boots.

Zach must have felt her anxiety, for he turned down a near-empty side alley and led her to a bench in a small open courtyard. Without saying a word, he sat her down, then joined her on the bench and held her tight until she stopped trembling.

His arms felt so safe and strong, but they didn't take away the nagging feeling that it had been a mistake to go off on their own.

"I'm sorry, I—" she started.

"Shhh," Zach whispered. "It's okay. It's not your fault. You didn't ask to be kidnapped and brought to a country where you don't speak the language."

"That's not it." Sofia pulled back and looked down at her hands in her lap, searching for the right words. Zach had rejected everything Will said, and he didn't seem to be in the mood to listen to her, either.

Before she could collect her thoughts, he said, "I heard from Liv."

Sofia's gaze jerked up to his. "How? ... When?"

Zach's cheeks turned pink. "Right when we came out of the apartment building." He looked away. "I know this is going to sound weird, but ... Liv and I have this special thing between us. I can sometimes hear her thoughts, and she can hear mine. That's how she contacted me ... in my head."

Sofia's heart skipped a beat. "I can hear your thoughts sometimes, too."

Zach's brow furrowed. *"Can you hear this?"*

*"Yes, I can."*

His mouth dropped open. "How—"

She put her hand on his arm. "Look, I know you don't want to believe Will ..." She felt him tense and hurried on, "... but too many things have happened that don't make sense. Like being able to hear each other's thoughts. And both of us being able to see UV light. Your jumping—"

Zach reared back as if she'd spit on him. "Nooo ..." He shook his head in denial. "I can't believe you bought into that bullshit!"

He jumped up and walked a few paces away. When he whirled back around, Sofia felt a blast of energy flow past her. Several pigeons that had been picking at the trash on the ground let out a squawk and took to flight.

"Do I look like an alien?" Zach didn't let her answer. "No, I don't! And neither do you." He raked his fingers through his hair and looked away. "This is messed up. I just want to find Liv and get the fuck out of here."

The look on his face when he turned back to her was a mixture of uncertainty and trepidation. "If you want to go back and play Alien Encounters with Will, be my guest. If you want to come and help me find Liv, that's cool too, but no more talk of aliens."

Sofia swallowed hard. She'd made the choice of Zach over Will when she followed him out of the apartment. Though she still wasn't sure they were doing the right thing, she had no intention of abandoning him now.

"But Daher isn't taking Liv to the pyramid until after dark," she said. "The complex will be closed to the public by then. How do you plan on getting to her?

"We'll have to go in early and hide out somewhere on the grounds and—"

"Can I be of assistance?" a voice said from the shadows.

Zach spun around as a twenty-something man wearing sunglasses stepped into the open. He was tall, and unlike almost everyone else they'd seen on the street, had dark auburn hair instead of black, though most of it was covered by a baseball cap.

He bowed. "You seem to be lost. Can I direct you somewhere?"

"Yes!" Zach exclaimed. "Thank you. We got turned around and we don't speak the language. We're trying to get to the great pyramid."

The young man's face lit up like a beacon. "Ahh, yes, it is our city's greatest treasure. It would bring me much pleasure to show you the way. And if you would be so kind as to bestow upon me the honor, I could also be your humble guide."

Zach stuffed his hands in his pant pockets and dropped his eyes. "Yeah, well … um, we don't have much money. I'm afraid we wouldn't be able to pay—"

"We'll not talk of money now. You can decide what my services are worth at the end. I am confident you will be very pleased, and a five-star Yelp review is what's most important to me." The young man smiled again, showing his remarkably white teeth.

Zach couldn't help but laugh at the man's hopeful expression. "I can definitely do a five-star review." He looked over at Sofia. "What do you say? Do you want to do this with me or not?"

Having already made her decision, she replied without hesitation, "Of course."

The look of relief on Zach's face was unmistakable.

The man bowed again. "My uncle has a taxi. I will go find him and be right back."

"Hey, what's your name?" Zach yelled as the man scurried back to the main street.

"You may call me, Kemen," he said, and disappeared into the crowd.

# TWENTY-EIGHT

S ofia's heart stalled for a beat when she heard the man say his name was Kemen. That was the name of the person in the room with Will, the one who was supposed to check the pyramid. Could they be the same person?

She cautiously stole a sidelong glance at Zach to see if he had picked up on the name. His pleased expression told her he hadn't. She twisted her hands in her lap and debated whether or not to say something. What if Kemen was just a popular name here in Egypt and this wasn't the same man at all?

As she chewed on her lip, trying to decide what to do, a voice popped into her head: *"Sofia, it's Will. Don't react. I don't want Zach to know I'm talking to you."*

Sofia froze.

*"Kemen is one of us. Don't be afraid. Just go with him and his uncle, Iker, and listen to them. They'll take care of you and see you get to the pyramid safely. I'll meet you there. Trust me. I'm only trying to help you get Olivia back and keep you all safe from Daher."*

"Sofia?" Zach asked.

She flinched and looked up. He was studying her with a look of concern.

"I'm sorry," she mumbled. "… what did you say?"

"Are you okay?"

Sofia felt her cheeks heat up and hoped they wouldn't give her away. "Yeah, you know, I'm just …" She sighed. "This has been a lot to take in."

Zach put his arm around her shoulders. "I know, but it's going to be all right. Look … we're already halfway there. We've got a ride to the pyramids. And once we find Liv, we're going to get the hell out of here. Then everything will go back to normal."

She looked away, not sure normal was even possible anymore, especially if it turned out they truly were aliens.

In no time at all, Kemen was back. "My uncle said he will come straight over after he has dropped off another fare across town." He gave Sofia a meaningful look. "While we wait, may I suggest we enjoy some cold refreshments, yes?"

"Did your uncle say how long he'd be?" Zach frowned, looking up at the sun, which was already low in the sky.

"Not long, I'm sure. He is worth the wait, you will see. There is no better driver in Cairo."

"It's just that we need to get into the pyramids before they close—"

"Oh, do not worry about that," Kemen cut in. "My uncle knows people. He will get you in after hours, and you will see the pyramids with no crowds. You will be very pleased, and I will get my five stars."

Zach looked at Sofia, his eyebrows raised in question.

She shrugged. "Well, we *were* wanting to see the pyramids at night. If his uncle can get us in, that's all the better. I'm kind of thirsty anyway," she added, guessing Kemen was wanting to get them somewhere safer.

"Good!" Kemen jumped in before Zach could respond. "Right this way." As he led them back into the congestion, he babbled on. "I know this little café. It is a short way up the street and has the best juice and Om Ali in all the city. You cannot say you have been to Cairo until you have tasted the Om Ali. It is so much better than American bread pudding." He brought his fingers to his mouth and made a kissing sound. "Almost like tasting a bit of heaven."

"You're sure your uncle will be able to get us into the pyramids after hours?" Zach asked again.

"Oh, yes. Don't worry about him. He is very good. Some think he is the son of Heka, who is the god of magic, because he can slip by people and no one sees him."

∠⋊Ɍ⋎ⲪⅢ◿⋉⅄

Liv felt the mattress dip as someone sat down on the bed beside her, but she didn't want to open her eyes and give up her dream. She, Zach, and Sofia were at the beach. It was an overcast, chilly day and no one else had ventured out except for them, which meant they had all the seashells to themselves. They had already collected enough to completely side the walls of a sandcastle they'd built, which was massive and impeccably done for three toddlers. They even had the insight to scrape out a deep moat around the castle to keep the surf from washing it away. Each time a wave rolled in and filled the moat, they would scream with delight.

A hand shook Liv's arm and a female voice said, "Olivia."

Liv stirred, but she held onto the dream.

"Olivia," the voice said a little louder, shaking her arm more forcibly.

"Hmm," Liv moaned and opened her eyes a slit. An unfamiliar woman's face came into focus. Standing behind the woman was a dark face she did recognize. She started to rise but could only lift her head a couple inches off the pillow. Her head felt like it weighed a ton and the nape of her neck was tender and sore as well.

"What happened?" she mumbled.

From the doorway behind Daher, Hannah said, "You fainted."

Daher's cold eyes sparked, but he didn't say a word.

The woman sitting on the bed rose, took Hannah by the arm, and escorted her out. The door clicked shut behind them. An uncomfortable silence followed.

Liv shrunk back into the pillow without realizing what she was doing.

"Are you feeling better now?" Daher finally asked.

"Yes, sir, I'm fine," she croaked, though in reality she didn't feel fine at all. She felt nauseous, and the sense of danger she'd been trying to ignore since arriving in Nice was like a giant elephant in the room.

Daher's cold gaze didn't move off of Liv's face. "What was that earlier? You appeared to be in a lot of pain."

Her hand went to the back of her head. She remembered feeling an excruciating pain after she saw the reptile man, but her instincts told her not to tell him the truth.

"I, um ..." Liv strained to come up with a plausible excuse, but with him standing there, it was hard to think. "I hadn't eaten anything all day and I tend to get hypoglycemia if I don't eat."

Daher studied her for another moment, then said, "I've decided to move up the next contest. We'll be leaving within the hour. I'll have Bennu bring you some food. I suggest you eat it. It would be a shame, not to mention an inconvenience, if we had a repeat of the earlier incident."

It was all Liv could do to keep her face blank under Daher's scrutiny. Thankfully, he turned and walked to the door before she broke.

As Daher reached for the knob, Liv called out, "Sir, can I ask what the next contest is?"

He didn't look back at her, but his voice carried a smile. "You'll see once we get to the Great Pyramid of Khufu."

Liv shuddered and closed her eyes. For first time in her life, she felt totally out of control and she didn't like it one bit. But Daher was just a man, and he'd already shown an interest in her. That was something she could use if she had to, even though the thought made her feel sick.

She inhaled a deep breath. *Get a grip. You've done this before. It'll be a piece of cake,* she told herself, channeling her inner bitch. *Nothing is going to get in the way of your plans for Zach.*

ᒿ✕ᖇ⅄ᗡIIIᐃ✕ᒧ

Zach looked at the dashboard clock and shifted nervously in the back seat of the taxi. The sun had already sunk below the horizon when Kemen's uncle, Iker, arrived at the restaurant to pick them up. Iker assured them he would get them to the pyramid in plenty of time, but Zach had his doubts. Not only did it seem like Iker was taking an exorbitant amount of time and the longest possible route to get out of the city, but he and Kemen didn't look related in any kind of way. Kemen was light complected, had auburn hair and blue eyes, and was friendly and outgoing. Whereas Iker was all business and looked more middle Eastern with black hair and dark eyes.

Zach eyed the three giant pyramids out the window, each lit up in a different color for the nightly light show. The music and announcer's voice, telling the history of the monuments, bled through the glass, but his attention was elsewhere.

"You're sure getting in at this hour won't be a problem?" he asked.

"No, no problem," Iker said in a heavy accent that sounded more Spanish than Arabic. "You're in good hands. I bring many fares to the pyramids at night."

Zach leaned toward Sofia. "Daher's supposedly not getting here with Liv 'til around midnight," he whispered. "So, once we're inside we'll have to ditch these guys and find some place to hide. Any ideas on how to do that?"

Sofia reluctantly tore her gaze away from the impressive structures. "Not really. From the photos I've seen of the complex, there didn't look to be a lot of places to hide. And I don't think these guys are gonna be that easy to lose. Maybe we should just ask them to help us? They seem awfully nice. They might do it."

"Yeah … I think it's better if we just handle this ourselves."

Zach turned his gaze back to the window and stared out at the desert and the pyramids that were getting farther away with each rotation of the tires. He frowned, then jerked up, suddenly alert, and flipped back to the front.

"Hey, we've passed the pyramids! Where're you taking us?"

Iker grunted, "You can't go through the front entrance after hours. Too many security guards."

"Uncle is taking us to the dunes at the south end of the complex," Kemen added. "Camels will carry us the rest of the way in. The best view of the pyramids is from the back of a camel … you wait and see."

Zach felt Sofia's hand slip into his, but for once her touch did nothing to soothe him. Too many things had gone wrong, and he couldn't shake the nagging feeling that Liv was in real danger. They were *all* in danger, but from what or whom he still didn't know. Daher seemed like the most logical suspect, but that didn't make sense. He was the richest man in the world and could get anything he wanted with the snap of his fingers. Why would he want to hurt the three of them?

As he shuffled the facts around in his head, searching for an explanation, something Will had said stuck his mind: Daher was supposedly an Anunnaki and wanted them all dead.

Zach shook his head to rid it of the notion. It was pure nonsense. Only nutjobs and freaks believe aliens were here on earth, and he was neither one of those.

All at once, an image of a man with lizard-like features popped into his head. It was the second time since he'd awoken that morning the man had appeared to him. And just like the first time, a cold sweat swept over his skin and his stomach clenched into a tight knot.

*What the hell did you get us into, Liv?*

# Twenty-Nine

S ofia stood a short distance away from the others, staring blankly at the line of saddled camels. She wasn't thinking about the prospect of riding a camel across the desert, even though it was not something she had ever dreamed herself doing. She didn't even know how to get up on one. But that was the least of her worries.

Her mind was roiling with the prospect that she might actually be an alien. It would explain so many things if it turned out she really was.

Her whole life, she'd been an outsider and different from everyone else in a weird sort of way. She couldn't cry real tears. She never got sick or hurt. And things had a habit of falling over on their own around her. But while all that set her apart and gave other kids a reason to tease her unmercifully, it didn't necessarily prove she was an alien. The strong magnetic pull of the pyramids, though, made it difficult to put two thoughts together, let alone try to figure anything out.

"Miss, your camel is ready," Kemen said, jolting her back to the present.

Sofia looked around just as Zach lifted his leg over the back of a kneeling camel. In one swift easy move, he was sitting regally on top of the creature.

"Come." Kemen lightly touched Sofia's arm to get her moving. "You will be riding Apollo. He is very gentle."

As if Apollo the camel knew they were talking about him, he let out a loud Chewbacca bellow and sent a stream of spit that smelled like a slimy compost pile in her direction.

She jumped backward into Kemen.

"It's okay," he reassured her, urging her forward. "He is just saying hello."

Sofia wasn't so sure, but it was either get on the beast or be left behind.

She reluctantly climbed onboard and immediately realized two things. First: she had been right to be hesitant. Being on the back of a camel was nothing like being on a horse. When the creature stood up, she was a good seven feet off the ground. Second: shorts were not the best thing to wear on a camel ride. The multi-colored blankets thrown over the saddle were stiff and scratchy and chafed the insides of her thighs. They did nothing to pad her rear end either.

A slight man in a turban took Apollo's reins and led the camel across the sand behind Zach's, who was being led by another camel driver. Kemen and Iker brought up the rear, riding their own camels without a lead.

Sofia hung onto the saddle's wooden handle for dear life as she rocked side to side and tried unsuccessfully to find a comfortable position. She had no idea how long she was on the wretched animal—it felt like hours—and she didn't care that they hadn't reached the pyramid when the handler stopped and coaxed the camel to the ground beside a dredged-out trench that led to the entrance of an excavated tomb. She just hurriedly slid off with a groan.

"No, this isn't right," Zach said to his camel's handler, who was tapping the camel's leg with a stick to get the beast to sit down. "Pyramid." He pointed to the huge stone structure at least a half mile away. "... Khufu."

The man said something Sofia couldn't understand, but the gesture he made was clear—he wanted Zach to dismount.

"No," Zach replied. "I'm not getting off. I want to go to the pyramids."

"This is as far as you go," Will said, stepping out of the shadows of the trench.

Zach's face darkened as he turned on Kemen. "You son-of-a-bitch, you set us up." He promptly slid off the camel and faced Will.

"What the fuck are you doing here? We don't need your help!"

"Yes, you do!" Will bellowed, then turned away as if to collect himself. When he turned back, his face was more composed.

"You think this is a TV reality show, but I can assure you it's not. The man you know as Daher wants you dead. Wants us all dead. And soon, he's going to discover that two of his chosen ones are imposters. There's no telling what he'll do then, but you can bet it won't be good … especially for Olivia. We have to get to her before it's too late."

Zach winced when Will said Liv's name.

Will suddenly jerked around to face the direction of the pyramids. He stared intently for a moment, then turned back and motioned to Kemen. "As I feared, Essol is early. His convoy is on the move now." He started toward the tomb's entrance. "We have to get going."

Sofia saw the look on Zach's face and knew he was torn over what to do. "Listen to him," she said, rushing to side. "He's telling the truth. I can feel it. You would too if you just gave him a chance."

Kemen took hold of Sofia's elbow to usher her toward the tomb, but she pulled back.

"But … that's not the pyramid!"

"No, but there's a secret tunnel inside that runs to Khufu and will get us there without being seen," Will answered, then looked over his shoulder at Zach. "This may be your only chance to get Olivia back alive. Are you going to cooperate?"

Sofia watched as Iker and the two camel drivers moved up and formed a wall behind Zach, and Will's earlier words echoed in her head: *"One way or another he is going to have to do his part. It'll be a whole lot easier on all of us if he does so willingly."*

She tugged on Zach's hand. "Come on. Let's go get Liv."

Zach's eyes narrowed as his gaze moved from Will to Sofia. "Were you in on this?"

She wished she could say no, but that would be a lie. "I—" She stumbled for the right words, ones that wouldn't make her look like a traitor.

His face screwed up with a look of betrayal and he yanked his hand out of hers. "I thought I knew you."

Sofia felt her heart crack.

Zach faced Will. “How are you going to get Liv away from Daher?”

“We’re prepared to do whatever is needed.” Will’s tone was ominous.

The corner of Zach’s mouth twitched. “Fine, I’ll go.” He turned to Sofia. “You’re staying here.”

“No,” Will cut in. “She has to come.”

Zach opened his mouth, but Sofia cut him off. “Hey, I’m right here!” she said, putting her hands on her hips. “And I can speak for myself if you don’t mind. I’m perfectly capable of taking care of myself, too.” She looked into the trench where Will was standing. “Count me in. I’ll help in whatever way I can.”

“Thank you,” Will replied. “I’m hoping we won’t need you, but Essol is desperate. It may take the force of you three to stop him.”

He eyed Zach. “I understand your concern for Sofia’s safety, but she has strengths you don’t understand yet. Trust me.”

“Sure, I’ll trust you about as far as I can throw you.”

Will’s golden aura dulled a little. “Well, if you don’t want to trust me, trust Sofia.”

Liv sat in the back of the stealth-looking black SUV, the same make as the one that had taken her to the maze. Her unseeing gaze was fixed on the window as she tried to think how she had gotten into this mess. And how she was going to get out of it.

She’d already tried feigning sickness, but the behemoth guard that had come to get her either didn’t understand English or had been instructed to bring her, no matter what. He just picked her up and carried her like luggage to the garage, by way of the private elevator, her kicking and squealing the whole way.

She was still pissed at being manhandled, but she was also scared. And she could no longer deny the sense that she was in danger, which she was starting to believe was from Daher. Wrapping her head around that idea was weird, but too many things about him and the TV show just didn’t add up. Like the fact that there were only three of them moving on to the second challenge. And the fact that the maze had obviously been rigged to make sure only certain people made it to the tower.

But why had she, Nick, and Hannah been chosen? She was just a girl from Texas who couldn't even afford her own college education. What was it about the three of them that would appeal to someone like Daher?

She had yet to come up with a way out of her current situation when the car pulled through the gates of the pyramid complex and three giant shadows, each in the shape of a triangle, filled the view out the window. She felt so alone and helpless, and the only tool she had with her was her charm. It had always worked for her in the past, but she'd never come up against anyone like Daher before either.

The driver barely slowed the car down at the security check points and drove straight up to the Pyramid of Khufu, stopping in front of the visitors' entrance. He hurried around the car and opened the door.

Liv took a deep breath, lifted her chin, and climbed out after Nick and Hannah.

The second she stepped into the open, a blast of intense electromagnetic energy hit her like a thunderbolt and nearly knocked her back inside. She struggled to catch her breath as her whole body tingled and the hairs on her arms stood on end. She looked down at her right palm, which was buzzing and felt hot, and didn't hear Daher walk up behind her.

"I have a special treat for the three of you," he said, sounding like a little kid on Christmas morning.

Liv jumped.

"I've obtained permission from the Ministry of Antiquities to enter the subterranean chamber of Khufu. No one has been permitted to go into the chamber for over a decade, so this is a great honor. Now, if you please follow these men to the entrance, and watch your step."

Hannah let out a squeak and clapped her hands together. Nick grinned like an awestruck Cheshire Cat.

Liv rolled her eyes in disgust. *God, these guys are totally clueless. How can they not sense something's wrong?*

She turned her gaze on the giant stones of the pyramid, which seemed to go up all the way to the stars. A feeling of vertigo washed over her, and a strong premonition told her not to go inside the pyramid. She swallowed hard.

"Olivia?" Daher spoke her name softly, but he couldn't keep the excitement out of his voice.

Liv's stomach dropped as she slowly turned. *Okay, you can do this.* She wet her lips and forced them into a seductive smile.

"Wow," she purred, batting her eyes at him. "It says a lot about you that they would let you in after-hours like this. I'm sure not many others would get this kind of opportunity. You must be really respected around here."

His look of a snake eyeing his prey sent a chill up her spine, but she didn't back down. She ran a fingertip down his bicep.

"It sure would be nice to see the inside of the pyramid, but you see, I'm claustrophobic. So, it's probably best if I stay out here with the car. If you don't mind."

Daher struck as quick as a viper and grabbed her forearm in a bone-crushing grip, sending a wave of shock and pain up her arm.

"I do mind," he growled and started up the pyramid steps, dragging her along with him.

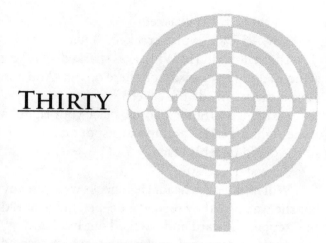

# THIRTY

The energy of the pyramid hummed in Sofia's head as she followed Will through a hole in the wall and into the tunnel that ran between the tomb and Khufu. Though, calling it a tunnel was a stretch. It was more of a narrow shaft that forced them all to bend nearly in half to keep from hitting their heads on the ceiling. The floor was uneven, too, which tripped her up more than once. But the worst part by far was the heat. It felt like they were walking inside a volcano vent, and the stale, almost non-existent air stank of mold.

Just when she thought her lungs would explode, the tunnel spilled out into a small chamber.

She straightened her back and inhaled a deep breath of stagnant air and dust, which sent her into a coughing fit. Once she got her breathing under control again, she looked around. The only light in the room was coming from Will's flashlight, but it was enough for her to see there were four solid stone walls and no door or passage other than the tunnel they had come through.

*Oh God no! It's a dead end.* Her stomach sank at the thought of having to go back through that suffocating tunnel from hell again.

Will waited until everyone had piled into the chamber before he spoke in a low voice, "There's one more shorter tunnel to go to get into the subterranean chamber of Khufu. The tunnel is smaller than the last, so you'll have to crawl on your hands and knees."

Zach suddenly jerked and stood straighter. Every eye in the room shifted to him.

"What is it?" Will asked.

"Liv …." Zach's voice cracked. "I just felt her. She's scared."

The yellow ring of Will's eyes sparked. "We've got to hurry. Try to avoid making any noise from here on out. And absolutely *no* talking. Sound carries inside the cavern."

He turned to Sofia. "Come, place your right hand flat against the stone right here." He pointed to a spot on the wall, then moved aside so she could take his place.

Sofia started. "Me?"

Will nodded his head. Her cheeks were already hot from the heat, but she was sure they turned a deeper shade of red. Self-consciously, she stepped forward and reached out her hand.

The wall was cool to the touch, which was odd considering the temperature in the room had to be at least one hundred degrees. A slight buzzing sensation ran through the palm of her hand, then, in the next blink of an eye, a large section of stone popped out from the wall. She jerked her hand back and the section slid silently to the side, exposing a square hole that was no bigger than the attic access at the Millers' house.

Will pushed her to the side and crawled into the hole. Kemen followed. Zach rushed in after them, and Iker motioned for Sofia to go next.

She took a big breath, steeled herself, and climbed in.

⟋⨉⌀⟍⌀∇⏐⏐⏐⌀⌇⟍⟍

Zach scurried through the tunnel like he was racing an avalanche. He didn't know what was going on with Liv, but he'd never felt her so scared. He crawled out into a lighted cavern on the heels of Kemen and blinked his eyes into focus.

Will and Kemen headed to the left toward a glowing rock formation at the back of the cavern.

Zach started to follow, then stopped short as a diagram of the room popped up before his eyes. It was similar to what had appeared to him during the semi-final's basketball game, except these series of dotted lines made paths around the chamber—one leading around the back of the rock formations on the west end, another around large piles of rocks on the east end, and one going to a square pit inside a metal railing in the center of the room that had a large X hovering over it.

Slowly, he turned in a full circle to take in the whole chamber, which appeared to have been manually dug out of the limestone bedrock. The diagram that was overlaid on his vision showed that the room measured twenty-seven feet wide by fifty-six feet long. The ceiling height where he was standing was thirteen feet but lowered toward the end with the stone formations, which looked as if someone had started to sculpt something, then gave up after making a couple long, rounded ridges. On the north wall, directly across from the opening he had come through, was the main entrance where Daher and Liv would be entering from.

Zach rubbed his thumb back and forth over his right palm to ease the small ache that had started up there and stared at the X over the pit. The last time the dotted lines had appeared, they were laying out basketball plays, but that couldn't be what these were for. This wasn't a game.

Or was it?

ᐯХᴚᐯᗡ‖‖ᐯKᐯ

Sofia clambered out of the tunnel and used her hand to shield her eyes against an expected light. She staggered forward a few steps as her eyes adjusted and bumped into Zach. She opened her mouth to apologize, then snapped it shut, remembering what Will has said about no talking.

"*The stone mounds to your left,*" Will's voice said inside Sofia's head.

She spun around. Will was nowhere to be seen. Neither was Kemen.

"*Go there and find a place to hide. Don't show yourselves unless I tell you to.*"

She looked left and saw two separate mounds with a trench and some crude steps between them. The mounds didn't appear to be a natural formation but were sculpted and shaped. A faint orange glow pulsed around them in the same rhythm as the hum in her head.

"*Go quickly,*" Will added, making her jump again.

Assuming Will had only spoken to her, Sofia tugged on Zach's sleeve and gestured for him to go to the mounds.

"I know. I heard," he murmured, and walked toward the mounds.

His words stabbed her heart, but that pain quickly turned to anger.

*What a jerk! Here I am trying to help him get his sister back and he's acting like a five-year-old. Maybe I should just leave—*

She couldn't finish that thought any more than she could abandon him. Deep down she knew this was too important, though she didn't know why.

She angrily swiped at a drip from her nose and stomped after Zach.

# THIRTY-ONE

Daher kept hold of Liv's arm, forcing her to go along with him until they were standing in front of the entrance to the pyramid. He didn't apologize or seem to care she was upset. He just released her and strutted over to the group of burly men who were waiting beside the door.

Liv glowered at him as she rubbed her hand up and down her arm, wincing at the tender spots where his fingers had dug in.

Daher's henchmen snapped to attention as he approached—except for one, who turned toward Liv. He was the same one from the penthouse, the one that looked like her nightmare reptile man, and his dark, malevolent glare sent an icy shiver straight through to her core.

Though she wanted to look away, she couldn't. Something about his disquieting vibrations and reptilian features seemed familiar, as if she had actually met him in person before. She couldn't imagine where that could have been, though. Plus, she had a knack for remembering everyone she'd ever met. And of all people to forget, it would not be someone like him. He looked like a lizard, and she *hated* lizards.

As Liv racked her brain to remember where she might have met him, another memory surfaced as clear as if it had happened yesterday—this same man standing over a woman's body, lying on the floor. She instantly recognized the woman as being Mommy, though it wasn't her mother in Texas who had adopted her, or even the one whose picture came up in her stone pendant—the one Liv had learned was her biological mom. This woman had been her Mommy for a short time when she was just a toddler.

The front of Mommy's shirt was stained with red Kool-Aid. A puddle of it was oozing out from under her, too, turning the carpet red. The man jerked around at the sound of the front door opening and hurriedly stuffed a gun into his coat.

Liv's jaw dropped as panic swelled in her chest. *Ohmigod, that isn't Kool-Aid!* Her skin suddenly felt as if there were spiders crawling over it.

*"Oh God, Z, where are you? I need you. I'm in trouble!"*

She looked around for an escape, but while she was lost in her memory, the number of Daher's men had multiplied and there was nowhere to go.

A man came up behind her and took hold of her elbow, grunting something unintelligible as he forcibly guided her to the doorway.

"No ... wait!" Liv screeched. "I can't go in there."

"Look, man," Nick said, stepping in the way. "Let her be. Can't you see she's scared?"

A second man moved in and forced Nick back.

Daher seemed oblivious to what was going on. "The descent's a little cramped," he said in an overly sweet tone, as if he was just a tour guide. "And I'm afraid the last few meters, you're going to have to crawl on your hands and knees. But if you watch your head and take it slow, you should be fine."

He didn't wait for anyone to comment but ducked his head and entered the tunnel.

"Hey!" Nick said as a man shoved him toward the opening.

The man growled and took a step forward. Nick's eyes widened and his face paled. The dude's biceps were bigger than his thighs. He gave the man a quick nod, then without another word, turned, and hurried into the tunnel.

Hannah, visibly trembling, rushed in after Nick as if he were her lifeline.

Two of the henchmen squeezed in after her. Another two came for Liv. Her stomach fell to her feet.

"Nooo!" She braced her hands on both sides of the entrance in a futile effort to resist, but the men had no trouble prying her hands off the wall. And the next thing she knew, she was stumbling down a sloping wooden ramp in the narrow passageway. Her toe caught on a raised horizontal board and she fell to her knees. She covered her face with her hands and whimpered, hoping that would get them to relent and let her go back.

The man behind her simply hefted her back to her feet and growled something she couldn't understand.

"Get your fucking hands off me," Liv snapped, yanking her arm free. She gave her hair a flip into the man's face and continued on down the long ramp.

The narrow passageway had no ventilation to speak of and the stale air reeked of body odor and something else she couldn't put her finger on. She slowly inched her way down the ramp thinking of the woman she had once called mommy lying in a pool of blood. She couldn't believe she had totally blanked that scene out all these years. Even more troubling was that she had completely forgotten all about the woman until a few minutes ago.

Liv strained to bring up other memories, but with the hum of the pyramid in her head and her body tingling the way it was, she could barely even think. And her right palm itched like crazy, distracting her even more.

As Daher had said, the tunnel went down to more of a shaft and the last 10 yards was claustrophobic. When it finally came to an end, she practically fell out into an open chamber and stood up to her full height with a groan.

As she tilted her head back to stretch her neck, an unbidden vision slammed through her skull.

> *She's on her stomach in the dirt, struggling to crawl to two stone formations that are glowing with a strange orange halo.*
>
> *Daher grabs a hold of her ankle and stops her progress. She screams and kicks as hard as she can, but she can't get free. She starts to slide backward toward Daher.*
>
> *Zach and Sofia appear and each grabs a hold of one of her hands.*
>
> *"Hold on!" Zach yells as he starts to lose her grip.*

*Sofia reaches for Zach. "Here, take my hand."*
*Their fingers touch.*
*A tremendous electrical charge flows through*
*Liv. She feels empowered, but a blinding light has*
*turned everything white and she can't see a thing.*

Liv jerked out of the vision, her heart beating a hundred miles an hour, and looked around. The stone mounds from her vision were at the end of the chamber to her right.

One of Daher's men roughly shoved her toward Nick and Hannah, who were standing next to a metal railing that encircled a hole in the ground.

"Dude, not cool!" Nick said to the man, then softly asked Liv, "Are you all right?" He actually looked concerned.

"No," Liv stated bluntly. "Something's horribly wrong with this whole thing. I don't like it."

"It's hard to breathe," Hannah wheezed. "I don't know why we're down here. This can't have anything to do with the show. If it did, wouldn't they be taping it?"

Liv did a quick scan of the room. A single lightbulb hung from the ceiling above the pit, but Hannah was right. There were no other lights, no techs, and no cameras. Her chest grew tighter.

"Excuse me, sir," Liv said to Daher, straining to keep the panic out of her voice. "Aren't you going to get footage of this for the show?"

"You're very perceptive," Daher replied smoothly. "But it was never my intent to film tonight's adventure. This is a trial run to tell us what kind of equipment we'll need to bring in later. As I stated before, I arranged this as a special treat—"

The rest of his words faded as Zach's voice came into Liv's head.

*"Livy, I'm here! Don't worry, we're going to get you out."*

She fixed her gaze on the sculpted mounds. With the energy of the pyramid beating in her head, she hadn't paid attention to other vibrations in the cavern. But now that she focused, she could not only feel Zach and Sofia's vibrations behind the mounds, but several other people hidden around the room as well.

Liv's relief was cut short when Daher barked, "Olivia!"

She twisted around. Standing beside Daher was Reptile Man. Her heart moved into her throat.

"Z, *that man next to Daher. He—*"

"I said to stand over there with Nicholas and Hannah," Daher interrupted her. "And join hands. Make a circle."

Nick and Hannah were no longer standing next to her but had moved to halfway between the pit and the stone mounds. Liv slowly shuffled to Nick's side and took his clammy hand.

Daher's men lined up next to their boss, two on each side. Reptile Man stood off to the side.

"What's this all about?" she whispered to Nick.

"Dunno. Just doing what I'm told."

Daher stood stock-still, his intense look rivaling that of a raptor homing in on his prey. "You have no idea how long I've waited for this moment. ... Go on," he urged Liv. "Take Hannah's hand."

Hannah was marshmallow white and trembling so hard Liv could barely keep hold of her hand.

"It's going to be okay," Liv whispered. "My friends are going to get us out of here." She glanced at Reptile Man and prayed with all her might that was true.

The chamber went silent, as if everyone were holding their breaths to see what would happen next, but nothing changed.

Daher looked around the room as if expecting to see something. When he turned back, his face was dark. "Why isn't it working?"

He clomped over and rearranged the three of them, pulling Liv to the other side of Hannah.

"Now hold hands."

They did as they were told.

Liv's stomach clenched tighter as the frown lines on Daher's brow grew deeper. "*Now would be a good time to get us out of here, Z.*"

"Ezafak!" Daher exploded, then yelled something to his men in the same strange language.

The men snapped to attention and pulled out what looked like sophisticated Nerf guns from packs on their backs. They all rested the weapons at their sides, except for Reptile Man, who pointed his at Liv.

Hannah whimpered and trembled even harder.

Daher took a step closer to the three and ground out through his teeth, "You're the designated Guardians, now act like it. Turn. Off. The grid!"

"What grid?" Nick's voice cracked. "I don't know what you're talking about."

Daher screamed something else unintelligible to the men. One of them raised his Nerf contraption and aimed it at Nick.

"Is that right?" Daher looked like he was about to explode. "You think you're so smart you can trick me? I *know* who you are and what you can do. You proved it when you made it through the maze to the tower."

"I was just f-f-following Nick," Hannah whined. "He had a guy directing him and t-t-telling him which way to go."

"Shut up!" Nick hissed.

Daher rounded on him, his nostrils flaring, his eyes almost solid black. "What does she mean you had help?" His voice was low but sharp as a knife.

"I didn't …" Nick shifted his weight to his other foot, then let out a resigned sigh. "There was a button camera and an earbud in my hotel room when I checked in. The note that was with them said to wear them in the maze and someone would guide me through. I didn't think it was a big deal, so …"

Daher let out a bloodcurdling howl, reared back, and slammed his fist into Nick's jaw. Nick stumbled backwards.

"You fools!" Daher roared. "You've spoiled everything."

A second gunman raised his gun and aimed it at the three. Hannah shrieked and fell to her knees, sobbing.

"Essol!" a voice from the other side of the mounds shouted. A man stepped out of the shadows.

Daher's head slowly swiveled and the dark energy around him flared. The mounds' orange light glowed brighter, too.

"Gilamu," he growled. "You're supposed to be dead."

"And you're not supposed to be on this planet, but here we both are." The man lifted his chin toward Nick. "Let them go. They have nothing to do with this fight."

Daher tsked. "Isn't that just like you to use humans as decoys, then declare yourself innocent when their situation becomes precarious." He narrowed his eyes. "But you didn't come here for the humans, did you? You're here because our little scheme caught one of your true Guardians, didn't it?" He gestured to Liv. "This one, perhaps?"

Gilamu raised his hand. Nick went flying across the room into to the wall a nanosecond before the rock mound behind where he was standing exploded in a thunderous boom and a cloud of granite projectiles sailed in all directions.

Three of Daher's other men turned at once and fired on the man. Reptile Man fired at Liv. She dove to the ground and covered her head with both arms.

The lightbulb over the pit shattered, throwing the room into darkness, but for the glow of the mounds.

The echo of exploding rocks rang through the chamber, but Daher's voice could be heard above the racket, "Don't hit the Guardian!"

*What does he want with me?* Liv thought as she inched her way toward the mounds. Something warm, wet, and smelling of copper suddenly splattered her skin and she felt Hannah's energy extinguish like the light.

*Ohmigod!*

She squeezed her eyes shut, refusing to look around and confirm what she knew had happened. "Zaaach!"

### ᏆᚷᏒ᛭ᏈᛁᛁᛁᚫᚴᏃ

All at once, rocks started falling from the ceiling just like they had in the cavern at the maze and the echo of them pinging off each other and the metal railing was deafening, but Zach heard Liv's scream.

He raised up, "Livy!"

*"Zach, stay down!"* Will shouted telepathically.

Zach bolted into the trench between the mounds. Sofia was right on his heels, her invisible bubble fully functioning this time, protecting them both from the falling rocks and flying debris from the blasts.

The dust in the air, thick as a smoke screen, cut Zach's visibility down to about a foot in front of him, but he didn't need to see. He had the diagram in his head to guide him.

He crouched low and followed the dotted line to where Liv was lying.

### ᏆᚷᏒ᛭ᏈᛁᛁᛁᚫᚴᏃ

Sofia's pulse raced as she blindly followed Zach to Liv, who was lying on her stomach, clawing the ground to get away from Daher. He had a firm clasp on her ankle, though, which was preventing her from making any progress.

Zach grabbed hold of one of Liv's hand.

Sofia took the other. An electrical charge ran up her arm.

*"Sofia, take Zach's hand and complete the circle,"* Will called to her.

Without questioning, Sofia obeyed Will's direction and waved her free hand at Zach.

"Quick, grab my hand."

Zach took it. The second their skin touched, a loud whoosh soared through Sofia's head, drowning out the noise of the battle. At the same time, a surge of energy flowed into her, heightening all her senses and filling her with a sense of power unlike anything she'd ever experienced before. Her hair stood on end and her hands began to buzz with a strange, but not uncomfortable, sensation.

Then three blinding beams of light shot up from the points where their hands connected, bathing the whole chamber in a brilliant white glow.

"Grab the other two," Daher yelled to his men as he clutched Liv's leg with both hands.

Two of the men immediately ran to a pile of rocks closer to Sofia and Zach as the others fired to cover them.

Sofia strained to pull Liv away, but Daher was stronger than he looked and even with her and Zach pulling together, they weren't making any headway. And Daher's men were getting closer.

The energy inside Sofia continued to build until she felt like her skin was going to split open.

"Direct your energy at Daher!" Liv screamed.

Sofia started as Liv's word clicked something in her brain. Of course! If they were truly Pleiadians as Will said, they should be able to throw someone across the room just like he did with Nick.

She looked over at Zach. His expression told her he'd had the same revelation. They gave each other a decisive nod and together, released their hand and pushed them forward, palm-side out.

Sofia felt a release of energy and Daher flew backward into his approaching men. The men's weapons blasted into the ceiling as the force picked them up and carried all three of them to the far end of the cavern and slammed them into the wall.

The whole cavern shuddered. Cracks appeared in the bedrock of the ceiling and spread like slithering snakes. Several chunks fell, then a larger, boulder-size one dropped between Sofia's group and the pit

*"Quickly,"* Will said. *"You must go through the portal. It's the only way out now. The ceiling is about to collapse."*

Liv jumped to her feet and ran to Zach, her face paler than usual. "A voice in my head told me to go to the portal."

Zach turned his head toward the pit. A circle of iridescent light swirled like a whirlpool over the opening right where the X had been in the diagram in his head. He raised an eyebrow at Sofia in an unspoken question.

"Will's been right about everything else," she replied.

"Who's Will?" Liv asked.

Nick crawled out of the dust. A purpling bruise covered his jaw and a deep gash on his cheek oozed blood. He flicked a wary glance from Liv to Zach, then Sofia.

The floor trembled as another large chunk of ceiling fell.

*"Go now!"* Will called. *"When the ceiling comes down, you'll be cut off from us. The portal's your only way out."*

"We gotta do what Will says," Sofia said to Zach.

"But we don't know where that portal goes."

"What portal?" Nick asked, scrambling to his feet.

An unearthly sound, like that of a hundred mummies moaning, echoed through the room.

"Does it matter where it goes?" Liv's voice was shrill. "As long as it's away from here, who the fuck cares?"

Zach blew out a breath. "Fine. But I want it noted I don't like this." He took Liv and Sofia's hands.

As they took a step toward the portal, Nick cried, "Wait! What about me?"

Liv gave Zach a look. "We can't leave him here to die."

She held out her free hand. Nick eagerly latched onto it the same way a first-time skydiver latches onto his ripcord.

The four ran toward the metal railing separating them from the portal and, as one, jumped.

As Sofia rose into the air, she felt something slam into her shield. The force propelled all four of them forward as if they were wearing a jetpack. Frigid air stole her breath away and streaks of light flashed around her for just a moment before she was thrown to her knees on a hard cold floor.

She immediately flipped around and looked back over her shoulder. She could see nothing through the swirling whirlpool of light, but she heard a gravelly voice say, "I've found you before. I'll find you …"

The rest of the words were drowned out by the thunderous roar of the ceiling collapsing. The circle of light then blinked out as the portal closed and everything went silent.

"Where the fuck are we?" Liv asked.

# EPILOGUE

*One month later*

Daher's assistant, Tabari, stopped in the doorway of Daher's office in Cairo and adjusted his tie. As had been the norm over the past month, his boss stood at the window, brooding as he looked down on the lush fairway of the Katameya Heights golf course.

Tabari cleared his throat, "Ahem."

Daher bristled, then harshly snapped, "I told you not to disturb me."

Tabari's instincts told him to run, but he stood his ground. "Yes, sir. But you also said you wanted to be informed as soon as we heard back from the Dracuzians."

Daher whipped around, his expression dark and dangerous.

Tabari shifted his notebook in his hands to hide his trembling. Daher hated signs of weakness. "They haven't been able to find any trace of the Guardians. They believe now that they've left Earth."

He could feel the heat of Daher's glare all the way across the room. And though the billionaire remained silent, his nostrils flared in and out, a sure sign he was about to explode. Tabari hurried on.

"However, Ukani is closing in one of the Sons of Ea and will bring him in for interrogation once he has secured him. He suspects the man knows the Guardians' location and he can get it out of him."

Daher pursed his lips. "And Gilamu?"

The name was spoken with such venom it sent goose pimples up

Tabari's arms. His Adam's apple bobbed as he swallowed hard. "He has not been found."

Tabari took a tentative step backward into the hall in case he needed to flee, but Daher just turned back to the window.

"I want to question the man Ukani brings in myself. Advise me when he arrives," Daher said.

"Yes, sir."

"And remind the Dracuzians that I swore a vow to the Elite that I'd reclaim this planet. If they fail me, their entire race is going to pay."

"Yes, sir." Tabari took another step back. "Right away, sir." He turned and sped down the hall.

Daher clasped his hands behind his back and stared out at the immaculately groomed fairway, dreaming of how he was going to torture Gilamu once the Pleiadian filth was caught. And he had no doubt that Gilamu would be caught.

A white-tailed eagle suddenly swooped out of the sky and snatched up a giant rat from a patch of tall grass. He watched it fly off with its prey squirming in its claws and smiled, knowing there would be no saving grace for the rat now.

*Saving grace* ... He stood up straighter. "That's it! I should have thought of this sooner."

*Pleiadians think themselves noble saviors of these primitive humans. They'd never just stand by and idly watch if I start killing hundreds of thousands of their pets. They'd have to come out of hiding and bring the Guardians back, too.*

A low rumble started in his throat, erupting into a malicious laugh. He turned back to his desk and punched a button on his desk.

"Tabari, get in here ... we have work to do!"

## THE END

# A Note From the Author

Thank you so much for reading,
## THE GUARDIANS' LIGHT
### THE RISE OF THE THREE
I hope you enjoyed it. It was great fun to write.

If you could take a minute to post a review,
it would mean a lot to me. I always love to
hear readers' thoughts.

To follow M.J. and stayed informed on new
projects, please 'like' her Facebook page,
MJ Bell Author, or go to her website:
www.mj-bell.com

*Happy reading!*

# ACKNOWLEGMENTS

I'd be remiss if I didn't take a moment to thank a few very special people.

First off, my daughter, Tiffany Lopo, and good friend, Lisa Moore. These two spent countless hours with me brainstorming and perfecting the characters and plot. They are by far my biggest fans and I don't know that I could have put this story together without them. I love you 3,000.

Sometimes it really does take a village, and I am fortunate to have Lourdes Bell, Brandy Bell, Charmayne Sobon, and Janie Gianotsos in mine! I could always count on these four being there for me to bounce off ideas and give me suggestions to fine tune the story. They helped make it the best it could be. Love you guys.

I'd also like to thank my editor, DeAnna Knippling. I so respect your knowledge of writing and appreciate your patience with me, even when I question your suggestions. (And you are seldom wrong.) I not only consider you one of the best editors out there, but a very good friend.

And, of course, none of this would happen without the support of my husband, who puts up with me and doesn't complain when I forgo cleaning the house to write. I love you more than you know.

Lastly, I would like to thank all my readers who have followed me and supported me on this long road. You make it all worthwhile and the journey would be very lonely without you. Can't wait to reconnect with you in person at future ComicCons!

# ABOUT THE AUTHOR

MJ Bell's love of reading and everything magical is what motived her to jump headfirst into a writing career. Little did she know that only a few years later she would be an award-winning author (Gold award from Mom's Choice Awards), and have five books published, with more on the way.

Though MJ grew up in Iowa, her home is now Colorado, where she lives with her husband and dog, Tallie. Her family is a source of pride and joy to her, as well as a great source of inspiration, which she uses to bring a little more magic into the world.

She loves to hear from readers through her FB page: **MJ Bell Author**, or on her website: **www.mj-bell.com**

CPSIA information can be obtained
at www.ICGtesting.com
Printed in the USA
FSHW020948080421
80284FS